1st IN THE 1st DEGREE

A NOVEL

Other Proteus Books Now Available

Hell: A Cyberpunk Thriller—A Novel

The Pandora Directive: A Novel

The 7th Guest: A Novel

Star Crusader: A Novel

Wizardry: The League of the Crimson Crescent—A Novel

How to Order:
For information on quantity discounts contact the publisher: Prima Publishing, P.O. Box 1260BK, Rocklin, CA 95677-1260; (916) 632-4400. On your letterhead include information concerning the intended use of the books and the number of books you wish to purchase.

IN THE 1st DEGREE™
A NOVEL

Dominic Stone

PRIMA PUBLISHING

Based on a story by Peter Adair, Domenic Stansberry, and Haney Armstrong.

Prima Publishing would like to acknowledge Bruce Friedricks at Broderbund for his special assistance on this project.

ISBN: 0-7615-0197-5
Library of Congress Catalog Card Number: 95-70133
Printed in the United States of America
96 97 98 99 AA 10 9 8 7 6 5 4 3 2 1

CONTENTS

FOREWORD

If someone had suggested to me as few as five years ago that it might take as long to write the story and screenplay for a computer game as it would to write the source code, I would have thought the individual an unfathomable risk to the schedule of a product development team. After bouncing this creative individual (for purposes of illustration, let's call said visionary our Writer) out of the building and removing his or her name from my then still manila-card rolodex, I would have met for a reality check with all said product development team members and made certain their focus had not been compromised by such notions of grandeur. All would be reminded that we were in the computer games business. Sure there had to be Text. Text was a necessary evil, a bit map here or there that got picked up for back of box copy and perhaps massaged for the occasional print ad. Our Writer spoke of Story and Character, but all we needed was Text.

How long could it possibly take to create Text?

And how involved did it really need to be? How complicated could it be? Did our Customer really want all that elaborate plot, setting, texture, mood, and humanity?

Thankfully, it has always been our Writer's job to dream.

Okay, so now we are all on the same page. We need more than Text. Our Writer can give us a Story. . . and Characters. . . and yes, if absolutely necessary, even humanity. Yet if someone would have suggested to me those same five years ago that a serious work of CD-ROM fiction could be created and adapted into a serious work of written, printed, published fiction, I do not think I could have responded. I would not have been able to revive myself from the shock of such a notion, let alone convince my product development team that this was a meaningful part of our future.

So who is this Writer? Why adapt a CD-ROM game as a novel? What is it with all this Text?

And there before us is the answer. It is not so much Text that has been integral in the life of the computer as it is the Idea. The software content business is not really about technology (well, it is sort of, but go with me on this for a moment). What we are is another form of Media. Be it television, film, a stage play, a cartoon strip, a short story, a radio program, Carmen Sandiego, it all begins the same way—with the written word. The Word, the Text, gives life to the new Idea. And once an Idea is born into Media, its life can assume almost any format. The more care given to the Idea at its inception, the more likely it is to have multiple lives. Shakespeare's plays are a wonder when read on paper, engaging entertainment on the stage (when adequately performed), they have been triumphantly adapted into big-budget feature films, they remain the subject of endless intellectual essays, and recently they have even found their way into the world of multimedia software. An idea well framed by our Writer inspires other interpretations and often begs to be expressed creatively in alternative Media.

So what about the computer? What is Electronic Media that it too calls for adaptation? It is very much rooted in the Text of the original adventure games we played on mainframes. It is very much alive in the Text we send to each other every day over modems and through e-mail. It is very much the Text that we read when we visit each other's home pages on the Web. It is truly the Text we write for the scripts that actors record to further enhance our multimedia games—Text we write but never even see! These are Ideas that are maturing every day, reflections of Stories and Characters we long to explore at many levels of resolution, levels that are not necessarily exhausted when the game is over. And so our Writer gives us more, and we are fortunate to have the Words.

Long before we were digitizing video, long before we were even recording voice-overs, the standard contractual language in a software development and publishing agreement referred to a Developer as an Author. Imagine that! Today a Developer can be a team of individuals, a company large or small, and only sometimes what it used to be: a Programmer—you know, the Person who develops (translation: WRITES) the program code. Do I mean to say all that strange, humanly unreadable Code is actually Authored? Perhaps that is why the Programmer must use a programming Language! Somehow all that Text has to be given meaning. It is as much Art as it is Technology. It is composed on a keyboard, sometimes initially even on a yellow pad (egad!) and then transcribed. And most importantly, when well written, said code displays flare. That's the kind of code we like. You know it when it compiles.

Years ago, a leader in our industry posited the question, "Can a computer game make you cry?" Yes, way back when we were crawling out of our industry's primordial ooze of blips and bleeps, back when it was the plain old Software Business and not the glamorous Multimedia Industry, the challenge of eliciting emotion vis-à-vis electronic interactivity had already been identified. The first time Peter Adair and Haney Armstrong showed me their prototype for what would become *In The 1st Degree,* I knew we had a shot at real tears. The first time I played the game in its Text engine, I had real hope. The first time I played the game in Alpha on CD-ROM and saw Ruby break down on the stand in the midst of reading Zack's letter, I knew we had achieved a real milestone. I believe our friends at Prima Publishing had a similar reaction and thus asked us at Broderbund if we thought a book could come out of this. Sure, they had contracted novelizations before, but not one with this expanse of emotional complexity. I felt proud. I knew that Text had become Writing. The Author had given us Text that could have multiple incarnations, multiple interpretations, meaning and value beyond its initial Media. The Author was again at the heart of the Idea, and so rewarded by the request for a command performance, an adaptation in the oldest tradition we know as media, the Book.

So here we are, a computer game has been adapted to become a work of written, printed, published fiction. A story becomes a CD-ROM game, a CD-ROM game becomes a novel. And beneath it all the written word continues to live.

May we continue to live in interesting times.

Ken Goldstein
Executive Publisher of Broderbund Software's
Education and Entertainment Products Studio
Novato, California

PREFACE

This entertainment is a retelling of a story. As in many retellings—especially adaptations across media—the original has been reshaped, partly by the demands of this old format, the novel, but also by the talent, limitations, and moods of the author. In a book like this, the reader inevitably enters a world created by one person, not a world developed, for better or worse, by a team of writers and designers working in fevered collusion.

My hope is that this story remains true to the Rashomon-esque spirit of the original while offering yet another spin, another augmentation. In here readers will find all the characters in the CD-ROM, but they will also find a few new characters, new perceptions, new twists and turns, new insights into the behind-the-scenes machinations.

In other words, this book is yet another version of the story told upon the CD-ROM, which itself offers manifold versions of the same events. Some may argue that it is the technology that has allowed such luxury of exploration, but it is also the oldest trick of the storyteller to nudge us into familiar territory from yet another point of view.

ONE

∾ ∾

INSPECTOR LOOPER

Sterling Granger slumped in the chair across from Julie
Ann Wong and looked at her through the rising steam
from his coffee cup. The district attorney looked back at
him calmly, her head framed by the high back of her
leather chair, which was, in turn, framed by a flood of morning
sunshine. Late spring in San Francisco and, for a wonder, not a
shred of fog in sight. But Granger was in no mood to appreciate
the weather.

"You didn't get me down here on a Sunday morning to
discuss the art scene," Granger said. "Come on, Julie, spill it."

She shrugged. "But you do know who he is."

"Yeah. Everyone in San Francisco knows. Zachary Barnes,
Barnes Gallery, represents James Tobin, who paints portraits of
the poor and sells them to the rich. Big time social conscience,
shows up at all the right fund-raisers."

"Barnes?"

"Him too, but I meant Tobin," Granger said. "So?"

Wong leaned forward, bringing her face out of the corona of
sunlight. She didn't look pleased.

"Zack Barnes is also the husband of Yvonne Barnes, the
mayor's press secretary."

1

"Nice work," Granger said. Yvonne Barnes, beautiful, sculpted, and black, was acknowledged to be Mayor Jack McKinney's major concession to the city's liberal voters, although around City Hall she was known, with respect but no affection, as the Ice Queen. "He's a lucky man."

"He's also a dead one," Wong said. "Murdered. This morning, at his gallery. And it looks, Granger, as though James Tobin pulled the trigger."

Granger sat forward. "Tobin? But he's world famous. You must be joking."

She simply looked at him. District Attorney Wong, having no sense of humor, never joked.

"According to Chief LoBianco, Tobin's got a gunshot wound to the leg. They're transporting him to SF General. Anita Looper from Homicide's got the case. I want you to go talk to her, get to the bottom of this." The district attorney paused. "I expect that this will be something simple. James Tobin, as you said, is a world-famous artist. And Yvonne Barnes is big-time politics. Something simple, quick, and quiet, Granger. That's what I expect."

Sterling Granger resisted the urge to tug his forelock as he stood. That, of course, was why Wong called him rather than one of the other attorneys on her staff. He had a reputation for thoroughness, hard work, and competence. And a deep dislike for publicity.

"One more thing, Sterling," Wong said. "If you take on this case, I want you to win. I don't want another Hayes Valley fiasco."

Granger didn't reply. Wong was referring to a case in which he had prosecuted a serial rapist who'd been working the lower Fillmore. The accused had been a black man, and two of the three women willing to testify had been white.

For reasons Granger still couldn't quite perceive, he'd lost the conviction. Instead of a criminal trial, the case had turned into a referendum on racial and sexual politics—a nasty bit of business. Losing the conviction had almost cost him his job. By giving him this case, the DA was telling him that he had another chance. And that he had better not blow it.

"Understood," Granger said, keeping his face still.

If something simple, quick, and quiet was what the lady wanted, Granger thought as he left the office, then simple, quick, and quiet was what she would get.

He didn't realize—he couldn't realize—just how wrong he was.

One of the officers on the scene had pulled open the drapes across the large gallery windows, and another made sure every light in the place blazed. In that brilliant wash of light, Inspector Anita Looper stood back to let the boys from Forensics crowd around the body of Zachary Barnes.

He lay face up, eyes open above the gunshot wound in his throat. In death his ebony skin had already begun to lose its luster; face, arms, body, clothes, all were covered with blood. The blood, mixed with tiny shards of glass, sparkled in the bright light and threw prisms onto the stark white walls, the slightly shabby paint job, the nail holes left from the last showing, the smudged carpet. The displayed paintings did not show well in this harsh light.

A siren started up outside, and Inspector Looper sighed, listening to it. That would be the ambulance, come to transport James Tobin to San Francisco General. Tobin had a gunshot wound in his leg—just a graze from what the sergeant had told her, but enough to hurt. Looper had arrived fifteen minutes after the responding officers; the fire department's emergency medical technicians swarmed around Tobin, and according to the beat cop, two witnesses, both of them women, had already been sequestered in separate rooms down the hall.

Fifteen minutes might be record time, Looper thought, glancing at her watch. Usually the drag time was longer, but Looper had happened to be at the downtown station when the call transferred over from Dispatch. The location, the Barnes Gallery, had generated a rush of excitement in the office. Yvonne Barnes herself had placed the call. Like her husband, Zack, and the artist, Tobin, she was well known in the city. Even Looper had met Tobin once, at one of his openings a few years back. A gala affair, full of politicos and artistes, hobnobbers and dilettantes.

Looper shouldered her way between the arriving paramedics so she could look down into the face of the wounded man on the stretcher. The beat cops had gotten some preliminary information, but she hoped to get in a few questions before the paramedics hoisted him away. She waited while the EMTs briefed the paramedics, then packed their equipment and faded away.

"How's the leg?" she asked.

Tobin grimaced. Shock had tinged his pink skin white, making a stark contrast with his black hair.

"It's not bad," he said, making a show of bravery—and knowing it. "It stings like hell, but the docs here tell me it's more blood than anything. I guess I'm lucky."

"You're James Tobin?"

"Yes."

"The artist?"

Looper was not sure why she asked. Maybe it was to see that little smile turn the corner of his lips, pleased that even the homicide cop knew who he was. His paintings hung on the walls all around them, the images of pain and poverty somehow sanitized. To view a Tobin, Looper thought, was to see homelessness and despair through pink-colored glasses—the sort of social conscience you could hang above your living-room couch without fear of offending the neighbors. After working Homicide in San Francisco for fifteen years, Looper hated the stuff. As far as she was concerned, sanitizing agony should be a capital offense. It was all a colossal fake—especially coming from an artist who, this Sunday morning, wore a Rolex watch and, tucked into one earlobe, a perfectly cut diamond stud. Besides, the bastard had flirted with Luisa—and Luisa had flirted back.

"I'm Inspector Looper," she said, showing him her badge. She wanted to be sure he knew she was a cop. "We met once before. At one of your openings."

Tobin smiled again, bravely. "You'd think I'd remember the hair," he said. Looper just looked at him, then deliberately pushed a lock of her wild red hair behind an ear. She turned to the lead medic, a young woman about thirty with blunt-cut hair dyed white as a sheet, a bright magenta streak down the center. Her nose had been pierced, and her ears too, in maybe a half-dozen places, so a row of tiny rings ran down each lobe. The sight of this angel of mercy, Looper guessed, had probably pushed a few coronaries over that last edge.

"Give me a minute with this guy?"

The medic hesitated.

"I'd like to talk to the Inspector," he said. "I don't think I'm going to die in the next few minutes."

He smiled at the medic, flirting with her, and the young woman smiled and moved back.

"What happened here?" Looper said, pencil hovering over her notepad.

"He tried to kill me."

"Who?"

"My partner. Zachary Barnes."

Looper's deadpan didn't change. "What were you doing, the two of you, here on a Sunday morning?"

"Talking. Business stuff. Then he came after me with a gun. He was freewheeling around, threatening me, and just as I got out of the chair, he fired."

"Was he aiming for your leg?" She didn't allow the disbelief to tinge her voice.

"My head. I got up so quickly, I didn't even know he had hit me, and I leaped across the table, to try to get the gun out of his hands. Then we came crashing down together, and that's when the gun went off. A second time."

Something about the way he talked bothered her. He was cooperative enough, but seemed pretty lucid for a man who'd just been shot. And a bit too eager to talk. "Did you have your hands on the gun?"

"I might have. But Zack did too."

"So what did you do after the gun went off?"

"I lay there on top of him, in all of that blood. I didn't know whether it was mine or his. Then I got up, thinking I had to get some help. I staggered a few steps before I realized I'd been shot too, all that pain in my leg. Then I must have fainted because the next thing I remember, Yvonne was over there," Tobin pointed to the dead man, "howling over Zack's body."

"Howling," Looper repeated, writing it down. "Yvonne Barnes?"

"Yes," Tobin said. "Zack's wife."

"This fight just came out of the blue?"

Tobin hesitated and reached toward his leg. Faking it, Looper thought, then bent her head toward the pad. Stop it, she told herself sharply. OK, you don't like him, you don't like his art-work, you don't like his style. It doesn't matter. You're a cop. Act like one.

"Zack was my friend," Tobin said, bewildered. "This shouldn't have happened."

The magenta-streaked angel stepped forward. "Enough," she said, grabbing the gurney. "We've got to take him in, he might be hemorrhaging."

Another medic moved to the foot of the gurney. Looper had to make a decision. She could ride with Tobin to the hospital, getting the rest of his statement on the way, or she could send somebody from Patrol. She did have other witnesses to see to.

"OK," she said. "I'm going to come up to the hospital, after the doctors look you over, and get a statement."

"Anything I can do to help," Tobin said.

The paramedics hoisted the gurney, but before they carried him away, his eye caught hers. "I know you," he said, and grinned suddenly. "Yeah. What was her name—oh yeah, Luisa. You're Luisa's friend. That's right." The grin widened. "And how is Luisa these days? Remember to give her my best." Then he nodded at the magenta angel, and the paramedics trundled the gurney away, leaving Inspector Looper staring. Soon, though, her shock gave way to outrage.

You're a cop, she told herself furiously. Looper sent one of the boys from the Mobile Crime Unit over to catch the ambulance before it drove off; it had occurred to her, almost too late, that she needed Tobin's hands bagged and checked for gunshot residue.

Then she stood for a moment, facing the wall, breathing deeply until she had bundled up her anger and pain, and stuffed it away. When her hands stopped shaking, she flipped back through her notebook until she came to the first page. Two witnesses: Yvonne Barnes and Ruby Garcia, Tobin's girlfriend. Looper took a deep breath, pushed fiery hair away from her face, and went to find them.

TWO

∽ ⌣ ∾

RUBY GARCIA

J emma Granger was not happy with her father, and
she made it pretty obvious. Granger watched unhappily
as his eight-year-old daughter marched, back straight
and stiff, into her grandparents' back yard. He had had
to promise one trip to the zoo, two to the Exploratorium, and a
new Barbie doll before she would begin to forgive him for
working on a Sunday. Spoiled, he knew, but ever since the
divorce he had found it impossible to say no to her.

"You never spend time with me," Jemma had complained,
when he returned from his early morning meeting with the DA.

"That's not true, punkin," Granger said. "It's the bad guys,
Jemma. I keep telling them not to get caught on weekends, but
they just won't listen to me."

Jemma tried to keep her glower, but the smile poked through
anyway, tilting all her freckles upwards. Her forgiveness hadn't
lasted very long, though, and now she let the garden gate slam
closed behind her.

Granger sighed, putting the vintage Mustang convertible in
gear and pulling away from his parents' house in the Richmond
district, he wondered if Marian, his ex, had the same problem

saying no to Jemma. Somehow he doubted it. Marian always seemed in control of everything. All the time.

Control, though, was something Granger was finding to be a scarce commodity these days. And this case, he thought, was simply another example. Wong wanted things kept simple, quick, and quiet, but he had already heard reports of Zack Barnes's death on the car radio, and speculation about murderer and motive. Quiet was already impossible, and he suspected that, given the cast of characters, quick and simple would be equally elusive. The case had politics written all over it.

He cut through Golden Gate Park, in no rush to reach his office at the Hall of Justice. Looper would still be hard at work; he had no desire to barge in on her initial interviews and too much respect for her professionalism to even think of intruding.

The park was lovely, decked in the flowers of early summer, although a few stubborn rhododendrons and azaleas still flaunted surreal, pastel blooms amid the dark trees. Bicyclists, picnickers, stylishly ragged teenagers on Rollerblades, grandparents in wheelchairs, grandchildren in strollers, and over them all the unexpected pleasure of a warm San Francisco morning. Granger frowned at it. He refused to think about the case already—not enough evidence, no real knowledge of the facts. Thinking about it at this stage could only prove frustrating at best. At worst, it could create presumptions, which in turn would create blind alleys, wasters of time and effort. No, he would get back to the office and start on the background, get the basics organized, and try not to think about how Wong had given him a case that promised to reek of publicity and politics—the two things that he, of all the people on her staff, disliked the most. That she had given him the case deliberately was not open to question. It made sense. She would step in and take credit for a good out-come and leave him, alone, to take blame for a bad one. He knew that some people considered him to be the best prosecutor in the DA's office, but it seemed that being a good prosecutor these days wasn't enough. And Granger, who hated Court TV and all that it implied, knew without a doubt that Wong considered him a liability.

It wasn't just a murderer whose fate depended on this case. Granger knew that his career, too, was on the line.

Ruby Garcia couldn't keep herself still. She couldn't sit, she couldn't stand, so she paced restlessly around the gallery's reception area, where the lady cop had asked her to wait. Past the cool leather sofa, all planes and angles; past the glass coffee table with its two artfully arranged magazines; past the metal kinetic sculpture that rose from the floor in the corner and tinkled at her whenever she passed. And back again, sculpture, coffee table, sofa, metal, glass, leather, and none of it warm. She could hear voices through the wall, not the words of course, but the sound, coming from Zack's office. Yvonne's eerie monotone and the cop's short grumbles. Then every once in a while Yvonne's voice grew louder—still controlled, like always, but lilting, sounding like the professional broadcaster she'd once been. The television voice that delivered the grimmest news in the same tone as sunny weather. She wondered what Yvonne was saying now.

This was all too strange. Ruby trembled, clutching at her gut as she paced back and forth. She couldn't believe, not really, that Zack could be dead, all crumbled up and lying in a circus of blood and glass on the gallery floor.

She wished she could get upstairs to their apartment, fix herself some coffee or a stiff belt of something. Jimmy's apartment, that is—he had always made that clear. Not her place, just Jimmy's, even if he did let her live there. But Zack had told her that it wasn't Jimmy's place either, not really. Not the way Jimmy made it sound. Zack owned the whole building, and he had let Jimmy stay in the apartment ever since Jimmy's divorce. But Jimmy didn't own any of it. Even if he made it sound that way.

Not that it mattered, not now. Not with Zack lying out there, and Jimmy shot. She'd gotten over being mad at Jimmy for not letting her go to Los Angeles with him. It was a publicity deal, he said, boring as hell, society snobs, no place she'd want to waste her time. She should stay home and work on her own paintings. Develop herself as an artist. But she knew the real reason Jimmy wanted her to stay behind. Some woman or other down in LA. A gallery type, maybe, floppy hat, sunglasses, print skirt, and a long scarf. Ruby and Jimmy had been together only a year, his divorce was barely final, and already he was skipping around on her.

But thinking of Jimmy's trip made her think of other things, and she pushed the whole subject away and paced again, rubbing at the knot in her stomach with her fists. Zack had been good to her, better than he'd had to be, better than Jimmy had ever been. Even if Zack was an art dealer.

"Ruby Garcia?"

Ruby turned suddenly. The cop had walked in quietly and stood in the open doorway.

"Yes," Ruby said. Her stomach knotted more tightly.

"My name is Inspector Looper. Homicide." The cop paused a moment, looking Ruby up and down. "Are you all right?"

"Yeah. I guess so." It was hard for her to breathe. "I'm just shook up."

"Why don't you sit down?"

"Sure."

Ruby sat down and Looper sat down too, and they stared at each other intently. Ruby didn't like this game, but she didn't know any way not to play it. She could think of nothing to say because every thought in the world had left her head except the image of Zack all bloody on the gallery floor. The cop took out a notebook and put one of those little tape recorders on the table between them.

"Age?"

"Age?"

"Yes, how old are you? I'm starting with the easy ones first."

The cop smiled a little bit. Ruby didn't know what to think of her. Looper was maybe forty. She had fiery red hair and thick features. A face like somebody from the old neighborhood, only no one from her old neighborhood had ever been a cop.

"I'm twenty-three."

"And what was your relationship here?"

"I'm Jimmy's girlfriend. We live upstairs. In the loft apartment."

"Did you witness the shooting?

"No."

Ruby paused. The cop just looked at her, waiting.

"When I came into the gallery, Zack was lying on the floor. With Yvonne over him. He was already dead, I guess. And Jimmy was shot, too."

"Did you see Zack earlier today, before the shooting?"

"Yeah, he came over this morning. Him and Yvonne."

"Social call?"

"Not really. He and Jimmy were going to talk business. And Yvonne and I were supposed to go to this arts commission thing down in the Mission District—a mural project, for the Bernal Street Dwellings—it was planned months ago. But we get out there, and it turns out the whole thing's been canceled just a week ago."

Looper wrote in her notebook. "How long did you expect to be there?" she said.

"All day."

"So you came back early?"

Ruby hesitated. "Yeah, that's right."

"Yvonne was still with you when you came back?"

"Yeah. I dropped her off out by the alley entrance. She was in a rush to see if Zack was still around, and I had to go park the car."

"About how long was that?" Looper asked. "I mean, between when you dropped her off, and when you got here yourself?"

Ruby shrugged. "Hey, you know what it's like, parking around here. I dunno, maybe ten minutes, maybe fifteen. There's a place we park around the block, but it was taken so I had to go a block over. You know San Francisco, you're never gonna find a place to park."

The cop smiled a little bit again, and Ruby felt herself loosening up.

"So then?" the cop said.

"I walked down Minna Street, then up the, you know, that little walk up the side there. We always go in that way because that's where the work space is—and the stairs to the loft. Anyway, I saw the gallery door was opened, and I thought that was funny. It wasn't the kind of thing Yvonne did, leaving doors open behind her. Then I saw her purse on the ground. Coins and money, lipsticks, all this stuff, scattered all over the alley—and I ran inside."

"When you were outside, did you hear a gunshot?"

"No."

"Are you sure?"

"Yes. When I got inside, I heard Yvonne, though. She was in the main gallery, leaning over Zack, trying to bring him back to life, giving him CPR. There was blood on her hands, and on her blouse." Ruby started to shake. "Then I saw Jimmy. He was bleeding, and I ran to him."

"What did he say to you?"

"He said he was hurt. That I should call 911."

"Anything else?"

"No. Not really."

"Are you sure?"

Ruby put her head down, and the shaking got worse. Against her will she said, "He said Zack tried to kill him." She caught her breath, hard, against the sobs.

Looper handed her a tissue and waited until Ruby conquered the sobs.

"How long have you known James Tobin?"

"About a year. I'm a student, down at the Art Institute, and we met last spring, one night after this guest lecture he did. I moved in here about a month later. Jimmy had just broke up with his wife."

"I see."

Ruby stiffened. Something in Looper's tone reminded her of Aunt Imelda, prophesying eternal damnation because Ruby was living in sin. Ruby's lips tightened.

"I'm on a scholarship," she said defiantly. "I'm from the barrio. Jimmy let me stay here free. My folks don't have a lot of money."

"Does Tobin?"

"What does that mean?"

"Were there financial problems at the gallery?"

"Does everything come down to money? There's a man lying dead in the next room!"

"I know. That's why I'm here." Looper stared at Ruby until the girl lowered her eyes.

"After Jimmy asked you, did you dial 911?"

"No."

"Why not?"

"Because Yvonne went out of her skull," Ruby said angrily. "She started kicking Jimmy, and when I tried to stop her, she came at me."

"Why?"

"She was upset, I guess. And she was still mad at me for what had happened."

She looked at Looper and wondered if Yvonne had told the cop about her and Zack. Ruby felt herself begin to smile. She couldn't help herself. She felt proud, even a little smug, that Zack had wanted her. For a minute anyway she'd outclassed Yvonne, and that pride overpowered her shame, even now that he was dead. "You know, between me and Zack. She was pretty jealous about that."

"So you were sleeping with both men?"

"Yeah," Ruby said, and she said it with finality, as though this were the tiny bit of information she had been rushing toward all along, only just now realizing it. Then she felt the shame worse than ever as the cop bent her head, expressionless, making a quick little jot in her book.

THREE

❧ ❧

YVONNE BARNES

Granger tossed the sheaf of papers onto the desktop and swung his legs so that his feet bracketed the papers. Across the desk from him, Anita Looper already had her feet up.

"OK," he said. "So much for Tobin and Garcia. Now tell me about Mrs. Barnes."

Looper gestured with the remains of a poor-boy sandwich.

"Gimme a minute," she said around a mouthful of food. "I didn't get any lunch."

"My heart breaks," Granger said, but he grinned at her. He tucked his hands behind his head and inspected the ceiling, seeing not the dingy acoustical tiles, but beyond them to SOMA and the gallery scene.

He could see how a girl like Ruby Garcia could be drawn to that world, especially a kid from the barrio, a kid with talent. Being part of the scene, having a lover or two there, was like being on the inside looking out, maybe for the first time ever. The gallery world was supercharged with money, excitement, sexuality, an illusion made by colors on canvas, by the smell of perfume, of money, of excited bodies pressed close on opening night in chic little spots all over South of Market. The sleek debutantes of Pacific Heights, the purple-headed stoners of the Haight, the clown-suited boys of the lower Mission, and of course women dressed in black and black and more black. All of them roaming around to the clink of glasses, the rhythm of shuffling shoes and close-handed comments, under-the-breath whispers, oh-my-darlings and look-at-this. The Art Scene, written up by Caen in the *San Francisco Chronicle*, visited by channel two, cherished by the dilettantes and glitterati and raved-out punksters and politicos with wine glasses in their hands and a fever in their eyes.

Ruby Garcia had been seduced by all this. Hers was an easy case to figure. A harder one was Yvonne Barnes, the wife of the man who died on the gallery floor.

As the mayor's press secretary, Yvonne was a cool customer, used to tough situations. Granger had seen her on the courthouse steps, dealing with reporters. A beautiful woman, dark-skinned, fine-boned, able to deflect an unwanted question with the turn of her cheek. Icy and charming at the same time, then smiling suddenly, taking the conversation where she wanted it to go.

"OK," Granger said when it looked as though Looper could talk without choking. "So Garcia drops Mrs. Barnes off at the gallery. And then?"

Looper wiped her lips with a soggy napkin. "OK, she says she's in the alley. She turns the corner and bam, there's Tobin at the door. He's got a crowbar, and he's got some kind of yellow bundle."

Granger raised his eyebrows. "Yeah?"

"It's what the lady says." Looper reached sideways and snagged her notebook. She flipped it open, paged through it, and paused. "She said he saw her and went back inside. And locked the door."

Granger just grunted. He closed his eyes, trying to envision the scene. Looper would leave him a full copy of her report, and he knew from past experience that she was perceptive and thorough, but this personal question-and-answer helped so much.

"She had a key, but he double-locked the doors, so she says she had to hunt for the second key. Ended up turning her bag upside down and just leaving it."

"Why?" Granger said suddenly. "She comes down the alley, she sees Tobin, he's got a crowbar and a bundle. He goes back inside and locks the door. So why does she panic? Why not assume that Tobin hasn't seen her and just bang on the door? Why dump her purse?"

Looper shrugged. "You think I wasn't curious? But the lady's smooth, and she's got practice saying what she wants to say, not necessarily what you want to hear. And we know about the dumped purse—Garcia mentioned it, and I saw it when I got there."

"OK, hold it," Granger said. He made a note. "Great. All right, so she's dumped her purse. Then what?"

"Bang," Looper said simply. "Just one, from inside. I asked. She hears it, gets the door open, and runs inside."

"One gunshot. She's sure?"

"She's positive. Garcia's still parking the car. She runs inside. The door opens right into the main room, so she's inside, and she says she sees Tobin first. He's lying on the floor holding his leg and yelling that Zack tried to kill him. That would be Zachary Barnes, Counselor."

Granger looked at her, and Looper grinned. "Just want to make sure you're awake," she said.

"Yeah, I'm awake. So how did she describe him?"

Looper frowned and looked out the window. "You know, I was all set to see a show, Counselor. I mean, the woman started out in broadcasting, she's got experience with acting, all that sort of stuff. And for a moment I thought that maybe . . . but I don't know." Looper shook her head, as if annoyed with herself. "I don't know. She says she ran to him, tried CPR even though she knew it wouldn't work. Her clothes were bloody in the right places for that."

Granger picked up the write-up of the Garcia interview. "Garcia says that Mrs. Barnes started attacking Tobin."

"Yeah, that's a follow-up question. I interviewed Mrs. Barnes first. Anyway, she says she's positive that the man she saw in the alley was James Tobin, and that he wasn't wounded when she saw him. And when she realized she couldn't revive her husband, she called 911."

Looper put her feet on the floor. Sandwich crumbs spilled off her shirt, but she ignored them. "So Mrs. B. thinks that Tobin deliberately killed Mr. B. Says that Tobin was having money problems, art problems, and that he blamed it all on Zachary Barnes."

"And didn't mention that her husband had been sleeping with Tobin's girlfriend?"

Looper shook her head. "No, she didn't mention it. And like I said, I interviewed Garcia second. Another question for follow-up."

Granger swung his feet down from the desk. "OK, so here's what we've got. Tobin claims that Zachary Barnes tried to kill him, and that he shot Barnes in self-defense. We've got one body, shot in the throat."

"Forensics ought to be back to me about that, real soon."

"Good. We've got glass under the body and a broken glass coffee table. What's the story on that?"

"Tobin says it broke during their fight. That they fell on top of it, and it broke."

He nodded. "OK. What else?"

"The cash box," Looper said. "Lying upside down on the floor, like it got tossed aside. Unopened. Forensics is looking for prints."

"Right. And the crowbar?"

"Just inside the door. Pry marks on the outside of the door. They looked pretty fresh."

"And the yellow bundle? The one Mrs. Barnes said she saw Tobin holding, along with the crowbar?"

"Aha," Looper said, raising one finger. "The mysterious yellow bundle. I don't know. The criminalists couldn't find it at the scene, but they're still looking. Just like they're looking under Barnes's fingernails for skin samples, and checking hands for gunpowder."

Granger looked up with interest. "Whose hands? Tobin's and Barnes's?"

She nodded.

"But not Yvonne Barnes's or Garcia's?"

Inspector Looper looked at him.

"Jesus, Counselor," she said finally. "How small a limb do you want to go out on? And you want me to cut it off for you, or you want to do it yourself?"

Granger stood and walked to the window, trying to straighten out a cramp in his back.

"You didn't bag their hands," he muttered, almost to himself. "Jesus Christ."

"Yeah, and so what? You get a shooter on a bus, you gonna bag everyone's hands just in case the guy with the smoking gun isn't the guy with the smoking gun? Gimme a break, Counselor."

Looper sounded angry, defensive. She knew she'd made a mistake. It was a crucial piece of police work, something that should have been totally routine—so routine that not doing it could, perhaps, constitute "reasonable doubt"—especially these days, when reasonable doubt seemed to lurk around every corner. But there was no help for it now, Granger thought, and no sense in losing her good will over it.

"Don't hassle me, Inspector," he said. "You're leading up to telling me that Tobin shot himself in the leg."

Looper shrugged. "I asked Forensics to look at Tobin's wound. You got a problem with that? It's been known to happen, Counselor."

"Yeah, maybe, but not to people like James Tobin."

"Really? Why not?" Looper said, with more than a touch of belligerence.

Granger turned to her, curious. "Because he's one of the golden boys, Inspector. I don't think that man's ever been seriously hurt for a moment in his life. That's why those paintings of his are shallow, and that's why nobody's buying them, or him, anymore."

"My my," Looper said, making her eyes wide. "So now you're an art critic, too?"

Granger ignored her. "I don't think James Tobin has the guts to shoot himself, any more than he has the guts to confront real social issues, or the guts to take the blame himself for what's happened to his career." He paused. "Have you got a problem with him, Inspector? Because if you do, I want to know about it right now. This case is sticky enough without that."

Looper was saved from answering by the phone. Granger picked it up, said his name, and listened for a moment, frowning.

"I have no comment," he said, slamming it down.

Looper rose, gathering her stuff. "TV or radio?" she said.

"Wire service," Granger replied sourly. "Where are you headed, Inspector?"

"SF General. I told Tobin I'd be back to interview him, and I think I've let him stew long enough." She favored Granger with her best grin. "You wanna come, Counselor?"

Granger declined and watched her leave. Five minutes later he also left, planning to salvage what he could of his wrecked Sunday with his daughter. The sound of his door closing echoed in the empty building.

FOUR

∼ ∽

A SHOT IN THE LEG

G ranger sat alone, ignoring the Monday morning office noises filtering through the closed door and the Monday morning street noises filtering through the open window. The weekend's sunshine had disappeared into San Francisco's more typical gray morning fog.

Anita Looper had arrested James Tobin yesterday for the murder of Zachary Barnes. The *Ten O'Clock News* on KTVU had featured her beaming her wolf grin into the camera and saying, "He told me he shot himself in the leg. Anybody crazy enough to do that, well, I just had to take him downtown."

KTVU may have been the first on the scene, but the line was picked up and rebroadcast on every TV and radio station in the city. It had bounced up from the front page of Granger's *San Francisco Chronicle* that morning and assaulted him twice on the car radio on his way into work.

Cynthia Charleston, Tobin's newly hired attorney, had a field day with the line. She, too, covered the airwaves and the newsprint this summer morning. Smart, attractive, glossy, expensive, and totally ruthless, Granger had butted heads with her before and respected her professionalism while privately wondering if the woman ever relaxed.

"Crazy? I didn't know the SFPD was hiring psychologists as cops," Charleston had told the press. "But their charges have about as much merit as their psychology."

Charleston had jumped the gun, though. Tobin had been arrested, but not yet charged. That was Granger's task this fine San Francisco morning. It was not a choice he'd be allowed to make by himself.

There were times, he thought, when the idea of private practice seemed really appealing.

Granger leaned forward and pushed a button on his tape deck. Once again his small office filled with the voices of James Tobin and Anita Looper and, behind them, the bustle of SF General's emergency room. Granger listened intently, leaned back, and closed his eyes.

TOBIN: The paintings. My paintings. They were stolen from the gallery. In February.

LOOPER: What's that have to do with it?

TOBIN: Like I said, Zack had a scheme going with the insurance. He was trying to frame me up on it, but I wouldn't go along. That's why he called the meeting this morning. I'm telling you, Zack brought the gun. Zack tried to kill me in cold blood. That man had a lot of people fooled.

Tobin sounded urgent, innocent, appalled—like someone who had just discovered that his old friend was a liar. Granger didn't trust him for a moment.

LOOPER: OK, but I got some confusion here. Yvonne says she saw you in the alleyway, just a few minutes before she got inside. She says she saw you run in the back door. That you locked it behind you.

TOBIN: She's mistaken.

LOOPER: She says she saw you very clearly.

TOBIN: That's not true. I was on lying on the floor, bleeding, when she came in the gallery. That's the way it happened.

LOOPER: She says she saw you outside the gallery, with a crowbar in your hand.

TOBIN: A crowbar? What would I be doing with a crowbar?

LOOPER: You tell me. I noticed some jimmy marks on the back door.

TOBIN: Those happened months ago. The break-in I was telling you about, when my paintings were stolen.

LOOPER: How about the cash box?

TOBIN: The cash box? I'm sorry. I don't understand.

Granger put the tape on pause while he flipped through the file and pulled out a large photograph of the gallery. He found the cash box and, with his finger, traced an aimless path from it to Barnes's body and back again as his other hand pushed the "play" button again.

LOOPER: It was on the floor. Upside down. Next to Zack's body. How did it get there?

TOBIN: It must have happened during our struggle.

LOOPER: Earlier, you told me it was kept in the drawer. How did it get on the ground?

TOBIN: I don't know.

LOOPER: Looks like somebody was trying to stage a break-in. That somebody wanted to make it look like Zack had been killed by an intruder. During a robbery. Isn't that what you were thinking, to make it look like a robbery?

Granger stopped the tape, backed it up, and listened again. Something in Looper's voice bothered him, something beyond her normal abrasiveness. He frowned and listened a third time, but couldn't put his finger on it, not precisely. It nagged at him, and he pushed it toward the back of his mind where his subconscious could question and poke at it and, with luck, solve this minor puzzle. He sat back to listen to the rest of the tape.

TOBIN: No.

LOOPER: That's nice to hear. But it's easy to think, just looking things over, that maybe you were caught in your own scheme. You had just killed Zack, you were getting ready to leave. Then maybe the dead man's wife shows up in the alley, and you run back inside.

TOBIN: I was never in that alley.

LOOPER: Let me explain something. At the crime scene, one of my people put some plastic bags over the hands of the victim. One bag for each hand. If I'm right, Officer Zuckerman did the same thing to you, just before they took you off in the ambulance.

TOBIN: Yeah.

LOOPER: Do you know what those bags are for?

TOBIN: Fingerprints?

LOOPER: No. There's a chemical inside. Detects gunshot residue. If Barnes fired a gun this morning, if he pulled the trigger, there will be residue on his hands.

For a moment Granger heard only the background ER noises, then a small sound that might, perhaps, have been a sob.

TOBIN: I lied.

LOOPER: What?

TOBIN: I lied. What I told you before wasn't true. At least not all of it. I was so scared. I thought no one would believe me.

LOOPER: Tell me what happened.

TOBIN: Zack and I were having problems in our business, that part is true. But I had no idea he was so desperate. He brought a gun to our meeting, like I said, and he pointed it right at me. I tried to grab the gun out of his hand, and it went off. It happened so fast, I didn't know what to think. I couldn't believe he was dead. I tried to stop the bleeding. There was nothing I could do.

LOOPER: I see. And your leg—how did that happen?

TOBIN: I thought no one would believe my story. I panicked. I wanted it to look more like self-defense. So I shot myself in the leg.

LOOPER: You shot your own self in the leg?

TOBIN: It sounds insane, I admit, but I held the barrel close so it would only graze.

There was a pause, filled with the distant sounds of an ambulance siren and someone shouting incoherently. Then Tobin's voice said urgently, "I'm telling the truth. You'll see."

LOOPER: What kind of problems were you and Zack having? What was the argument?

TOBIN: I think I better see a lawyer.

LOOPER: Yes, I think you better.

The tape went dead, and Granger leaned back in his chair. Each time he listened to it, his gut reaction was the same. He guessed that Looper had felt it too, hearing it all in person. Tobin was lying. He was guilty as hell.

But of what? Manslaughter would be easy to go for. In fact, it was probably what Tobin and Charleston were praying for. Heat of the moment, self-defense, all that—Tobin would be out in record time and more famous than ever. But Wong and Mayor McKinney were pushing for murder one and so was every black leader in the city. After the recent Southern California celebrity murder trials, after Rodney King and OJ Simpson, any inter-racial crime was big news, big politics. Hell, according to KCBS Radio this morning, even the local, seldom-seen neo-Nazis had rung in, demanding that Tobin be freed immediately. If nothing else, the support of that group should make the artist and his attorney profoundly uncomfortable.

Something else rode on this case, and a few of the reporters were savvy enough to make the connection. Wong was a good DA, but she was also a politician, conscious of image. She'd gotten elected by a coalition of minority liberals and white conservatives, appealing with her ethnicity on one hand and by hard-nosing the crime issue on the other. The Hayes Valley fiasco had hurt her with both constituencies, and she was smart enough to realize that this case could make up some of that ground—if it went her way. And Granger was smart enough to realize that if he lost this case Wong would save her political hide by sacrificing his. After all, he might be one of the city's leading prosecutors, but in the long run he was just a flunky, an expendable cog in San Francisco's political wheel.

In the meantime, Mayor McKinney had put Yvonne Barnes, his press secretary, on "compassionate leave"—an unrequested leave, if cafeteria gossip was accurate, and it usually was. This might be very embarrassing for the mayor, committed as he was to being tough on crime in this, one of the country's most liberal cities. Even Yvonne Barnes, adroit as she was at deflecting unwanted questions, had had to toe a few of his lines in the recent past. She was on record, for example, as disapproving of affirmative action, and her background revealed nothing about her opinion of such political hot potatoes as abortion or family values. Cafeteria gossip portrayed Mrs. Barnes as very cool, very tough, and very ambitious.

Granger tried to put politics aside and concentrate on the evidence. Hard facts, hard conclusions, would make his case. He had to prove the charges beyond a reasonable doubt while Tobin and Charleston had only to evoke that shadow, had only to create in the mind of one juror a small, niggling feeling of uncertainty.

And what, really, did the prosecution have? A handful of possible motives: money, jealousy over the Garcia girl, an argument about the handling of Tobin's career. But none of these motives really stood out. There had to be something else.

In the end, as in most self-defense cases, it would come down to whether or not the prosecution could present enough evidence to force the accused onto the stand. The defendant had no obligation to testify, of course, but if the evidence was strong enough, the jury expected to hear an explanation. Then it was between the prosecutor and the accused.

To win that battle, Granger needed to know more. About the crime itself, yes, but also about Tobin. The artist had been visible enough these last years. Profiled in the paper, in a magazine, on the television news. A good-looking man with an aw-shucks smile, but there was a darkness there, too. He had the ability to be self-deprecating one minute, full of wild vision the next. A real chameleon.

A guy like that could be trouble on the witness stand. He could disarm you. Worse, he could charm the jury and leave you looking like a fool.

Wong wanted a decision now. The law said they could only hold Tobin for forty-eight hours without charging him, which gave them a solid day left. But politics spoke louder than the statute books. Another twenty-four hours of Cynthia Charleston's public sniping would leave everyone, from the mayor on down, in the middle of a full-fledged crisis. "We don't want to look indecisive," Wong had said flatly, in her "won't brook discussion" tone of voice.

"You don't want to look wrong, either," Granger had retorted, but it hadn't helped.

In the end, he knew he'd go with his gut reaction. Tobin was guilty—guilty of premeditated murder, murder in the first degree, guilty as hell. Now all he had to do was prove it.

FIVE

～ ～

JOSALYN WILLIAMS

I'm giving you Williams," Wong had said coolly. "She's good, and you'll need the help. Get a couple of clerks, too. I don't want any technicalities on this one, Granger." With that, the district attorney had turned around, dismissing him. But not, Granger knew, dismissing the case. She'd be on the phone to Mayor McKinney and Patti Cronen, his interim press secretary. Well, let them work the publicity angles, Granger thought as he left the DA's office. Sterling Granger, Josalyn Williams, and two clerks would make an adequate team. It would have to.

Josalyn was still out wrapping up the Spangler case. Granger left a message in her box and headed back to his office, momentarily filled with envy. Spangler was neat and easy: the defendant, an unemployed waiter, had killed his wife, a topless dancer, on the busiest intersection in North Beach, at the height of tourist season, in front of fifteen delegates to the Forensic Scientists of America's national convention. Nine of the delegates had been sober, and of those, three had actually seen the crime take place.

It was almost noon. Granger picked up a sandwich at the cafeteria and took it back to his desk. He turned on his computer and began a database search. He listed "Tobin" and "Barnes" as

31

the key words, and wasn't surprised when the computer gave him a preliminary hit list of more than 300 citations. Laboriously, sandwich in hand, he started to refine his search strings.

Half an hour later, he had refined the list to twenty major hits. He finished his sandwich just as someone knocked on his door, and Josalyn Williams stuck her head in.

"Say 'way to go, girl,'" she demanded.

Granger grinned. He didn't know Josalyn very well, but he liked what he did know. "Way to go, girl," he said obligingly. "The Spangler verdict come in?"

"Yeah." Without invitation, she slid into the visitor's chair and rummaged in her briefcase. "We got him, but what do you expect, you murder your old lady on Columbus and Broadway, 7:15 on a Saturday night in front of every damned tourist in Northern California? I could have got him for littering, too, if I'd wanted to." She pulled a sandwich from her briefcase and centered it before her, then gave Granger a wide look.

"Wong says I'm your co-counsel on the Tobin case," she said flatly. "That OK with you?"

Granger stared back at her. A year ago, it might not have been OK with him, but perhaps he'd changed. Or perhaps Josalyn had. Last summer she'd been cocky and abrasive and ambitious, just out of law school, the bar exam successfully behind her, hungry and eager and ready to take on the world. The horrible, unceasing caseload of a DA's office had beaten much of the cockiness out of her without diminishing her energy or her competence, and Granger liked the results. Her ambition might be a problem, but it meant he could saddle her with some of the tasks that he hated, and she loved. Like dealing with the press.

He also liked the package. Josalyn Williams was petite, with skin the color of cinnamon and chiseled, North African features. She wore her hair in sleek cornrows that looked both stylish and professional. Wong had been right: Josalyn would be an asset to his team, and not only because of her race.

"Yeah, it's OK with me," he said, and turned the computer monitor around so that she could see it. "I just finished a media search. Here's the results."

"So what do we really have?" Williams said, half an hour later. The media information hadn't added a lot: gallery openings, reviews, magazine write-ups. Nothing really juicy, no prior convictions on Tobin, Garcia, or either Barnes.

The best things they had found were reviews of Tobin's show last February. The snootier art critics had been sniping at Tobin for years, but with this last opening, they let him have it with both barrels. No longer afraid, Granger guessed, of losing their own credibility by attacking an artist of such popularity. "Antiseptic agony for the walls of the wealthy," according to *Art World* magazine, which went on to assure its readers that antiseptic agony was now hopelessly trite. *The Examiner's* critic called Tobin's recent work "the triumph of kitsch over content." Even though Granger disliked the man's work, the reviews made him flinch.

In addition, the coroner's office had delivered a bag containing the contents of Zachary Barnes's pockets, and the attorneys had gone through it. A wallet with money, cards, and photographs; two key rings, one heavy with keys, one with only a Porsche key on it; a laundered, monogrammed handkerchief; and the real prize, a computer disk. It held a mailing list and a bunch of bookkeeping files, but near the end of the listing Granger found something called RUBY.LTR. They brought it up on the screen, but it held only a salutation and the first two enticing lines of a letter:

Dear Ruby Red,
    After what happened last night, and the unexpected passion between us, I find myself struggling for words and remembering your body. If I were to speak the truth. . . .

"So where's the rest of it?" Josalyn demanded, and Granger only shrugged and added that to the list he was compiling of unanswered questions, missing evidence, and the like.

He took the disk from the computer and slid it into an envelope. "We'll have the computer wizards check this stuff out. Barnes might have a complete version on his hard drive," he said. "In the meantime, we've got another problem." He reached into his desk drawer and brought up transcripts of the initial interviews with Ruby Garcia and Yvonne Barnes.

"I want you to read these, first thing. Read Garcia first, then Barnes. There are some questions here, some stuff Barnes doesn't mention that she should have."

"OK." Josalyn took the papers. "And then?"

"I want you to interview Yvonne Barnes."

Josalyn Williams looked at him skeptically. "Major witness in the case? Political hot potato? Why me, Granger? That ought to be the lead attorney's job, and as far as I know, I'm not."

"That's right, you're not," Granger said. "But Barnes is a major witness, and I want to keep her cooperative. There are enough questions about her interview that I think maybe she's not being entirely open. I don't want to give her any excuse to clam up on us, or to hold anything back." He paused, looking at Josalyn calmly. "I think she'll talk more easily to you. You're young, you're a woman."

"And I'm black," Josalyn said, making it a challenge.

"And you're black," Granger agreed. "Do you have a problem with that?"

Josalyn stared at him and then began to laugh. Granger, immensely relieved, laughed with her.

"OK, boss," she said. "I'll interview the Ice Queen. What else?"

"The gun," Granger said immediately.

"The gun?" Josalyn echoed, balling up her sandwich wrappings. She made a perfect three-point shot into the garbage can on the far side of his desk. Granger ignored it.

"The gun was registered to Daryl Barnes."

"Daryl? I thought the deceased's name was Zachary."

"His cousin. A security guard for Tiffany's."

Josalyn pursed her lips and whistled silently. "What was Tobin doing with it?"

"That's the question. If Tobin's supposed to have planned this murder, then how'd he get his hands on that gun? According to police personnel, Daryl Barnes took an eight-month unpaid leave to do volunteer work in Central Africa. Something his church put together. He's been gone for four months."

Josalyn thought about this. "Would he have given his gun to Tobin? Did he even know Tobin?"

"I don't know," Granger said. "But I'd guess he did, if Daryl had anything to do with his cousin. Check it out?"

"Sure thing." Josalyn made a note. "He must have a house sitter, or maybe he rented his place out until he comes back. I'll see what I can find."

"Then there's the matter of motive," Granger said. "When Looper pressed him in the hospital, Tobin said Zack tried to kill him to cover up an insurance scam. Regarding some paintings that were stolen from the gallery back in February."

"He's just spinning stories," Josalyn offered, speculatively. "Looking for a way to blame it on the other guy."

"We checked into it. There was a theft at the gallery. And there was an insurance claim."

Josalyn cocked her head. "And . . ."

"Tobin says he's got a corroborating witness, some kid named Simon Lee. Looper's trying to track him down, but he's hard to find."

"How important is he?" Josalyn asked.

Granger frowned. "Very. The way I see it is I've got two major problems with murder one. First, I need a stronger motive because the ones we have just don't sit right with me. And second, I need to see that gun in Tobin's hands, I need to know how it got there, and why, and when. Unless I have both those, I don't think I'm going to get a jury to buy murder one. And if they don't, then James Tobin is going to walk."

SIX

❧ ❧

SIMON LEE

imon Lee slept on a futon in the back bedroom of a third-story walk-up on lower Haight Street. He didn't hear the knocking at first. It took a while for the sound to penetrate. But when it did, he sat bolt upright, and he flashed that he shouldn't open the door. Ruby would say that a flash like that was a premonition, maybe, but most likely it was just his roommate and his roommate's girlfriend. Out all night zoning through the rave clubs in South of Market, with all those hipster kids hugging each other, dripping with love. Now they were back, probably after a long roam around town, thinking they had lost the key to the apartment. But really that key was just buried down in the pocket of What's-her-name's print dress. Or in her bra, or her shoe, or some damned place.

Even so, he kept the chain linked and just cracked the door, peeping down the hall. It was a woman with flame crazy red hair.

"Yeah?"

"I'm looking for a young man named Simon Lee," said the redhead. "That you?"

The sleep was leaving him, and he knew better than to answer that one straight out.

"Who can I say is calling?"

"The police," she said, and showed her badge. "I'm just look-ing for some information."

"I'll go get him," he said. He tried to shut the door, but the lady cop stuck her foot inside.

"Will you let me in?"

"Sure," he said. "I need to shut the door to unhook the chain."

"Are you Simon Lee?"

He didn't answer the question, but rather gestured down to his naked legs. "Let me put on my pants."

Simon gave her his best puppy dog look, eye-to-eye, and he could see she didn't trust him but also that she didn't have much choice unless she wanted to push the door in. She withdrew her foot, and he shut the door and hurried down the hall. He put on his pants and clambered down the fire escape. He hopped on his Kawasaki—there in the alley, with the bedroll still tied on—and wailed out in the streets while that lady cop outside his door just waited around.

It wasn't the thing to do, Simon realized as he drove away; it wasn't smart at all. But when he first came to the city, three years ago, it had been as a runaway, and his old man in Florida had sent the cops after him. Because he looked younger than he was, and they had his picture on file down at Social Services, or someplace, he kept having the same kind of trouble. So his first impulse had been to ditch.

Simon rode out into the Richmond district, taking Balboa Street past all those little houses that looked as though they were made of sand, then stopped in a hamburger joint to get some breakfast. He was still foggy-headed from the night before and hungry as hell, cursing himself because he had a baby face and a jerk for a father who wouldn't leave him alone, not even now that he was going on twenty-one.

While waiting for his burger, he rummaged through a stack of old newspapers some customers had left behind. Nobody had bothered to sort them, or to toss the old ones out, so he came up with one from last Sunday. He'd been gone a few days, and it didn't much matter to him anyway which one he read.

He was settling down to his burger when he happened to glance at the lower corner of the front page. His eyes caught a picture of Zachary Barnes, then a headline that made his heart feel like a big drum in his chest: GALLERY OWNER SHOT DEAD.

The article told what he had missed while he was out of town. How Zachary was killed beneath all those paintings. Found lying there in a big, colorful pool of blood. And now James Tobin was being held for murder.

This freaked Simon, freaked him bad. He wondered what the police really wanted to talk to him about. It didn't matter, he told himself, because he really didn't know anything. He just worked at the gallery. He didn't know anything about Zack and Tobin and their crazy lives.

Tobin had hired him off the streets, and the artist had taken him under his wing in some ways. That had been just after Simon had quit his job doing motorcycle delivery, skidding like a maniac on one of those two-stroke aluminum death machines, taking little packages of paper and whatnot all over town for lawyers and other assholes.

That scene had gotten old, and working with Tobin had its kicks. Simon stretched canvas for him and pushed brooms and washed paint from brushes. Though Zack hadn't been too crazy about him at first, after a while the guy had warmed up and given him this and that to do around the gallery.

Then there was Ruby. Tobin's girl. She was closer to Simon's age, but she had a thing for the older guys. Even so, they got to be friends. Getting silly in the back room. Walking down those SOMA streets through that crazy traffic, the white noise blasting in their ears. She'd told him a few things about Zack and Tobin. He'd learned a few more on his own.

It was fierce stuff, the gallery, at least the way those two did it. Like there was an electric moon casting its light all over everything.

He had to admit that it got him off, especially the way it seemed everybody in town wanted to stand inside that glow, and there he was, Simon Lee, a cool shadow leaning against the wall.

Now everything had exploded. Zack was dead, and Tobin was in jail.

The cops had probably talked to Ruby by now, and maybe she could tell him what to do. There was no answer at her place, just the machine with Tobin's voice on it, and he didn't want to leave a message. He didn't want to go back to his apartment, so when it got dark he rode out to Ocean Beach. The city was building a new sea wall, and he unrolled his bedroll behind a cement mixer the workers had left parked in the sand.

It was a miserable night, partly because of the cold, but also because he kept thinking about Tobin and Ruby and Zack, the whole scene at the gallery, trying to figure out what had happened.

Things had just gotten too lively, he guessed. Like one of his old man's crazy schemes back in Florida. Always drinking beer and lifting cars. Talking baseball in between. Except with these guys it was cabernet and Renoir, or some such thing. And instead of his mother hanging out, it was Ruby. Flipping back and forth between Tobin and Zack. With himself caught in between.

When you got down to it, every place was the same damned swamp. Simon didn't like to think so, but he guessed it was true.

And what was he going to do for work now, with the gallery closed? They'd screwed everything up good, those guys, with their fooling around.

In the morning, Simon had nowhere to go, so he headed for the Crazy-Z.

He spent a few dollars drinking, and while he did he thought more about Ruby. One day, when they were alone in the gallery, he'd tried to put the moves on her. She'd just given him a big blank face, like she didn't understand, and he'd felt like an idiot. She was sleeping with Tobin, but she was all hung up on Zack and those two were all she wanted to talk about. He tried to let it go, but sometimes it still got to him, the way she didn't seem to really see him. Then about two weeks ago Zack had asked him to come over to deliver some letter he'd written to Ruby. Use a stamp, Simon had thought, but he'd agreed to it anyway. Later, though, his jealousy got to him. When he ran into Tobin on the way downstairs, Simon told him about it, just for spite. Then Tobin went up there and gave it to Ruby pretty good.

Simon still felt bad. He didn't want Ruby to know he'd double-crossed her the way he did.

After draining the last of his beer, Simon went back to his apartment. He didn't know what else to do, and he just had to get some real sleep or he would drop. His roommate and What's-her-name told him the lady cop had been by a second time. Then the two of them went out again, raving the town, all dressed up in their hippie beads and rose-colored glasses.

Simon sat in the chair by the window, watching the streets. Just as he decided the cop had given up for the day and that it was safe for him to sleep, he saw that wild shock of red hair coming toward his building. He waited until he heard her clumping up the stairs and then he climbed out the window again and headed back to the Crazy-Z.

Seven

~ ~

Ruby at the Loft

On the other side of town, Ruby Garcia had agreed to meet with Granger. She was still living in Tobin's place, in the loft apartment above the Barnes Gallery in South of Market. The neighborhood was one of the oldest in the city, dating back to the 1870s. It had been called South Park then, laid out by a group of anti-abolitionists who built stately houses and staffed them with Chinese servants. Those old houses were gone now, and the neighborhood was filled with decaying industrial, converted warehouses with lofts upstairs and four lanes of traffic out front.

Upstairs, in Tobin's loft, the noise from that traffic seemed distant. Ruby Garcia sat on a stool across from Granger, regarding him warily. She had obviously been packing; half-filled boxes and bags lay against the walls.

"Why are you going after Jimmy?" she asked. "Can't you see it was self-defense?"

"I wish I could," he said.

"Cynthia Charleston, Jimmy's attorney, she told me I didn't have to talk to you if I didn't want. She said I have no obligation to cooperate. That I can cut this off any time I please."

"Legally, that's true. I appreciate your taking the time."

43

"I figure the truth can only help Jimmy." Her voice was tentative, as if she didn't quite believe what she said. "That's why I'm talking to you."

"Yes," Granger said politely, and nothing more. Like most police officers, he knew that the best way to get someone to talk was to say nothing at all. Most people felt an almost desperate need to fill a silence, and he very much wanted to hear what she had to say. If Charleston had warned her about this meeting, then Ruby must have her own, very strong reasons to talk to him.

She wore a bright T-shirt and pair of shorts, both stained with paint. On all sides they were surrounded by paintings, some of them still in progress.

"That painting behind you, it's one of Tobin's?" Granger asked.

He knew that it was and waited for her reaction. The painting was something of a departure for Tobin, less realistic than his usual work. It showed a man rendered from several angles, in the style of the cubists. Receding in the background was another figure, on a hilltop, laughing.

"Yeah. He calls it *Self-Portrait*. It's part of that series *The World Is Burning*. It was a big change in direction for him. Harsher colors, darker forms, more haunted."

"I see."

"It was his best stuff," she said flatly.

"*The World Is Burning*? Isn't that the series that debuted last winter? I heard they were all stolen."

Ruby shook her head; dark, unruly curls bounced along her shoulders. "Not all of them. He'd brought a couple up to the loft, just the day before. That was one."

"Do you mind if I ask you a couple of questions about the theft?" Granger said casually, as though he were just filling time, as though the subject wasn't vitally interesting to him.

Ruby shrugged, taking the bait. "All right. But I don't really know much about it."

"You were here when it happened, weren't you?"

"Yeah. But I didn't see anything. Nobody did. We came down one morning, and somebody had broken in. They used a straight razor to cut the paintings right out of their frames. Rolled 'em up and walked right out the door, I guess."

Granger looked puzzled. "Wasn't there an alarm system? I thought I saw some company's sticker downstairs, on the front door."

"Yeah, but it's not so great. Sometimes there are false alarms, other times it won't ring at all." She brought up her legs so that she sat cross-legged on the stool, looking suddenly like a vulnerable girl.

"Was anything else taken?"

"No," she said.

Granger frowned again. "Why would someone steal Tobin's artwork? I mean, it's not like a TV set, or jewelry. It wouldn't be easy to fence. Besides, how much would it be worth?"

"It's worth a lot," Ruby retorted. "Those paintings, Zack had stickers on them, you know. The cheapest was five thousand dollars. Yeah, it may not be a Sony or shit like that, but a real collector, someone who knows modern art, they'd pay a lot for an original Tobin."

"OK," Granger said. "I'll take your word for it. You know more about it than I do. But there was insurance, wasn't there?"

Ruby grimaced. "I guess. But it takes time, you know, all that kinda stuff. I don't know what happened to the money, or even if they sent it yet, or what." She grabbed her ankle and bent forward over it. "Listen, see, Jimmy, he said I'm an artist, and I gotta pay attention to that. I mean, not get all tied up with gallery stuff and all the other shit, cause an artist's gotta make art, no matter what."

"Gallery stuff?" Granger echoed.

"Oh, yeah," Ruby said intently. "Listen, I know I wasn't supposed to pay attention, but everybody knows about it, how gallery owners, and dealers and stuff, they just rip off artists. I mean, you hang around at the Institute, you hear all kinds of stories. Owners, jeez, I mean, like they tell you all this stuff they're gonna do for you, like hang your stuff out front, or in a special place. Or how they're gonna guarantee you money. I mean, they'll say anything just to get you to sign an agreement."

"An agreement?"

"Yeah, a consignment agreement," Ruby said. "That's what happens with artists and dealers or galleries. You sign this agreement that says that you'll let this guy handle your artwork, and they're supposed to do all this stuff in return, but they don't gotta, you know."

"They don't?" Granger said. "But the agreement."

"Oh, yeah, sure," Ruby said sarcastically. She gestured with her free hand, the other still clutching her ankle. "What you gonna do, sue? Where you gonna get the money to do that, especially if the dealer won't pay you? And that's what a lot of them do, you know. They sell your stuff and don't pay you for it until you make a real stink. Or there was this one guy around here, he'd start a gallery, sign up a bunch of artists, sell their stuff, then he'd file for bankruptcy and the artists would never see a dime." She bent forward.

"And you know what?" she demanded in a large whisper.

Granger also bent forward, shaking his head.

"His brother would go buy the gallery assets from the bankruptcy judge, you know? Like they were partners." She sat back. "Dealers are scum," she said with finality.

Granger looked fascinated. In fact, he really was. "What about Zack Barnes?" he said. "Was he scum, too?"

Ruby, looking suddenly nervous, dropped her legs. "No. Not really," she muttered.

"Tobin said he and Zack were partners."

Ruby's mouth twisted. "Naw, they weren't. Not like real business partners, they weren't."

"Then I'm confused," Granger said. "What was their relationship? Do you know?"

Ruby said she did, or at least she knew part of the story. Barnes and Tobin had met at college in Santa Barbara, Barnes the transplanted Berkeley boy from the upper-middle class background, Tobin a military brat whose longest stay, growing up, had been in New Orleans. Both interested in art, both ready to shock their families by taking up careers that would almost guarantee financial disaster and, together, rising above that gloomy prediction. Tobin's artwork had hit at just the right time, and Barnes's genius for promotion had made sure the hit stuck. For more than ten years, the two seemed to represent the ideal relationship between best-selling artist and best-selling dealer.

"But they were never partners," Ruby said positively. "They always had a consignment agreement."

"What about recently?" Granger said. "Weren't there some financial problems?"

"No," Ruby said. "People liked Jimmy's work. Yeah, his stuff was selling. No problem."

Granger didn't respond. He had taken a preliminary look at the bookkeeping files on Barnes's disk, files indicating that, financially, matters between him and Tobin were pretty desperate.

Then along came a thief to steal Tobin's paintings, and an insurance payoff to save the day.

"You were here the night the paintings were stolen, right?"

Any friendliness on Ruby's part disappeared, replaced by distrust. "I already told you, I was in bed. What's this gotta do with Zack's murder?"

"I'm just curious. Where was Tobin?"

"He was in bed too. He was on his side, and I was on mine. At least at first."

"Then what happened?"

"Do you really want to know?"

She gave him a sly smile. Ruby was playing games, he realized. He stood and sauntered over to a pile of half-finished canvases. Unlike Tobin's, these were obviously rough, the work of a talented beginner. Color and energy fairly vibrated off the canvas.

"Yours?" Granger said. "I like them."

"Yeah, that and a buck will get you a coffee," she said, but she'd stopped smiling. "You gonna talk about my artwork? Or the theft? Or you gonna talk about Zack?"

He turned back to her.

"You think Jimmy's innocent?"

"I know he is."

"Then what happened downstairs the day Zack died?"

"Like Jimmy said. It was self-defense." Her voice rose, as if for emphasis.

"You were fond of Zack, weren't you?"

"This is hard for me to talk about," she said, almost whispering. "Jimmy wasn't a perfect person, you know, but that didn't make it right for me to go and sleep with his partner. It's just like my mom used to say, I'm always only thinking of myself. If it hadn't been for me, none of this would've happened. Zachary would still be alive. Jimmy wouldn't be in jail. And Yvonne would still have a husband."

Granger waited in silence. When she didn't go on, he said, "Did Jimmy ever find out about the affair?"

Another long silence, before she said, "Zachary wrote me a long note after we slept together. Simon Lee, the gallery assistant, had just delivered it to me when Jimmy came in and took it."

Granger looked surprised. "Did Jimmy usually take your mail?"

She shrugged and looked away. After a moment, Granger said, "What did Jimmy do then?"

"He got mad. I only got to read the top, you know, just a little bit." She bit her lip, then looked at him sideways. "Charleston said that you had a copy. From Zack's computer. And you were going to use it in your case."

"We might. If it's relevant." Granger took a moment to thank his stars that Charleston already knew that they had the whole letter.

"Tell me, Ruby, when Tobin found out about you and Zack, what else did he do?"

"Nothing."

"Did he yell?"

"A little."

"What did he say?"

"I don't remember."

"Did he hit you?"

"He didn't hurt me." But she winced as she said it, and her hand moved, as if unconsciously, to massage her ribs.

"Did you hear him threaten Zack?"

"No."

"What else did he say?"

"Nothing. It wasn't a big deal, I told you."

"Not a big deal?"

"No!"

Granger did not believe her. Ruby had been on the verge of letting go her loyalty to Tobin, but she couldn't take that final step.

"Ruby, the circumstantial evidence says your boyfriend killed Zachary Barnes. Can you show me otherwise?"

She did not answer. Instead, she reached down and held her ankle.

"I don't want to prosecute an innocent man," Granger said.

Ruby shrugged. "If I knew something, I would tell you."

"How about the murder weapon? You ever see either man with a gun?"

She met him straight on with those brown eyes of hers, a little tearful, a little smug. She had let go of her ankle, and the leg was swinging now as though the rocking of her body on that stool was supposed to be some kind of answer in itself.

"The murder weapon was registered to Daryl Barnes, Zachary's cousin," Granger said. "Did Tobin have access to that man's house, or to his guns?"

"Please leave me alone. I don't want to talk anymore."

"Did your boyfriend have access to any gun?"

"I said *leave me alone*," she said angrily, and buried her face in her hands. Her shoulders shook.

Granger let out his breath and put his hand on her shoulder. She didn't look at him, but she didn't shrug him away either. He kept his hand there for a minute, then he put his business card on the table.

"Call me when you're ready," he said.

On the way out, he happened to notice Tobin's painting again, the self-portrait. He figured Tobin had started hanging out with Ruby because she was attractive, yes, but also because she was younger. Maybe he thought he could manipulate her. She hadn't been so easy, though, and that must have bothered him, in the same way that the many-sided man in the self-portrait seemed bothered by that laughter from the tiny figure on the hill.

EIGHT

❧ ❧

THE CRAZY-Z

Two days later, Looper was still in pursuit of Simon Lee. She had taken over a booth at the back end of the Crazy-Z. It was a good vantage point. She could see the television up over the bar. She could see the front door that swung open to Valencia Street. Better yet, she could see without being seen, and she had hidden her unruly red hair under a black beret. She wasn't much worried about being recognized at first glance, at least not by Simon Lee.

She'd figured out on the first visit that he was jumping out the back window and revving away on his motorcycle. A couple more, and she'd figured out where in the neighborhood he was going.

Here, to the Crazy-Z, where he probably guessed the scene was too weird for cops to go, with lesbians and gays and straights mixing, but not quite, along the high-polished bar and down the skinny dance floor. Except this was San Francisco, after all, and even the cops made the scene. Especially cops. Anyway, she'd decided to catch him here for a little chat.

She glanced at her watch. At this moment, Molly from Meter Patrol should be marching up the steps of Simon's building. Looper had asked her friend to knock on the kid's door. Molly had bright red hair, like Looper, and no doubt this would send

Simon scurrying. He'd be out his window and on his bike in the next minute or so. If he were running true to form, he should walk through that door sometime in the next few minutes, thinking he'd outwitted the lady cop again.

In the meantime, everyone in the bar was watching Court TV, like everybody else in the city. There was a break in the action while a no-brain reporter profiled up-and-coming cases. A mother who drowned her children in a car. A man who executed strangers on a train. A wife who cut off her husband's genitals, then fed them to the family dog. At the end of this sequence, up came a story about the Barnes murder, with file footage of a gallery opening last year, Tobin smiling, arm around his buddy Zack, Yvonne in profile, haughty, beautiful. Then to a morgue shot, Zachary Barnes under a blanket, identification tag hanging from his toe.

Cut to Cynthia Charleston, Tobin's lawyer, standing on the steps of the Civic Center.

"He's not guilty," Charleston said.

Charleston was a delicate-faced woman whose features took well to the camera. She dressed in an edgy, almost fashionable way, in straight-cut skirts and loose blouses, her hair cut blunt and tinted just a shade, a perfect auburn. Looper had had to testify in another case where Charleston was the defense attorney, and she knew how good the woman was at using the press. In a case like this, she would try to attract as much publicity as possible, all the while screaming that the press made a fair trial impossible. In truth, a fair trial was the last thing on Charleston's mind. She wanted to try the case in public. To stir up issues of race and politics, of class and social animosity. To do it loudly enough so that no potential juror was untouched, and a hung jury was the best verdict you'd ever get.

"This is a case of sloppy work by the homicide detective, using poor judgment at the scene, acting rashly," Charleston said.

"Jesus Christ," Looper responded, but she should have seen it coming. Police incompetence was the first accusation the defense always made.

"The DA's office leaped on the case without thinking. They responded to public pressure before considering all the suspects. Now they realize the evidence is shoddy, but it's been turned into a political issue. They are backed into a corner and have to prosecute. And the person who suffers through all this is James Tobin. An innocent man in jail."

Looper was so disgusted she almost missed Simon Lee walking through the door. He stood there, backlit, a dark figure in the light that poured through the open window, and then went over to the bar, underneath the television. As he glanced up at the set, Looper placed her hand on his shoulder.

He jumped about fifteen feet.

"Take it easy, honey."

"I just came in for a beer."

"My treat. Let's go to the back table."

Simon looked at her without recognition.

"No. You wouldn't want me. I'm a man," he said. "I'm not in drag or anything. I really am a man."

Looper shook her head. Despite the tattoos, the greased hair, the leather jacket, the medallion through his nose, in the end he was nothing but a kid, and this whole thing was over his head. She tightened her grip. "You know me."

"Yeah?"

"Yeah." She took out her badge. "Inspector Anita Looper. Homicide. Why don't we go to the back table and talk? Or would you rather do this downtown?"

"Can I take my beer?"

"Sure. Take your beer."

As she guided him to the back, Looper took a last desultory glance at Court TV. They had gone back to live coverage, a Cuban euthanasia specialist on trial in Miami. Looper turned her attention to Simon.

He was trying to play it cool, but he was shaking as he drank from his glass. Looper figured it wouldn't be long before everything came tumbling from this little boy's mouth.

NINE

⮂ ⮀

SIMON SAYS

The cop had almost scared Simon out of his skull when she pulled the badge on him like that. It was the last thing he'd expected. He had to admit, though, when she took him back to the booth he felt not fright but relief. At least he wouldn't have to play hide-and-seek anymore. And this cop didn't seem so bad. He figured he could pretty much run-the-rosie on her.

"I'm glad you caught up with me. I've been wanting to tell somebody this stuff. That murder, it's really got me bummed."

"You haven't told me anything yet."

"What do you want to know?"

"Let's start with the theft."

He gaped at her. "Huh? What theft?"

"The theft that took place at the art gallery. Last February."

"I don't know anything about that," he said automatically, but he started to sweat.

"That's not what your friend Tobin told me. He said you stole the paintings."

"Me?"

"Zack engineered it, but you did the rummy work."

"Why would I do something like that?"

"For the money. Zack paid you."

"That's not true."

"It's what Tobin told me. I have it on tape, if you want to hear."

Simon felt his heart again, all wild in his chest.

"Tobin never said anything like that," Simon said.

The cop was quiet. She just went on looking at him. She had taken off that beret, and her wild red hair seemed to be everywhere. Her mouth was turned up into a smile, like she knew something he didn't know. Tobin was off his rock, thrashing in deep water. Simon didn't want to yank the guy's paddle, but he didn't want to go to jail for him either. Just the memory of the Dade County lockup, and his gap-toothed cellmate down there in crocodile land, that was enough, almost, to set him talking.

"You're lying. Tobin wouldn't make up a story like that. He wouldn't do that to me. We're friends."

"Let me show you something."

Looper took out a picture of Zachary Barnes, the one the police photographer had taken at the scene. It was a close shot, so you could see the gaping wound to the throat, the ghastly expression on Barnes's face. One eye was open, the other closed, and there was blood everywhere. It wasn't a picture that would be released to the press, but the jurors would see it all right.

It was not the most gruesome photo Looper had ever seen, but it seemed to have its effect on young Mr. Simon Lee.

"Your friend Tobin held the gun to Mr. Barnes's throat and pulled the trigger. We know that. The evidence tells us that. The fingerprints. The powder burns."

"This doesn't have anything to do with me."

"You know, Tobin claims self-defense. Zack tried to kill him, he says, because Tobin had found out the truth about the theft. About Zack's scheme with the insurance. Now, maybe that's true and maybe it's not, but I'll tell you this: if Tobin gets off, then we'll charge you with theft. We'll get Tobin to testify against you. He's already agreed."

"You can't prove anything," Simon said, close to panic. "I never got any money."

"A month ago, Simon, you bought yourself that Kawasaki. It's a nice-looking bike—not cheap, either. I could find out how you paid for it. Shouldn't be too hard." She looked at him with sympathy. "Do you want to go to jail, Simon? Or are you going to tell me what the hell happened?"

Simon caught a glimpse of himself in the mirror over the bar. He was taken aback, as he sometimes was, by the tattoo he'd gotten some six months back. A snake, just below his neckline. It showed more clearly in a tank shirt, like he was wearing now. He felt like that snake was wriggling up his neck, whispering in his ear.

Fuck Tobin, it said. Save yourself.

So he told her about it, about the Mardi Gras party, the dancing, the lousy food, the Dixie beer. They'd been hungry, he and his friends, unwilling to eat the fake jambalaya and soggy shrimp, hungry and broke. Simon decided to stop by the gallery and borrow some money from petty cash. Barnes let him do that, provided he left an IOU. He had a key to the side door; Tobin had turned off the alarm system the day before, saying that it kept pulling false alarms.

He'd seen a light, Simon said. And when he went in, he saw Tobin in the main gallery.

"He had a razor in his hand. And some of his paintings were on the floor. They'd been cut out of their frames, and rolled up."

Looper looked happier now. "Did you talk to him?"

"I tried, but the way he is, you know, he was my boss, and he says, 'What the hell are you doing here?' I guess I took him by surprise, and he was pretty shook up, the way I came behind him. Anyway, so I told him I just came by to borrow some money from petty cash."

Tobin gave him twenty bucks and told him to keep his mouth shut about what he'd seen. They were his paintings, he said, and he could do whatever the hell he wanted with them.

"Then a few days later I got a bonus in my pay envelope. Cash. Fifteen hundred bucks. I figured it was from both of them—you know, him and Zack—that they were in on it together and just wanted me to keep shut."

For a moment, Looper looked wistful. "I don't suppose you got a receipt for that? Or put it in your bank account, and I could find it on a statement?"

Simon looked at her blankly. "Receipt? Hell, I wasn't gonna put it in no account. I spent it, before they could change their minds and ask for it back."

Looper sighed, shaking her head.

"A detective's life is not a happy one," she said philosophically. "Did Zack ever mention the theft to you?"

"No."

"Did Tobin ever mention it to you again?"

"Not exactly."

"What do you mean?"

"Well, when he lost his temper with Ruby that time. After he found the letter Zack had written her. That love letter."

"Tobin knew about the letter?"

"Yeah."

Simon didn't want to talk about this anymore, but he knew what he wanted didn't matter. Looper was looking at him with those cop's eyes, and he'd come too far already.

"I showed it to him. I delivered it to Ruby—Zack asked me to. But I saw Tobin right after I gave it to her and . . ."

"Why?"

He shrugged uncomfortably. He didn't want to talk about being jealous. "I felt bad afterwards, though."

"Then what happened?"

"You're not going to tell Ruby, are you?" Simon heard the furtive note in his voice and was disgusted with himself. This cop was leaving him with nothing.

"Ruby's the least of your worries. Tell me what happened. What did Tobin say?"

"He said something like, 'That son of a bitch. First the paintings, now he goes after Ruby.' Then Tobin stomped up the stairs and started wailing on her. He smacked her around pretty good, I think."

Looper stood up. "Come on," she said. "I want to get this on tape."

Simon hesitated. "What if I don't cooperate?"

"Then I beat the shit out of you."

Looper smiled as she said it, like it was a joke, but then she came over and took him by the arm. She had a strong grip, he thought, and she held him like she would break his arm if he tried to get away. He bet that she could do it. She put him in the back of the cop car, inside that iron cage, and he was already thinking ahead to that gray room where they would interrogate him with the tape machine spinning, and how that snake would be all the way up inside his throat for sure, spitting out the words, betraying anybody and everyone, including Simon himself, anything not to spend a night inside a cage like this.

TEN

❧ ❧

WHO WAS ZACHARY BARNES?

J emma Granger's hair had not changed substantially since her first soft fuzz of baby hair had been replaced with this tangle of short brown curls. When she shook her head, the curls flew and bounced and her entire head looked like the very definition of an emphatic negative—and Jemma Granger liked to shake her head.

This time, shaking it, she grinned at her father.

"I don't want to eat out," she said flatly. "I want to eat at home, with you. We always eat out. It's no fun anymore."

"Oh, come on," Granger said, groaning. He'd put in at least ten hours today, staring at his computer screen, at his legal pad, and at the pile of case law books and statutes that his two clerks kept building at the corner of his desk. His head hurt, and his eyes felt like sandpaper; to be honest, the last thing he had needed was the five-fifteen call from Marian, his ex, telling him that she had to work late that night and asking him, with cool politeness, to take Jemma overnight and deliver her to school the next morning. Since the divorce, Marian hadn't bothered with politeness, but these past weeks she had seemed even angrier than normal. Granger didn't have time to worry about it. Normally he would have loved an unexpected extra evening with Jemma, and even now he tried to smile as he turned to her.

"We could go to Amaretto's," he said, hoping that mention of her favorite Italian restaurant would change her mind. "Tortellini soup? Ravioli? Cannoli for dessert?"

"Oh, Dad," Jemma said with eight-year-old exasperation. "You're trying to bribe me."

"Bribe you?" Granger put the car in gear and pulled away from the after-school child-care center. "You don't even know what that means."

Jemma heaved a sigh. "It means to give somebody something so that they'll do something that they might not do unless you give them something so that they'll do it," she said patiently. "Like you letting me have cannoli for dessert."

Granger looked at her sideways. "That's a pretty good definition. What about 'perjury,' can you define that?"

Jemma frowned terrifically, then brightened. "It's like how you figure something out," she said. "Like, you get one courtroom perjury."

"How do you figure . . ." Granger muttered, then laughed. Of course, per diem, per cent, per jury. "Pretty good there, kid. So you don't want to eat at Amaretto's?"

"I didn't say that," Jemma said. "I said it was bribery. That doesn't mean I won't take it."

By nine o'clock, Jemma was tucked into bed, and Granger had spread the contents of his largest briefcase over the dining room table. Photographs, old news clippings, printouts from online information services, magazine articles—his clerks had accumulated quite a pile of information about the principals in the case. Granger fixed himself a drink and stood over the table frowning.

Just who was Zachary Barnes, the handsome, dark-skinned man who stared back at him from the cover of *Image* magazine? Five years ago, at the height of Tobin's popularity and Barnes's success, a flurry of articles had been published about what one writer called "the art scene's dynamic duo." Of the various write-ups, this one seemed the best. Now Granger took it, and his drink, to his favorite chair. He sat and put his feet up. Across the room, the big corner windows showed the San Francisco night.

Fog enshrouded the great arches of the Golden Gate Bridge, and the lights of Marin were already becoming obscured. In a little while, that low bank of fog would be here too, up the city streets, smothering the sound of traffic and giving everything an ethereal glow. Granger took in none of it, thinking instead about Barnes and Tobin, about Ruby Garcia and Yvonne Barnes, and young, frightened Simon Lee. Then, shaking his head sharply, he picked up the magazine.

Zachary Barnes grew up in a professional family in Berkeley. His father was a doctor (general surgery, Alta Bates Hospital), his mother a college teacher (art history, California College of Arts and Crafts in Oakland). Both parents were slightly disappointed when their only son chose a career in the arts, but they sup-ported him nonetheless. He attended Berkeley High School and UC Santa Barbara (it was tough, the article quoted him as saying, being a black kid in that white environment). He met James Tobin in college; together they took a trip to Mardi Gras in New Orleans during their senior year. Tobin had gone to high school in New Orleans and introduced Zack to a young Creole friend named Yvonne; they immediately fell in love. She trans-ferred to San Francisco State to continue her studies in media, and after her graduation they married. She began her career in television, and Zack opened his gallery.

OK, Granger thought. That's where he came from, but who was he? Granger knew from long experience that if he really wanted to understand why a person had been murdered, he had to look at who that person was.

He put down the article and turned to another one about Yvonne Barnes. In newsprint, City Hall's Ice Queen came across pretty much as she came across on television: cool, collected, and always in control.

Thirty-seven years old, two years older than her husband. Raised in New Orleans. Creole on her mother's side. Her father taught at Southern University, a black school, and Yvonne had gotten a scholarship to the Tuskegee Institute. She'd studied communications law there before moving to San Francisco State. After college, she landed a job as a reporter at KIVE in San Jose. She was good.

According to the clerks' Post-it notes—which flagged, explained, cross-referenced, and commented on all the papers—Mrs. Barnes had covered City Hall first, then state politics. Eventually she caught the eye of Jack McKinney, who brought her on to handle his press campaign when he ran for mayor of San Francisco. It was a good choice on his part: he desperately needed someone on his staff to counter accusations that he represented the worst of old-fashioned, sexist, racist, pro-business, anti-abortion, conservative politics. According to the local liberals, all these accusations were quite true, but just the appearance of political correctness went a long way, especially when you hired PR people to keep that appearance before the public. And Yvonne Barnes had a nice, clean background: hard working, good parents, no affirmative action taint there.

Yvonne and Zack had married about twelve years ago, Granger read, when Yvonne was still at the TV station. The Barnes Gallery was just breaking then, and Tobin was the hottest young artist on the West Coast. His openings were wild affairs; everyone wanted to go. But even then there were rumors about the two men, Zack and Tobin, and how their partnership was a stormy one.

But storms didn't seem to affect Zack and Yvonne Barnes' marriage. Granger dropped the magazines and picked up an 8x10 glossy photo taken at a political fund-raiser last year by a photographer from the *Examiner*. Zack and Yvonne stood together at a crowded party, each facing in different directions, each holding a wine glass, each laughing, intent on separate conversations, wholly within their own skins and their own moments. What the photographer had caught, in the small space between their bodies, was their two hands, fingers interlaced, casually and completely together.

Granger lifted his glass as he looked at those twined fingers. You could talk forever about someone, he thought, but it was this, a silent moment—unheralded, unbroadcast, possibly even unnoticed—that defined a relationship. Whatever else may have been true between them, he had no doubt that Zachary Barnes had loved his wife—and that she, in turn, had loved him back.

Could that have changed so quickly in the eleven months since the photograph was taken? Yvonne Barnes was still hiding something, and Granger almost didn't want to know what it was. But could two people that much in love change so much, so fast?

Then he thought of Marian, and drained his glass.

Eleven

⌒⌒

A Funeral

Yvonne Barnes kept herself under tight control at the funeral, with the cameras whirring all around. In the station newsrooms later that evening, she knew, busy reporters would write the voice-overs for the evening broadcast. After all the delays caused by the coroner—the autopsies and tests, the waiting for Zack's heartbroken parents to return from their interrupted vacation in France—Zachary Barnes would finally be put to rest, but the maudlin pawing of the corpse had only just begun.

She knew the story being told; it was on radio, television, splashed across the front page of every newspaper in the Bay Area, impossible to avoid. A love triangle. A young woman at the center. Two men. Jealousy out of control.

None of it, she thought, was even close to true. And she couldn't do a thing about it.

The preacher said what had to be said; dirt and roses shook on the top of the coffin, and Yvonne stood staring into the grave. She looked not at a coffin, but at her memories of Zack's body, his angular, solemn face beset with unexpected smiles. Her skin ached, and her arms felt empty, as though nobody, ever again, would fit within them, would be there to hold her, to comfort, and to give comfort in return. Perhaps if they had had the children Zack wanted so much—she shook herself hard to keep the tears at bay and turned away from the grave.

"Mrs. Barnes?" Yvonne Barnes looked up at a black woman, maybe five years younger than herself, wearing a black shift, cornrows in her hair.

"Yes."

"I'm Josalyn Williams. With the district attorney's office."

"Oh."

"I've left a few messages for you. . . . I don't want you to think I'm being pushy."

"Pushy," Yvonne echoed. "Pushy." She almost smiled. "If only you people were being pushy."

Josalyn nodded. "I know it can be frustrating. But I'm part of the team that Ms. Wong put together on this case, and I would really like to talk with you."

Yvonne looked around. The photographers and news crews had left, trailing after Zack's parents, and for the moment she and Josalyn Williams stood alone.

"Why?" Yvonne said bluntly. "You have your case. You have your murderer. You even have your smoking gun."

"But we don't," Josalyn replied. "We don't have a witness, so the case is circumstantial. We could try Tobin for manslaughter and probably win, but we don't want to."

"Good," Yvonne Barnes said.

"If we're going to prove intent, it's not enough to have a smoking gun; we have to show how it got there. And it's not enough to say the men argued; we need to know what they argued about. We need a strong motive, Mrs. Barnes. That's what I'm trying to find here."

Yvonne Barnes shook her head. "I can't help you," she said.

Josalyn looked at her for a moment. "All right," she said finally. "But let me tell you something. If it was your husband charged with that murder, or if it was me, or you, then yes, maybe there's enough evidence already. There are fingerprints. There's blood. There's gunshot residue. But it's a white man who's been charged. And it's one of us who died. You and I both know what that means."

The young attorney turned away. She left Yvonne standing in the middle of the cemetery, staring down a long line of graves.

Yvonne Barnes cursed suddenly, thoroughly and viciously and without moving her lips. She knew why James Tobin, that selfish, womanizing, thieving leech, had killed her Zack. Knew it beyond any shadow of a doubt, knew that it was a strong motive, a color-wouldn't-matter motive. A motive for murder in the first degree.

And she knew that she could never, ever tell.

Twelve

⮌ ⮎

At the Jailhouse

Ruby Garcia went to see Jimmy down in the general lockup, in a little gray room with gray walls and a gray Formica table and hard plastic chairs, the kind they put in bus depots so nobody gets comfortable or is tempted to curl up and fall asleep.

Before she came in, a guard patted her down and made her walk through a detector. When the buzzer screamed, they made her unbuckle her shoes and her belt, and when it went off a second time they sent her back to the ladies' room to take off her bra. The underwire was setting off the alarm.

Each time she had to wait in line all over again with the other jailhouse widows visiting their men, and it was this last time, when she was in her bare feet, braless, her skirt riding too low around her hips, that one of the other women said to her, "Tennis shoes, sports bras, elasto-snap, baby. Honey, that's the only way you get to see lover-boy with your clothes still on." Then she stepped through the machine once more, and the lady guard patted her down again, with a look in her eye as dull as Milpitas, or Gilroy, or any dud town away from the city's action.

She hadn't seen Jimmy since the arraignment, when he'd been wearing an elegant blue suit. He had held his head with dignity and said the words "not guilty" in a loud, clear voice that muddled her heart.

The next day she'd met with Charleston, who'd taken her back and forth through her testimony, pretending that she was Granger and out to nail Jimmy. When it was all done, the last thing she'd said was, "I don't want you talking to the prosecution."

"All right," Ruby had said.

The truth was, she'd done the opposite. She wasn't sure why. Maybe because she did not like Charleston. Or maybe because she still felt guilty over what had happened between her and Zack. Or maybe for some other reason, one she did not think about except in the early hours of the morning, when she was lying alone in her new apartment thinking about things that only she knew, only she and Jimmy.

While Ruby lay there, wondering if she could keep the truth to herself, she thought of the kiss Tobin had given her just after he'd come out of his paint closet the morning Zack was killed. It had been a long kiss, very intense but very cold, and it had left her with an ugly feeling that would have taken all morning to shake—if the murder hadn't been even uglier.

When Ruby walked into the visitors' room, Jimmy was standing by the table in his prison blues. He had a fevered look in his eyes, a pale cast to his cheeks. She had hoped that when she saw him again all the ragged doubts she held in her heart would fall away. No such luck. She hugged him but could not bring herself to kiss him as passionately as he wanted. Instead she brushed her lips against his and buried her head in the hollow of his neck.

"What's wrong, Ruby?" he said. "I miss you like a maniac."

She lowered her eyes, not knowing what to say.

"They keep me in a small room with nothing but a basin. It's stone, and it's gray—like everything around here. I feel like I am in a goddamn Edward Hopper painting."

"Not Hopper," she said, showing off a little, like she'd always done for him. "He gave things more dignity."

"You don't think I have dignity?"

"That's not what I meant."

"You don't understand Hopper," he said.

Then he pushed her away, suddenly, as though he had remembered something more important.

"Listen, baby, you gotta do something for me," he said, and went on without waiting for her response. "Cynthia Charleston, my lawyer, she's not cheap. And you know Barnes cheated me, so there's no money, so I made this deal with her. She gets some of the artwork—I made a list of it, and she'll give it to you. You gotta make sure she gets it, OK? She'll give you the list, and you take her through the stuff." He turned then and twinkled at her, turning on the charm. "But you gotta keep an eye on her, sweetheart. Make sure she doesn't take anything . . . you know, extra, right? I mean, yeah, she's working for me, but she's still a lawyer, right?"

He caught her up again and squeezed. "You'll do it for me, baby, won't you? Talk to Cynthia, get that list?" His arms tightened uncomfortably around her. "Keep an eye on her, make sure she doesn't, oh, help herself?"

"Jimmy, please," she said, wriggling. "That hurts."

"Say you'll do it, baby."

"Sure, Jimmy, of course."

His arms didn't loosen. "And you won't think of taking anything for yourself, right, baby? You won't touch my stuff?"

"Please, Jimmy," she said, almost in tears with the pain. "Yes, of course, please, Jimmy, please let me go."

"That's my sweetheart," Jimmy said, suddenly opening his arms.

Ruby staggered and caught herself against the wall, but Jimmy didn't seem to notice.

"You never did understand Hopper," he said, as though nothing had happened. "But you're right about the other thing. I don't have any dignity. If only I had some paint. And a little bit of canvas. Even in here things catch my eye."

He glanced at the room, and something in his manner invited her to look around, too, as though she might be able to share in his perception.

"You know, I had an image. A kind of a vision. This prison world. Its stark colors. And the sky opening up above, a very flat sky, and ragged, and in that opening was another opening, and beyond that yet another. You know, if I get through this, my life here, this horrible thing that's happened to me—I think then I can pull my work to the next level. Hell, I don't even have to get out of here. I just need some paint. How can they torture a man like this?

"But other times the whole thing goes over and over in my head. I see Zack. I see the old times. I see us, you and me, and I just want to go back to the way things were. I can't believe this has happened to us."

Ruby didn't know what to think. Jimmy always skipped from one subject to the next. When she had first met him, at the Academy of Art, she had thought him an inspired artist, and she'd been flattered when he took an interest in her. Now inside this gray room, looking at him in his prison blues, it was harder to get swept up. Still, Jimmy had many sides to him. He could be charming as hell, all the time laughing at himself with that faint little smile. But you better not laugh, too.

"You betrayed me," he said suddenly, speaking softly and looking her in the eyes. Her stomach chilled, and the smile on her lips felt stiff.

"No. That's not true."

"Cynthia told me you're on the prosecution witness list."

"I might be on their list. But that doesn't mean I'm on their side."

"Then why did you talk to them?"

"To tell them you are innocent. To see, you know, if I could find out what they were thinking."

"Goddamn it, Ruby, can't you see what they're trying to do?" The pitch of his voice rose, and Ruby tried not to wince, tried not to put her hands up defensively. "They're running this smear on me. If they can drive a spike between you and me, it will be like a dagger in my heart."

"I didn't say anything to them."

"You know Yvonne works for the mayor. They're all tied up. The mayor, the prosecutor, the cops. The political pressure's on for a conviction. They're out to crucify me." He was almost shouting.

"I'm sorry," she said.

"Did they bring up the theft?"

"They tried to."

"Did they ask you where I was that night?"

"Yes."

"What did you say?"

"I said you were in bed next to me. All night. That we made love and fell asleep in each other's arms."

A vague smile came over Jimmy's face. "That's good," he said. His voice lowered. "It's the truth, you know."

"Yes," she said. But it wasn't, at least not completely. Because he'd gotten up in the middle of the night, she remembered, and had been gone for a couple of hours.

"I didn't steal those paintings. You know that. It was Zack. It was Zack and Simon."

"I know."

"I was just out for a walk."

"OK, Jimmy."

Something else bothered his mind, she could see that. He drummed his fingers on the table.

"I love you," he said.

"I love you, too."

"They can't tie the murder weapon to me. It belonged to Zachary's cousin. I didn't even have access to it."

"I know."

He studied her, trying to read her face. She kept it like a stone.

"I love you," he said again.

"Me, too."

They were both lying now. Because there had been a gun, Ruby knew. She'd seen it in the closet where Tobin kept his paint and brushes. She'd seen it there two days before the murder. And she'd thought about it the day of the murder, when Tobin had kissed her in front of the closet. Maybe he retrieved it right then, she thought. Maybe he'd been carrying it in his pocket when he went downstairs with Zack.

Jimmy didn't know for sure whether she had seen the gun. No one knew except her. Not Charleston, or Granger, or Looper. Not anyone at all.

"I didn't kill him," Jimmy said. "I hope you believe that. He was my friend, my partner."

"I know."

"I just wish this never happened."

"I know," she said again.

"You don't sound as if you believe me."

"I believe you."

He came forward like he wanted her to prove it. He kissed her, pressing her lips hard, and she pressed back. His kiss was unconvincing. Still Jimmy pressed harder, and she did too, maybe wanting something, but it just wasn't there. Jimmy pulled back, smiling, and she wondered if the deception was as plain on her face as it was on his.

"I believe you," she said softly.

Then he put one hand on her blouse, sliding it between the buttons, up onto her naked breast. With the other hand he intertwined her fingers, guiding them down beneath the elastic of his prison blues. His breath was fierce in her ear. She was crying now because she was afraid of the horrible thing that had happened, and she wanted to push him away. She did not want to believe he had gone downstairs with that gun. Maybe he hadn't. Her arms felt numb. His breathing grew wilder and would have grown wilder yet if the guard hadn't come in just then. Then she left, hurrying down the long gray hall, astounded by the chill that had seized her heart.

THIRTEEN

❧ ❧

THE WORD FROM ABOVE

A nd you are to leave Yvonne Barnes alone, is that understood?"

Granger gave up on maintaining a polite expression and simply glared at the district attorney. "Leave her alone?" he echoed with fury. "She's a major witness, she can speak to motive, and opportunity, she's the victim's wife, she's—"

"A member of Mayor McKinney's personal staff, and if he wants her left alone, you'll leave her alone." Julie Ann Wong glared back at him. "And it doesn't make me any happier than it makes you."

"Julie."

"Don't even start," she said. She opened a manila folder she'd been carrying and pulled out a sheet of paper, the folder's only contents. "This is from Mrs. Barnes. She gave it to McKinney when she called to complain about Ms. Williams's talking to her at the funeral."

"I can't believe this," Granger said, still furious. "Who the hell does she think she is? Who the hell does McKinney think he is?"

"Sterling, shut up," Wong said, not unkindly. "Here. This is the best you're going to get for now, so calm down and take it." She put the paper in his hand, dropped the folder on his desk, and headed out the door. "It's better," she said, "than a kick in the head."

Granger glanced at the paper, then threw it down. "But not by damned much," he muttered.

When Josalyn came in a few hours later, he handed her the letter and let her read it by herself.

FROM THE DESK OF YVONNE BARNES
15 Brannan Place
San Francisco, CA 94107

Dear Mr. Granger:

I am writing in regard to the murder of my husband, Zachary Barnes, and the case you are prosecuting against James Tobin. I have no wish to be disturbed, as this is a very trying time for me. However, I understand that I will be called to the stand either during the preliminary hearing or during the trial itself. I want you to know that I am willing to testify to the following:

First, I would like to remind you of the well-publicized theft which took place in the Barnes Gallery a month before the murder. I think it important to note that this theft was presaged by the accused himself, in insidious remarks he made at a gallery reception several weeks before.

Second, not long after the theft, my husband became suspicious of Mr. Tobin. His suspicions were fueled by several irregularities, not the least of which was Mr. Tobin's insistence that the alarm system be disabled in the days prior to the theft.

Third, when my husband confronted James Tobin regarding his suspicions, the painter admitted his crime— and threatened my husband with his life if he went to the authorities. I myself was witness to the above threat, which took place less than a week before the murder.

I do not think it takes a genius to see the facts behind this case. James Tobin is a puerile, self-absorbed man who will stop at nothing to advance his own interests. Though I have little faith in the righteousness of the world these days, I am still more than willing to take the stand if it will help convict my husband's murderer.

Please let me know when you have scheduled my appearance in court. In the meantime, I do not wish to be disturbed.

Sincerely,

Yvonne Barnes

"Understood, Ms. Williams?" Granger said when Josalyn threw the letter onto his desk.

She stared at him. "What are you going to do?"

He grimaced. "For the record? Precisely as the lady asks. I'm not about to tangle with the mayor, and I suggest that you don't, either. But privately . . ."

"Privately?" she echoed.

"Isn't it a pity," he said, picking up the letter, "that I only gave you a summary of the proposed testimony here, and didn't mention the last paragraph at all?" He looked up at her, making his eyes as wide as he could. "Gee, I really messed up on that one, didn't I?"

Josalyn looked at him for a moment, then started to laugh.

FOURTEEN

༄ ༄

PRELIMINARIES

I t promised to be the trial of the decade so in the best tradition of San Francisco perversity, the preliminary hearing was held in the ugliest room available. Granger put his briefcase down on the prosecution table and looked around at the low ceilings, white walls, aluminum trap windows, and the fluorescent lighting that tinged the skin of the principals an unhappy yellow. Court TV's minions, behind their nests of equipment, looked sour, and Granger felt a smile tugging its way to his lips. He hated Court TV.

So, it seemed, did the Honorable Harvey Wagner. The best, and worst, to be said of him was that he was old-fashioned, competent, and tough-minded, and he glared at the cameras as he mounted the bench. The lighting made the old man seem even more sick than rumor had it he was, and Granger wondered suddenly if the judge could make it through a lengthy trial. He glanced at Cynthia Charleston, but she was busy settling herself and her client at the defense table.

The point of a preliminary hearing is only to establish probable cause, not to establish guilt or innocence. All Granger had to do was show that there was enough evidence against the defendant to warrant a trial. He had little doubt that he could not do it, and he knew that Cynthia Charleston realized it. She occupied her place at her client's side, the two of them smooth, sleekly dressed, and calm. They made Granger feel rumpled, a feeling that he liked. Beside him, Josalyn Williams looked cool and professional and as polished as a fine gemstone. That, too, was a feeling Granger liked.

He kept his opening remarks short and to the point and called Inspector Anita Looper. Her shoes clicked against the ugly linoleum tile as she walked toward the witness stand. Taking the oath, she towered over the short court clerk, her wild red hair inadequately restrained with clips, her business suit neat and conservative. She sat, and Court TV's cameras swung between her face and Granger as he rapidly established her identity, her title, her years on the force, and how she had been called to the scene.

"And when you entered the gallery, where was the defendant?" Granger turned to look at Tobin. There was no jury at this point, but that didn't matter; he wanted Tobin to know this was going to be no easy business. Tobin, in his tailored suit, seemed unfazed.

"The paramedics had him on a gurney," said Looper.

"Did you talk to the defendant at this time?"

"Yes."

"In your own words, what was the substance of the conversation?"

"I asked him what happened to his leg."

"How did he respond?"

Inspector Looper paused, then said, "He told me he had been shot by Mr. Barnes, during an argument over business. He said that Mr. Barnes had tried to kill him."

Granger nodded, glancing at his pad of paper.

"Did you ask him to explain what had happened to Mr. Barnes?"

"Yes, he told me that after the first shot—the one that wounded him—that he and Mr. Barnes had struggled for possession of the gun. That's when the gun went off a second time."

"And this second shot was the one that killed Mr. Barnes?"

Cynthia Charleston came to her feet, as Granger knew she would.

"Objection. The witness wasn't present at the shooting, Your Honor, and is at any rate not an expert in medical matters." Her voice sounded as smooth and determined as she looked.

"Withdrawn."

Granger kept the pace rapid. He took Looper through the crime scene: to Zachary Barnes's body and the glass shards that lay across it, to the pry marks on the door, to the crow bar and the upturned cash box.

Josalyn Williams handed him a sheaf of papers which he introduced into evidence as the transcript of Looper's taped conversation with Yvonne Barnes. He had the detective read from them as he sought to further establish the contradictions between the evidence and Tobin's initial rendition of events.

"So according to this transcript, Mrs. Barnes told you that she had seen the defendant at the alley door. Did you ask her if she noticed a wound to the defendant's leg?"

Inspector Looper lay the transcripts down and nodded.

"I asked her. She told me no."

"At this time, you had talked to the defendant, the deceased's wife, and a young woman named Ruby Garcia?"

"Yes."

"And you had also completed a preliminary examination of the physical evidence?"

"Yes."

Granger nodded. "What did you do next?"

"I went to the hospital for a second talk with Mr. Tobin."

"When you asked him to describe the shooting during this second conversation, did his response differ in any way from the one he gave you initially?"

"Yes."

"In what details was it different?"

"This time he told me that the wound to his leg was self-inflicted. That he shot himself after the struggle with Mr. Barnes."

Granger paused and turned again to Tobin, and Tobin met his eyes in the same dispassionate way. His eyes were ocean blue and reflected a studied confidence. It bothered Granger: most defendants in a murder case looked more worried, either because they really were or because they thought they had better look as if they really were. Since the reinstatement of the death penalty, murder in the first was serious business whether you were innocent or not.

"Did he offer you any explanation as to why he shot himself?"

"Yes. He said he did it because he was afraid that unless he were wounded, no one would believe he had killed Mr. Barnes in self-defense."

"Did you draw any conclusions as a result of what Mr. Tobin told you during this second conversation?"

"Yes."

"What were those conclusions?"

"That at least one of his stories wasn't true. And neither of them was in agreement with the physical evidence."

Granger paused to let this sink in. He kept Looper on the stand a while longer. Her testimony was deadpan as hell, but it was also damaging, and he didn't see any way Charleston could prevent this from going to trial. He suspected that Charleston's goal today might be to probe Looper, to draw her out of that deadpan manner, though any real heat would come later, during the trial.

Still, it was with some trepidation that he turned Looper over to Charleston for cross-examination.

Charleston walked around to the front of her table. While other attorneys dressed conservatively, in grays and browns and blues, Charleston shattered the mold. It was a risk she almost always seemed willing to take, so much so that it was routine for journalists to mention her wardrobe in their articles. Today she wore a plum-colored shift cut at the knees.

"Good afternoon, Detective Looper," said Charleston with deliberate, almost insulting politeness, and Granger could see the inspector bristle.

"Good afternoon," Looper said frostily. Granger tried to catch her eye, but she concentrated on Charleston almost fiercely, and he felt a quick stab of alarm.

Cynthia Charleston wasted no time at all. "Where were you when the call came in regarding the incident with Mr. Barnes?" she said, as though she already knew the answer.

"In my office," said Looper.

"Is it normal for you to be in your office on Sunday morning?"

"I was catching up on some work."

Charleston's eyebrows rose for the benefit of Court TV, and Granger realized that she would, of course, be playing this as much for the public as for the bench. Unnerve the prosecution, pressure their witnesses, assess their strategy, and rake in publicity at the same time. Charleston, an ambitious woman, was no dummy.

"Is it normal," she said, "for you to arrive at the scene within minutes of on-duty patrol?"

"No."

"Then how did it happen in this instance?"

"Someone in the next office had the scanner on. I heard the call come in and decided I better go down."

"Did they mention that the call was from the Barnes Gallery?"

"Yes."

"Did this have any significance to you?"

Looper shrugged. "Not particularly."

"No one mentioned that the Barnes Gallery was owned by the husband of Yvonne Barnes, the mayor's press secretary?"

"Someone may've mentioned it. I don't remember."

"In fact, wasn't the office pretty much buzzing with this news?"

"I don't know if I would phrase it that way."

Looper's eyes passed over Granger, as if to tell him she was in control, not to worry. Even so, he could not bring himself to relax.

"When you first talked to James Tobin, was that the first time you ever met him?" she asked.

Looper hesitated, and the hesitation grew longer. Granger thought at first it was just the usual hesitation, drummed into detectives from their earliest training. Think before you answer. Take your time. Don't give anything to the defense. Except this question should not have required much deliberation.

"No," Looper said at last.

Granger's stomach tensed. Looper had never mentioned any earlier meeting with him. His legs tensed, ready to lift him into an objection.

"When did you first meet my client, James Tobin?"

And here it came. "Objection," said Granger, on his feet. "Relevance?"

Granger hoped only to slow things down, knowing instinctively that Charleston would argue that the cop's prior knowledge of the suspect was indeed relevant. Wagner agreed.

"It was three years ago," she said. "At a gallery opening."

"Were you alone when you met him?"

"No."

"Who were you with?"

"A woman named Luisa Brown."

"What was your relationship with Luisa?"

"We were lovers," Looper said stiffly.

In another city, in another time, this response may have caused a little rumble of shock. Perhaps it still did, out there in the heartland somewhere, on the other side of Court TV. In San Francisco, here in the courtroom, a man yawned, and Granger winced inwardly. Luisa had walked out on Looper not all that long ago. This had to hurt.

"Did your lover and Mr. Tobin talk?" asked Charleston. She seemed to delight in Looper's discomfort.

"Yes."

"For how long?"

"I don't remember. Maybe fifteen minutes."

"Where were you?"

"I was standing next to Luisa."

"Are you still lovers with Luisa Brown?"

Granger objected. Wagner sustained, but something shifted in the courtroom. Looper had flinched.

"Did you participate in the conversation with Mr. Tobin?"

"Not much," said Looper.

"Based on that conversation between your lover and my client, did you draw any opinion of Mr. Tobin?"

Looper paused. The smart thing, of course, was to say no. Walk away from the question. Looper had to realize that. But Charleston stood there with her back arched, playing it up, and Looper was still stinging. The antagonism between the two women had its own kind of electricity. Granger glanced at Tobin: the man looked pleased, as though a small mechanism he had made was playing out satisfactorily.

"I wouldn't defend him in a murder trial, if that's what you mean."

A funny answer; it got the courtroom laughing. But it wasn't the right answer, and Charleston had made a damaging point, establishing a prior relationship between Tobin and the arresting officer. It suggested some kind of grudge.

Charleston nodded, graciously accepting the quip, and changed the direction of her questions. She had Looper take the transcript of the interview with Yvonne Barnes again.

"Detective, you've shown us a crowbar and a cash box, is that correct?"

"Yes," Looper said with caution.

"The transcript of your interview with Mrs. Barnes mentions those items, I believe. And one more. Can you find it for us, detective?"

Looper gave Charleston a suspicious look but obligingly paged through the transcript.

"Mrs. Barnes mentioned a yellow bundle," Looper replied. "Here."

Charleston read the page citation into the record. "And tell me, Detective, were you able to locate that yellow bundle?"

Looper shrugged. "No."

"You did look for it, I assume."

"Objection," Granger said, rising. "Badgering."

"Sustained."

Charleston took it graciously and changed direction again.

"Where were you the night before the murder?"

"Relevance, Your Honor?" Granger said, objecting. "Inspector Looper is not on trial here."

Wagner nodded. "Explain yourself, Counselor."

Charleston spread her arms. "I'm trying to establish the officer's state of mind the morning of the arrest."

"I'll allow. Overruled," said Wagner. "Inspector Looper, please answer the question."

Granger sank into his seat. Looper was on her own now. There was little he could do.

"I was at home," she said. "I went to bed early, about ten o'clock."

"Before this, didn't you spend several hours at a bar called La Rondala?"

"I ate dinner there."

"But you sat at the bar?"

"Yeah."

"Alone?" Charleston demanded.

"I was alone," Looper shot back, just as abruptly. Granger bit his lip.

"How long were you there?"

"A couple of hours, I didn't keep track. I was trying to relax."

"Did you have anything to drink?"

"Beer."

"How many beers?"

"A couple."

"A couple? How many precisely? Two? Four?"

Looper opened her mouth, then obviously thought better of it. She took a breath before saying, "Three, maybe. I don't recall."

"You don't recall. Was it five then, or six?"

"Objection," protested Granger. "The witness has answered."

"Sustained," Wagner said, frowning. "Don't badger the witness."

"My apologies, Your Honor."

Charleston strung it out a little longer, agitating Looper for agitation's sake. The tactic irritated Wagner, Granger guessed, though for the time being that didn't matter. Charleston had planted the seeds.

Then, just before lunch, Charleston struck a solid blow. She had once again switched directions and, with breathtaking direct-ness, took Looper back to the crime scene.

"So let me get this straight, Detective," Charleston said. "The criminalists bagged Zachary Barnes's hands to test for gunshot residue. That was their responsibility. You were responsible for bagging James Tobin's hands, correct?"

"Yes," Looper said warily, and Granger remembered her com-ment, on that long-ago afternoon, about going out on a limb.

"And you had Officer Zuckerman bag Mr. Tobin's hands before the ambulance took him to the hospital, is that correct?"

"Yes."

"Did you bag Yvonne Barnes's hands?" Charleston asked in a very conversational tone.

"No," Looper said.

"No?" Charleston sounded amazed. "Did you arrange to have someone else bag Yvonne Barnes's hands?"

"No," Looper said, and Granger could hear the tension in her voice. Beside him, Josalyn madly scribbled notes on her legal pad.

"I see. What about Ruby Garcia's hands, Detective. Did you bag Ms. Garcia's hands?"

"No."

"Or arrange to have someone else bag them?"

"No."

Charleston looked surprised—the way, Granger thought sourly, that an alligator might look surprised at the unexpected gift of a side of beef.

"So of the three living people at the crime scene, of the three possible suspects, you bagged only Mr. Tobin's hands. Not Mrs. Barnes's. Not Ms. Garcia's. Is that correct, Detective?"

Looper paused, staring hard at Cynthia Charleston, who stared back.

"Yes," the detective said finally. "That's correct."

"I see." Cynthia Charleston paced away from the witness stand, and the cameras followed her every move. "So, Detective Looper, we have a strange bunch of evidence here, don't we? We have a mysterious yellow bundle that may or may not exist. We have a common crowbar and no indication of where it came from. We have broken glass, we have a cash box, we have all sorts of stuff." She turned to face Looper. "But we don't know whether Ruby Garcia or Yvonne Barnes would have tested positive for gunshot residue, do we? So either Ms. Garcia or Mrs. Barnes could have fired that gun that morning. Either Ms. Garcia or Mrs. Barnes could have shot Zachary Barnes. And Mrs. Barnes could have lied about that bundle. Isn't that true, Detective?"

"Objection, Your Honor," Granger called.

"Sustained. Counselor, don't do it again."

"Of course not, Your Honor. No further questions," Charleston said. Looper gazed across at Granger, who gazed back. The press would have a field day with the implications. What had happened between Luisa Brown and James Tobin? What was Looper's grudge against Tobin? Did Looper have a drinking problem? Was she hung over when she arrested Tobin? All nonsense, of course, but it generated noise and confusion and publicity, and that's why Charleston liked it. Still, she'd surely be out in front of the cameras tonight, complaining that the media was tainting the trial, a real pro, playing both ends against the middle.

And she had unerringly put her finger on one of the largest holes in the prosecution's case.

Fifteen

❧ ❧

Ruby on the Stand

Ruby Garcia had been told not to talk over the case with anyone other than the lawyers, to avoid reading about the case, and to not watch it on televiion. The judge had so instructed her, in her capacity as a valuable witness in a very serious case. She ignored it. It was her life, after all. When Looper's testimony aired on Court TV, she watched, propped on a mountain of cushions in her new studio apartment, surrounded by a clutter of boxes and bags and secondhand furniture. Jimmy's paintings, what remained of them, were in a warehouse in Daly City. She was still amazed, when she thought about it, by the number of Tobin paintings Cynthia Charleston had taken.

Arms and legs akimbo, unconsciously tugging at her brown curls, Ruby watched Court TV, scarcely daring to breathe.

She knew she was supposed to be the prosecution's witness, but she couldn't keep her eyes off Tobin. He seemed so tiny, sitting there on the TV screen, decorated with static. She pressed her palm against her ribs and shuddered as she watched Cynthia Charleston nag and pick and fray at the edges of Inspector Looper's confidence. Charleston's directions had been so clear, so friendly, so helpful—and Tobin seemed so harmless, sitting there in his neat suit, one lock of hair falling over his forehead, his expression so calm. She pressed her ribs again and repressed a shudder. What if Jimmy Tobin went free?

The next day, when Granger called her to the stand, Ruby felt Tobin's blue gaze on her and, for a moment, couldn't look away. Charleston had briefed her again that morning, and the words repeated themselves as she settled into the witness chair. Don't volunteer details. Stick to "yes" or "no" or "I don't know." Charleston had not said to lie; she had made it clear that she was not instructing Ruby to tell a lie, or what to do if she was caught in one. What Charleston did say, though, was that if anyone made Ruby feel confused, to tell them that she didn't remember. Ruby crossed her fingers and hoped that nobody would make her feel confused.

Granger, by taking it gently and with sympathy, didn't make her feel any better.

"At the crime scene," he said, after establishing her identity and connection with the case, "you told Inspector Looper that you'd had an intimate relationship with Zachary Barnes?"

Ruby turned her head away. "I'm not sure what you mean."

"Did you ever have sex with Zachary Barnes?"

"Yeah. Just once."

"When was that?"

"I'm not sure of the exact date. A Wednesday night, I think. About ten days before Zack died."

"Did James Tobin know about the incident?" asked Granger. He looked at her sympathetically, and she resisted the urge to touch her ribs.

"Ms. Garcia?" he prompted softly.

"Yes."

"When did the defendant find out?"

"Not long after it happened. About a week, maybe."

"Did he express jealousy or anger?" Granger asked the question with the same soft voice, a little sleepy, prompting her.

It made something shift inside of her, something that made her trust him, made her want to tell him the truth, get it out in the open, get rid of all the pretense—and then she glanced away and saw Jimmy, lips parted, beseeching, but his hands rested on the table in front of him, tense and flat and hard. She faltered. "No."

"Did you ever discuss that affair with him?"

"Yes."

"What did he say?"

"I don't remember."

"You don't remember?" Granger repeated. His eyes widened.

"No."

"You had an affair with your boyfriend's long-term friend and business partner, correct?" Granger's voice was suddenly business-like, the gentleness gone. Ruby was glad. It made it easier what she had to do.

"Yes."

"Your boyfriend discovered the affair?"

"Yes."

"How did he discover it?"

"I'm not sure."

"He didn't tell you?" Granger asked. Angry now. Insistent.

"No," she said, lying, holding her ground.

"When he talked to you about the affair, what did he say?"

"That it didn't matter. That he still loved me." It was another lie.

"A minute ago, you said you didn't remember."

"I remember that part."

"Objection," Charleston shouted. "Harassing the witness."

The testimony continued. They went round and round like that. The whole time, Ruby felt the cameras on her, and she thought about the people looking at her on TV and wondered if they could tell the game she was playing. She felt all those eyes on her, especially Tobin's, and she felt ashamed. Ashamed, and terrified.

*   *   *

Eventually Granger let her go, and Charleston approached for the cross-examination. Plum was becoming a theme with her. A plum-colored skirt and a plum-colored jacket. Matching hose, spiked heels, a quick little toss of the head. Though Charleston was on Jimmy's side, Ruby couldn't help herself—she didn't like the woman.

"Did Zachary Barnes ever discuss the theft that occurred at the gallery?" Charleston asked.

"Yes," answered Ruby.

"Did the deceased mention the insurance settlement he anticipated as compensation for that theft?"

"Yes."

They were going through it just like they'd scripted it. Meanwhile, Jimmy smiled at her, and she felt that same awful coldness in her chest that she'd felt visiting him in jail. Only there was something else, underneath, welling up.

"Did Mr. Barnes say anything more?"

"Yes. He said the gallery was broke." Ruby hesitated. That part was true, but there was something else Charleston wanted her to say. It was true too, though not in the way the attorney wanted it to sound.

Ruby had difficulty finding the words.

"Zack told me, sometimes, he hated Jimmy," she said. "He told me. . . ." She burst into tears. "He told me, before this was all over, somebody was going to end up dead."

It didn't sound right to Ruby. It didn't sound like Zack had said it—in a moment of fear, seeing how crazy Jimmy had become. Ruby put her head down now. She began to sob.

"No more questions, Your Honor," Charleston said.

As Ruby stepped down, touching the handkerchief to her eyes, she caught Charleston's smile and knew it had gone the way the lawyer had wanted.

The reason she had broken down, though, was not how it looked. She had cried because she could not get Zack out of her head. Because even when she spoke the truth, it came out a lie. She didn't know any way to make things come out any different.

The next day Ruby watched Yvonne's testimony on television. They went over the day of the murder again, and the fact she'd seen Jimmy walking around at the back of the gallery. It was designed to make Jimmy look like a liar. Only Yvonne came off poorly, cold and brittle, bitchy. Toward the end of the day, Charleston got her to snap.

"Yes, I dislike James Tobin, and that's been true for some time," Yvonne said. "I would do just about anything to see that bastard suffer."

For an instant Ruby sympathized, because there were times she wanted to see Jimmy suffer too.

SIXTEEN

∽ ∽

NEWS ANALYSIS

The preliminary was not going as well as Granger had hoped. He had gotten in the important physical evidence, but each of his witnesses had stumbled, and Ruby had been a disaster. Still, he had more than established probable cause, he thought. The evidence at the crime scene, together with Tobin's contradictory stories, these alone should be enough. Regardless, it was all over except for the attorneys' summations—and the media analysis. The latter never seemed to end.

It was going on here too: on a television screen inside Tommy's Joynt, a meat and potatoes joint a few blocks up from the Civic Center. It was dark and noisy inside, full of people just off work. Granger ordered himself a roast beef. Josalyn, declaring she intended to work through dinner, had disappeared into the courthouse law library. Overhead, on the TV, two legal analysts in blue suits talked over the case.

The heavier of the two men, a city prosecutor from Oakland, filled the screen. "Charleston has raised some pretty serious doubts about the prosecution's case. But, rather surprisingly, she passed up grilling Yvonne Barnes on a couple of key points. First, the murder weapon. Second, what was Mrs. Barnes doing, alone at the murder scene, after Ruby parked the car? There are about fifteen minutes that, so far, the prosecution can't account for. Combined, of course, with sloppy police work, you have to ask yourself whether this case has any chance of success at all."

Granger took his plate and sat down. He, too, had serious questions about Yvonne Barnes, based for the most part on an uneasy feeling that the Ice Queen was keeping secrets. Important secrets, secrets that could make his case. Or break it. He and Josalyn had gone round and round on this one, trying to figure out just what Mrs. Barnes was concealing. Josalyn had even gone so far as to wonder whether Yvonne had done something that long ago morning, something she was desperate to hide. Granger shook his head impatiently. He couldn't worry about that now. He had his summation to get through, and it would demand his full concentration.

Meanwhile, the second analyst was responding to the first, disagreeing.

"No. Charleston deliberately avoided pushing Mrs. Barnes on these issues. Rightly so. There's no advantage in raising sympathy for the deceased by attacking the widow."

The two analysts analyzed on, prodded by the news anchor, while Granger spread horseradish on the roast beef. In the old days, Marian would have yelled at him for his carnivorous tendencies, and she had trained Jemma to do it now. He smiled, thinking about his small, fierce daughter and her zealous guardianship of his health. Then he took a huge bite.

"How would you rate the prosecution's performance? Will this go to trial?" asked the news anchor. The fat analyst guffawed into the mike. Almost unwillingly, Granger listened. "I know there's a lot of public pressure to bring this to trial, but Judge Wagner, when he takes this one to chambers, will have to be wondering if this is really worth the state's time. Or money."

"Oh, there'll be a trial. Don't doubt that," said the other analyst. "But unless the DA's office gets a little smarter, the city's going to lose this case. Charleston's got Mr. Granger outclassed."

The hell she does, Granger thought. He thought about his two law clerks and Josalyn Williams, about the mountain of research and case law he'd read, about the many times he and his crew had gone over the evidence, then over it again. Ms. Charleston's suits might outclass his wardrobe, but that was about the only kind of outclassing that would happen here.

After dinner, he headed down to his office. Despite all the legal pontificators, he still felt the preliminary would go his way. In the meantime, though, he needed to read through his summation one more time.

SEVENTEEN

❦ ❧

RUBY'S SECRET

Ruby was a little drunk. Tequila had gotten her into this, and maybe tequila could get her out. Except she really didn't want to testify against Jimmy. He'd been good to her, mostly, and the longer she went over things in her head, the less clear they seemed.

How could she really know what had happened in that room between Zack and Jimmy? How could anyone really know? She'd even heard rumors that Yvonne had been involved, or Simon, or some other person, a killer who somehow had managed to tie this all to Jimmy in some way that he was afraid to speak out.

It didn't make sense, she knew. She didn't believe those stories, but there were times, alone at night, when she flinched at the simplest noises, the creaking of floors and the rattling of old pipes. She told herself she was right to go along with Charleston. Jimmy had to be innocent.

Still, the truth was bothering her. The attorneys were to give their closing statements tomorrow. After that, the judge would make his decision about whether or not the case should to trial.

What if the case did not go to trial? What if Jimmy had killed Zack? What if Jimmy went free?

It was late when Ruby finally walked up to the Hall of Justice. There were still some lights on in the upper floors where the lawyers worked. She had no idea if Granger was up there, but she had his business card, and she stepped into the phone booth.

Chances were that he wasn't there, she told herself. He was at home, or out for dinner, or doing whatever it was that lawyers did the night before they made their closing remarks.

A shadow moved behind one of the windows, Granger maybe. Ruby still hadn't decided whether or not to tell him what she knew. She picked up the phone. She would let fate decide. If he answered, then she would talk. She sipped tequila from a small flask, then dialed.

Three rings, four. Ruby waited for the phone to click over to the answering device. When it did, she would hang up. It didn't. Instead it rang again, five times, six, and then Granger picked up.

"District Attorney's office."

Ruby waited.

"This is Ruby Garcia," she said at last.

"Ruby." Granger's voice had that same gentle quality it had when she first took the stand. She imagined him up there behind the lit window, his head tilted, listening to the phone, while she was down here in this small booth, hidden in the dark of San Francisco. It reminded her of when she was a kid and would go to the confessional, whispering in the darkness. There was always a light in the priest's little booth, and she could see the dim outline of his head.

"Do you think this will go to trial?" she asked.

"It's up to the judge, Ruby. Why have you called?"

"You make closing statements tomorrow?"

"Yes."

"There's something I didn't tell you before."

"Would you like to come up to my office?"

"No. I'm afraid."

"Afraid of what? No one can hurt you."

"It's not that. I'm afraid of doing the wrong thing."

"The wrong thing," Granger said, "would be to hide the truth."

"How do you know what the truth really is?"

"It's easier to know if we have all the facts."

"Maybe. Or maybe we just twist the facts. To make the truth look the way we want. That's your job, isn't it? You and Charleston?"

"That's not the way I see it. I try to have a little more faith in the process, if not myself," he said. "Ruby, what is it you wanted to tell me?"

Ruby had the urge to hang up. She didn't want to betray Jimmy, but then she thought of the cold chill that had filled her chest that last time she had seen him, and she thought of Zack, and his sweetness, and how Charleston had managed to make it seem, through Ruby's own mouth, like he was a different kind of man than he really was.

"The gun," she started, but she couldn't finish.

Granger was quiet. She could hear him breathing softly, the way the priest used to breathe. A young priest. She'd had a crush on him. Later, when she saw him walking the grounds of St. Julian's, she'd been embarrassed by the things she had told him in the confessional.

"It was in his painting closet. In his studio."

"The studio in the loft? Where you lived?"

"Wednesday, before the murder, I went in there to get some brush cleaner. That's when I saw it."

"Could you describe the gun for me?"

"I don't know. I don't know much about guns."

"How big was it?"

"Small."

"A derringer?"

"No. Bigger than that."

"Could you fit it in a jacket pocket, do you think?"

"Yeah, it was about that size."

"What color was it?"

"Silver-colored, with a black handle."

"Could you tell me again, where did you see it?"

"In Jimmy's work closet. Where he keeps his paints. But it's not there anymore," she said. "Are you going to tell the judge?"

"It's not that easy, Ruby. Tomorrow we're scheduled for the closing statement. I'd have to ask him to reopen, and I don't know if he would. Before I make a request like that, you have to tell me, Ruby, are you willing to testify to this in court?"

Outside the phone booth, on the dark street, a homeless man walked by, and sirens wailed down Market. When the homeless man had passed, she took out the flask and pressed it again to her lips.

"Ruby?"

She took another sip of the tequila. It was hot and burned and tasted like hell. Zack was dead. No one cared about that. The case was about other things now. About city politics. About lawyers and their careers. She felt her eyes going moist, and the lights of the building blurred.

Then she heard her name again, and in disgust—with herself, with Granger, with everyone—she hung up the phone.

EIGHTEEN

⌒⌒ ⌒⌒

BOUND FOR TRIAL

The next morning, Granger delivered his closing remarks. Four days later, he was still waiting for a decision. He had expected an announcement early Friday, but the judge reported that he was feeling ill. The decision did not come down until Monday, after a long weekend in which Granger had plenty of time to doubt himself. The reporters and analysts and television commentators played armchair lawyer, many of them puzzling over why Granger had been so sketchy in the prelims. The city's Black Caucus issued a statement criticizing the DA's office, claiming the prosecution seemed to be holding back. Harsher voices charged that Granger was part of a conspiracy to let Tobin walk.

Monday morning, the judge's decision was postponed again, until 1:30 that afternoon. Then at 1:30 the judge kept them waiting. One rumor said he was ill, another that he was in a last-minute meeting with the mayor. Finally, close to an hour late, Wagner appeared in the courtroom. He looked disgruntled and displeased, uncomfortable as hell. He made his announcement as brief as possible.

"In the case of the people versus James Tobin, the court rules that there is probable cause. The defendant will be bound over for trial."

105

An ebullient noise rushed through the courtroom, and
Granger sighed in relief. He glanced over at Charleston. Though
she'd had to expect this—and had accomplished almost everything she could have expected to (and more than he would have
liked)—she nonetheless looked displeased. Like many lawyers,
particularly expensive ones, she thought herself more brilliant
than humanly possible.

Yvonne Barnes, on the other hand, sat quietly, a look of intent
triumph on her face. Granger glanced at her, wondering once
again what secrets the Ice Queen kept so jealously concealed.

Meanwhile, Tobin's eyes were downcast, his lips turned in a
young man's smirk. The bailiff was already moving to take him
away. Before this could happen, though, Tobin turned to Ruby
sitting in the first row behind him. Ruby reached over the balus-
trade, wrapping her arms around her man. She crushed herself
against him. A calculated moment, whether for his benefit, or
Tobin's, or the cameras, Granger did not know. No matter,
because in that moment he'd happened to catch her eyes. Those
eyes told him that this was an act she had not quite convinced
herself to give up. Sooner or later, though, she would give it up,
he was all but sure. When she did, he wanted to make sure it
happened on the stand, for all to hear.

He could almost feel the jubilation pouring from the Court
TV people and the radio and print reporters. Another circus, he
thought with disgust, another opportunity for people like
Charleston to subvert justice, to bring the entire thing down to
the level of a carnival sideshow. Come see the two-headed
defendant, come see JoJo the dog-faced witness, come see the
bloody evidence, come watch the pain. Come see justice's
stuttering progress. Justice is not scripted, Granger thought
angrily. It does not have a convenient climax just before you cut
to commercials. It's long and tedious and awkward and usually
boring, full of procedural issues and technicalities and not a chase
scene in view. And it was still, he believed, the best way society

had for determining guilt or innocence—in essence, for preserving the glue that keeps society together.

But how much longer would the courts be allowed to stutter and arrive, with painful slowness, at some judicial truth? Yes, there were mistakes and yes, there were problems, but turning the entire process into a daytime soap opera was not going to help.

Granger gathered his papers together and glanced at Josalyn Williams, who stood at his elbow stuffing her own briefcase. Josalyn glowed, ready to leap into battle, all prepared for the media feeding frenzy that would greet them on the courthouse steps.

And thank the Lord she loved it, he thought with sudden weariness.

"Do me a favor," he said, putting a hand on her forearm.

"Sure," she said, curious.

"You go deal with the reporters, would you? Just the usual stuff, you know the drill. We've got a good case, confident of victory."

"Racka racka racka," she said. "Yeah, I know the drill. Don't you want to do it?"

"God, no," Granger said. "I'm going to sneak out the back. Wong's sure to be out there. Tell her I had to get back to work or I broke my leg or something. And grab as much glory as you want, kid."

Josalyn started to grin. "Sure thing, boss."

"Just one thing, Ms. Williams. Don't you dare put my ass in a sling."

Laughing, Josalyn went out the front while Sterling Granger, already planning his opening statement, waited a judicious fifteen minutes before sneaking out the back.

Nineteen

୧୬ ୧୬

The Jury

I
n the end, the television crews won the battle over venue. Judge Wagner agreed to move the proceedings from that shabby room in the basement into one of the dignified old chambers higher up in the building, chambers smelling of polished wood and black-robed solemnity.

Wagner sat behind the judge's podium looking disgruntled, displeased, bearish, and surly in front of the whirring cameras. Granger, standing while the judge took his seat on the bench, couldn't blame him.

It sometimes seemed, in the days between the end of the prelim and the opening of jury selection, that every form of media in history had concentrated on the San Francisco Hall of Justice. Cynthia Charleston appeared nightly in snippets scattered from the start of the ten o'clock news broadcasts through the end of the eleven o'clock shows, and sometimes later if Leno or Letterman or O'Brien had a juicy shot. Granger, on the other hand, had been spared such attention, mostly by creating the impression that he was made of wood. "About as animated as the vice president," some comic had deemed him, and Granger was tempted to have the line framed and mounted on his office wall. He liked it that way.

Josalyn Williams, however, flourished in the glow of the media. Pretty, tough, quick on her feet, and quicker with her tongue, she came across as extremely competent and convinced, beyond a shadow of a doubt, that the prosecution would prevail.

Granger wished he were half so certain.

Despite Charleston's best efforts, the jury selection went fairly quickly. Judge Wagner promised that he wouldn't sequester the jury unless it was absolutely necessary and even threatened a media blackout if need be. This, Granger thought, was enough to put Charleston and some of the more wild-eyed television legal analysts on their best behavior.

After only a week, a jury was impaneled. Twelve good folk spanning the San Francisco range of color, religion, age, gender, and sexual orientation. A remarkably diverse jury, given that Charleston wanted to cram it with women (thinking they'd never convict the handsome artist) and Granger wanted as many minorities as he could find (hoping they'd nail Tobin good). Granger and Williams, in a wicked moment after court one day, came up with names for all of them, from Madame Defarge with her distrustful expression to Moonchild, a young man with pierced ears, tie-die shirts, and a wistful look about the eyes. Dudley Do-Right, shovel jaw and all, seemed to have emerged as the jury foreman; Josalyn swore that Dudley had it in for Moonchild, was Madame Defarge's illegitimate child, and yearned for the favors of Brenda Starr, a sleek professional woman. She and Granger giggled madly over their coffees before collecting themselves and never using those nicknames again. If you didn't respect your jury, each and every one of them, you couldn't expect them to respect your case.

The trial began on one of those June days typical of early summer, when the outlying areas were filled with a bright, illusory sunshine but the city itself was in fog. Not the romantic fog of postcards, but a gray, everyday fog that hung low over the valley of the Hall of Justice. The building sat stolidly, a gray maiden in the center of the city, far from where that famous singer left his heart.

Inside the courtroom, the Honorable Harvey Wagner banged his gavel and intoned: "The court will come to order."

The jury snapped their heads to attention.

Charleston wore plum again, a color that had become a trademark of hers these last weeks. The camera was drawn to her now. It lingered over her face, then pulled back to show the good-looking defendant beside her. The director cut to the prosecution team while the announcers dwelled over each side's strengths and weaknesses as though this were a tennis match.

Then the camera focused on Granger alone.

"Ladies and gentlemen." He turned to the jury, knowing these first moments were among the most important. "On March twentieth of this year, James Tobin shot Zachary Barnes to death. No one, not even the defendant, disputes this fact.

"The defendant, and his attorney, will claim self-defense. They will blame the victim, they will blame wild emotion. But the People say: no. The People say: let's examine the facts."

Granger paused. He held his hand up and used his fingers to count off the evidence.

"Fact. Five days before the murder James Tobin threatened the life of Zachary Barnes.

"Fact. James Tobin then secured a weapon in preparation for a final meeting with his partner.

"Fact. James Tobin brought a gun to that final meeting.

"Fact. James Tobin thrust the barrel of that gun beneath his partner's chin.

"Fact. James Tobin pulled the trigger.

"No, ladies and gentlemen, the facts do not suggest that the shooting of Zachary Barnes was self-defense. The facts tell us something different. This killing was premeditated, brutal, ruthless. And because of this," Granger turned. He pointed a long finger at the accused. "Because of this, the People charge the defendant, James Tobin, with murder in the first degree."

The jury turned its attention toward Tobin. So did everyone in the courtroom, and the court camera too, along with all those people on the other side of the lens, in their living rooms and kitchens, in the metro stations and bar rooms. All eyes were on the handsome, arrogant face of James Tobin.

That's the way Granger wanted it—away from the pretrial monkey business and on the accused and his horrible crime.

TWENTY

❧ ❧

DISCUSSIONS WITH THE DA

I t was a ceremonious start. That it was also a Friday pleased Granger because it gave the jury the weekend to ponder his opening. Charleston would deliver her opening statement Monday morning, and they would move right into the prosecution's case. All in all, for a case that made him feel as though the bottom would drop out at any moment, and one bedeviled with cameras and microphones, it wasn't too bad an opening.

Josalyn assured him that it played well on television and helped patch over some of the difficulties of the last weeks. That evening Wong joined the prosecution team to talk over strategy before the trial began in earnest.

"You're using jealousy as the primary motive?" Wong asked.

"No," said Granger.

"Why not?"

Wong always did this on important cases, challenging him on his basic premises, taking him on. He enjoyed the intellectual exercise. A good way to prepare, to hone his thinking.

"Jealousy had something to do with it, I'm sure of that," Granger said. "But there's something else beneath the surface. Insurance fraud."

"You're talking a dual motive. Juries don't like dual motives. Too subtle."

"Not if you play it right."

"How's that?" Wong asked.

"Focus on the jealousy, but keep reminding the jury about the possibility of larceny. A deal gone bad. In the end, we show jealousy was just a trigger, a flash point. Part of an angry competition between the two men."

"What do you think, Josalyn?" asked Wong.

"I agree," she said, tapping an elegantly manicured fingernail against her notepad. "But there are things I'm still worried about—that we're both still worried about. Boss?"

"You go ahead," Granger said.

Josalyn nodded. "OK. First, ever since my initial interview with Yvonne Barnes, I can't shake the feeling that she's covering something up, hiding something, and I'm not sure what it is, or how important it is. It could be just that she doesn't want her husband's reputation damaged, and something she knows could do that. Or it could be something with more weight, something speaking directly to motive. We don't know, but it bothers me."

"Has she been cooperative?" Wong asked.

Granger nodded. "Sure, to a certain extent. She answers questions, she's willing to testify, she's a good enough witness. But Josalyn is right, and Charleston's going to pick up on it because she's no dummy." He blew his breath out. "I hate surprises," he muttered.

"Can we do anything about it?" Wong said.

"No," Josalyn replied. "Short of going through the mayor, there's no way to pressure her. And she made it real obvious to me last week, when we were going over her testimony again, that anyone who tried to get to her that way was making a big, big mistake."

"OK," Wong said. "You've tried and you can't. Let it go. What else?"

"The gun," Josalyn said.

"I thought it belonged to Daryl Barnes." The DA looked from one to the other.

"Yeah, it did," Granger responded. "But I can't move it from his place to Tobin's hand—I can't prove a trail. I'm not even sure what the trail is."

Wong thought about that. "OK. You've got someone working on it?"

"Yeah, and Ruby Garcia, Tobin's girlfriend, called me during the prelim. She said she saw the gun in Tobin's paint closet in his apartment before the shooting. But I can't nail her down, and I don't want to examine her about it on the stand unless I'm sure what she'll say." He slumped in his chair. "She lied at the prelim," he said with a trace of anger. "I'll be damned if I'll let her sucker me again." He stared at Wong. "I don't like it, Julie Ann. I don't like secrets, I don't like not knowing, and I really hate being pressured with murder one."

Wong just shrugged. "How hard is Zachary Barnes going to take it in this case?" she said.

"He's dead," said Granger. "How much harder can it get?"

"You know what I mean, Sterling—his reputation. Are you going to have to drag him through the mud to get to Tobin?"

"I don't understand your worry."

"It's always a good idea to make the victim look as wholesome as possible, you know that," Wong said. The DA's voice was wry, full of that irony that prosecutors developed in regard to courtroom tactics and the manipulation of juries. "Besides, Yvonne Barnes has suffered enough."

"Oh, come on," Josalyn said sharply. "The deceased was having an affair with his partner's girlfriend. You know Charleston's going to drag that one around. If we pretend it didn't happened, if we act like Zack was some kind of saint, then we'll look pretty silly."

"I understand, but this thing's being politicized in certain ways," said Wong.

"What are you trying to say?"

"I'll be blunt. Yvonne Barnes is a very visible woman in the mayor's administration. I want the prosecution to be delicate. Also, Zachary Barnes was well-liked in the black community. If we sully him in the process. . . ."

Josalyn wouldn't hear it. She kept her voice down, but the edge was still there, palpable. "If we don't prosecute this in the way it should be done, exploring the links and whatever animosities existed between these two men—no matter where they take us—then we run the risk of losing this case altogether. That would be a much bigger political fiasco, don't you think?"

"She's right," said Granger.

"OK," Wong said finally. "If that's the way it is, then any stuff that has to come out against Zachary Barnes I want Josalyn to handle. To present it to the jury."

"I think we all understand what my role is, and why you put me on the case," said Josalyn. "To make certain things palpable to the jury. And to the public."

For the first time Granger saw her vulnerability. She had heard the media analysts: that she had been brought into the case because she was black, and she was a woman, and her presence brought balance to the team. But she was also hard-nosed and practical enough to know that such considerations were the reality of the world. She would like nothing better, Granger guessed, than a shot at examining the witnesses in a case like this, with all the lights on her, center stage. He began thinking that perhaps it would be a good idea to let her.

"Who are you putting on the stand first?" asked Wong.

"Looper," said Granger.

"Do you think she'll hold up against Charleston?"

"She'll handle herself," Granger insisted.

Wong grimaced. "Does she know that Luisa Brown's on the defense witness list?"

Granger and Josalyn shook their heads. It had been a distinctly unpleasant surprise, finding the name of Anita Looper's former lover on that list. They knew why Charleston had put her there.

She had something. Something about that conversation, so long ago, between Tobin and Luisa Brown at the show opening—something that might, combined with the failure to bag hands, cast doubt on Looper's testimony, and could cast reasonable doubt on Tobin's guilt.

"No," Granger said finally. "It would only shake her, keep her off balance. That's what Charleston wants."

The district attorney looked unhappy.

It was dark now. Light from the arc lamps outside fell through the slatted blinds in wide slants. Wong did not seem convinced about Looper, but it was a moot point. Looper had been the lead detective, and they had little choice but to put her on the stand.

Wong rose from her chair and looked down at him coldly. "You'd better be damned sure of that," she said, and left the room. She hadn't once mentioned the Hayes Valley fiasco, but it hung over the conversation like cigar smoke.

Granger and Josalyn shared a poker-faced glance, then went back to their paperwork.

TWENTY-ONE

༄ ~ ༄

CHILD CUSTODY

It was close to midnight when Granger got home. He dropped his tie and briefcase on the chair in the hallway and fixed himself a nightcap before playing back the messages on his answering machine in the kitchen.

"Sterling, it's Marian," said the cool voice of his ex. "I need to talk with you—it's urgent. Call me when you get home. It doesn't matter how late."

The machine clicked off, but Granger was already dialing Marian's number, his fingers stumbling over the buttons.

"Is Jemma okay?" he demanded as soon as the call connected.

"And hello to you too, Sterling," Marian replied. He obviously had not wakened her. "Jemma is fine, physically."

"Thank God." He sat on the stool beside the kitchen counter and rubbed his forehead. "Don't scare me that way, Marian. I'm under enough pressure as it is."

"So I understand," she replied. "Jemma tells me that she'll be spending lots of time with Grandma and Grandpa Granger. Do you believe that this is part of our shared custody agreement, Sterling?"

"Ah, come on, Marian," he said wearily. "You read the news, you must know what I'm up against here. I'm in court all day, and the only time I have to do research and paperwork and all that is in the evenings or weekends. I explained all that to Jemma. I thought she understood."

"She may understand, but I don't," Marian said. "Do you really believe that you can drop her like that, just dump her whenever you feel like it, and pick her up again when your schedule permits?"

"That's not the—"

"Because you may have forgotten, Sterling, but I know what that's like. I've been there. And I am not going to let the same thing happen to my daughter."

"Damn it, Marian, she's my daughter, too," Granger shouted into the phone. "Do you really believe, for one second, that—"

"What I really believe hardly matters," Marian said coldly. "Tomorrow I'm meeting with my lawyer, and I'm going to file for sole custody, and to revoke your visiting rights."

"But . . . you, you can't do that!"

"Watch me," Marian said. "If you believe that persecuting people—and don't correct me, I used that word deliberately—if you believe that using sloppy police work to jail an innocent man is more important than your daughter, then I think I should make sure she stays well away from you. That's not the sort of influence I want."

"Don't you dare," Granger said furiously. He took a deep, shuddering breath to calm himself. "Marian, can you at least give me some time? Please?"

Marian was silent, but he could hear her even breathing.

"Look," he said, pleading, "we've just impaneled the jury, I've just made the opening argument. You know I can't ask for a continuance at this point. If you could just wait, wait until this trial's over."

"No," she said flatly.

"No?" Granger echoed, disbelieving. "No? Marian, this is our child we're talking about here. This is Jemma, her well-being, can you really throw all that away out of spite? Marian?"

But Marian had already hung up.

*   *   *

Meanwhile, Simon Lee was lying low. The last time he'd seen Looper, she told him the prosecution would be in touch and that he shouldn't talk to the defense. He'd done like she said. As the trial wore on, he hoped maybe they'd all forgotten about him. After all, he was a nobody in this world.

In the interval, he'd gotten his old job back down at the New World Order Delivery Service, driving a two-stroke scooter up and down the canyons of the financial district, dodging yellow taxis and Muni buses and yuppies in Mercedes, weaving through digital designers and bankers and she-girl secretaries wearing bang-bang clothes that made him want to reach out and touch. Instead he kept dodging. He'd been dodging one thing or another ever since he could remember.

Then the Saturday after the trial started, a woman attorney showed up for him down at the New World Order.

"My name's Josalyn Williams," she said. "You're testifying for the prosecution, and my boss wants you to come down to the office."

"What for?"

"To go over your testimony."

She was somewhere around thirty. Her skin was a soft copper, and she had high cheekbones and a very cool, professional way of looking at him. Simon didn't want to visit the DA's office, but he enjoyed walking through the parking lot next to this woman, even if she frightened him some.

They didn't head straight downtown. Instead she took him to the men's section of one of those big department stores along Union Square.

"What are we doing here?"

"You need clothes for court."

"I got clothes."

She looked him up and down. He wore a shirt cut off at the sleeves and jeans the color of asphalt. The slightest trace of a smile crossed her lips.

"You need something more appropriate."

"I can't afford it."

"We'll pay."

She took him into the store and picked out a brown jacket from the rack. Then she hunted up a clerk who fitted him out with a dress shirt and some slacks. When Simon strolled out of the dressing room all decked out like that, Josalyn Williams examined the material and smoothed down his collar with her long fingers. She nodded to the clerk.

"This'll do fine," she said.

"I'm not a doll," Simon said. "I'm not some kind of puppet on a string." The truth was he enjoyed the attention. Josalyn paid the cashier, and Simon followed her to the car carrying his old clothes in a paper bag.

When they reached the Hall of Justice, she took him up into her office and started going over his testimony. Every once in a while the other attorney, Granger, would come in, sit, and listen. Mostly, though, it was just Josalyn Williams and him. She drilled him on the art theft. About how he had seen Tobin cutting out the paintings. About the letter from Zack to Ruby, and how Tobin had lost his temper when he found out about Ruby and Zack.

She went over it all a number of times, asking him the same questions over and over. She had him sit in a chair next to her desk, and she stood up, posturing like she was in court. She wore a gray skirt, a white blouse, a string of pearls. She felt him looking at her, he guessed, but it didn't seem to matter to her either way. She kept hammering at him, and he kept answering the questions the same way he'd told Looper, more or less. Finally she seemed satisfied there wasn't some other version of events kicking around in his head, waiting to pop up the moment he got on the stand.

"I guess we're done," she said.

"Oh."

He was disappointed. He had begun to enjoy this game, and he liked being in this room with her. Maybe she liked it too. Her expression had a certain open quality that had not been there before, and he noticed the deep brown of her eyes.

"Simon?"

"Yes?"

"Did you ever see a gun in the Barnes Gallery?"

"Yeah."

"Yes?" Her voice raised a little. Her eyes engaged him yet more intensely, and his eyes wandered from her face down her neck, into the soft white of her blouse. "When?" she asked.

"I don't know exactly. It was that week, you know, before Zack was killed."

"You never mentioned this to Inspector Looper."

"No."

"Why not?"

"She never asked me."

"Just a minute. I'll be right back."

Williams left the room, and Simon felt a rise of excitement. He wanted the interview to continue. When she came back, though, she was with Granger, the other attorney. He felt his heart sink like a stone in dirty water.

"What's this I hear about a gun in the Barnes Gallery?" Granger asked.

Simon stiffened. "Nothing," he said. "I don't know nothing about it."

Granger glanced down at the floor, as if studying the tips of his shoes. Simon thought the man would get in his face; instead he was low-key and slow.

"Take it easy, Simon. You're not a suspect in this case, OK?"

"No problem," said Simon, though he wasn't going to be taken in. Maybe it worked with the girls, but Simon could see through the guy. He looked at the two attorneys, Williams and Granger, standing around in their uptight suits, and he wondered what was going on between them.

"Good," said Granger. "Now, can we continue?"

"Sure. But like you said, I just worked there. I don't know everything that went on."

"I understand. Now tell me, where did you see this gun?"

"In Zack's desk—the cash drawer."

Granger looked at him, an expression of absolute surprise on his face. Simon glanced uncomfortably at Williams. She too stared at him, but she looked skeptical. That skepticism scared him. It was the same expression that Mrs. Barnes used sometimes, the times Simon knew his butt was about to be whipped. She doesn't believe me, he thought. "That drawer," he said. "It's locked. About a week before the murder, though, he started keeping a gun in there. A short barrel. A thirty-eight, I think. It had a silver facing and black grips."

"The desk drawer?" she said, just as Granger said, "Not the paint closet upstairs?"

"Naw, the desk drawer. You know, where he kept the cash. Downstairs, in his office in the gallery."

The two attorneys shared a glance, then Granger said, "How did you happen to run across this?"

"I saw Zack with it."

"When?"

"It was early one morning, just after I got in. Nobody else was there, downstairs I mean. Then I heard the door open. I went back to see who it was, and there was Zack, standing at his desk. The guy unsnaps his briefcase and slides a gun into the drawer."

"What did you do next?"

"I just turned and left. I don't think he even saw me."

"Did you talk with anyone about what you saw?"

"Nobody."

Until now, Granger had done most of the talking. Now Williams stepped forward again. She gave him that same direct look she'd given him before, with those wide and earnest eyes. He swallowed and turned his head. He wasn't going to be taken in twice.

"You didn't tell Tobin?" she asked

"No."

"Did Zack ever explain to you why he'd brought a gun to the office?" asked Granger.

"No. He didn't know I knew."

"You didn't think it was strange?" she asked. They were alternating now, one sweet, the other sour. Granger circled around behind him, hovering, waiting for his answer.

"I just worked there. Like you guys said. I didn't question stuff."

"Come on, Simon," barked Granger. "You told us before there was a lot of tension in the air, those last days. Didn't Tobin ask you to keep your eyes on Zack? Isn't that what you told us?"

"Yeah, but I didn't do everything he said."

"You told him about the gun, didn't you, just like you told him about the letter?" asked Williams.

Her voice was reserved and careful, almost gentle, but she stood with her arms folded. Granger did too. They stood there like a couple of mugs in an FBI movie, and Simon realized how easy it would be for people like them to send someone like him to jail. Without hesitation. Without the tiniest ache in the heart. Without a worry about poor Simon.

"Simon," Granger said. His voice was harsh now. Any trace of reasonableness was gone. "Did you tell Tobin about the gun?"

A wrong answer, and they would screw him. Or maybe they were just bluffing. Williams moved closer to him, as if this would prompt him to answer. Simon smelled her perfume and studied her face, her smooth skin, the curve of her lips.

"Did you help Tobin plan the murder?" she asked.

"That's crazy."

"We'll prosecute if you don't tell the truth," said Granger.

"Look, I'm not stupid. The police say Tobin killed Zack with that gun."

"So?"

"Everybody knows I was Tobin's assistant. If I go to court and testify that I told Tobin about the gun, they're going to think I was in on it."

"Were you?"

"No!"

"There's a good chance, before this thing's over, Tobin will tell us the whole story. What will you do then?" asked Granger. He had taken over now, and Williams stood back, watching.

"I don't think that's a problem," said Simon.

"He'll confess and tell how he got the gun."

"He'll never confess."

"You're lying, aren't you Simon? You told Tobin about that gun. Just like you told him about the letter."

Simon averted his eyes. He was afraid.

"It's true, Simon, isn't it?" insisted Granger.

"I didn't know what the hell he was going to do," said Simon. "I didn't have any idea."

"So you told him?"

"Yes," he said. "I told him about the gun. I didn't know what the hell Zack was up to, bringing a gun into the gallery. Things had been pretty strange around there. So I told Tobin. He was my boss. I thought he should know."

The room was quiet. They had gotten what they wanted. "Yeah, I told him," Simon repeated. "I guess that makes me the dumbest fuck around."

"I don't know about that," said Granger. "I've seen dumber." He looked at Simon, his expression unreadable. "When I get you on the stand, Simon, are you going to cooperate?"

Simon glowered. "What choice have I got?"

"Maybe you've been talking to the defense."

"I haven't said a word to them."

"Then you'll tell the truth? You'll tell the story the same way you told it today?"

Simon stared at him, and then the little snake, the one tattooed on his neck, the one that sometimes told him things, told him something now. His mind flashed to Court TV and watching Ruby at the prelim, on the witness stand, lying and lying. These guys need me, he realized, and he saw a way to salvage something, maybe, for himself.

"I guess," he said offhandedly. "But you don't have to bring up that stuff about Ruby, do you?"

"What stuff?" Williams said.

"The letter, you know. How I was the one who gave it to Tobin."

"Why does that matter?"

"Because Ruby and I were friends. And because after I told Tobin about it, he beat her around. I don't want her to know I double-crossed her like that."

Granger and Williams exchanged a glance, and then Williams said, "OK, Simon, I'll make you a deal. You tell me the truth on this gun business, and I'll let you loose on that. We'll try to avoid it. We might have to mention the letter, but you won't have to say you gave it to Tobin."

She didn't look at Granger, but Simon did. The man's face suddenly looked like it was carved from stone.

"All right," Simon said.

"OK. Now go home. Get some sleep."

Simon stood up to leave. He got as far as the door.

"Wait a minute," Granger said.

"What?"

"The suit."

"What about it?"

Granger bent over and grabbed the bag with his old clothes in it. He tossed it to Simon. "Change into these. I want you to leave the suit behind."

"Yes," Williams agreed. "Leave the suit. Stop in before court, and you can get changed here."

"We'll hang it somewhere nice," said Granger. "That way it'll still be clean."

"Damn it, Josalyn," Granger said. "You lied to him. You know we have to ask him about that letter."

"Yeah, I know," she said, raising her chin. "But do you think we're going to get him to talk about the gun otherwise? Do you?"

Granger had to stop himself from wrenching open his office door. "I don't like it," he said. "It stinks." He almost threw the clothes bag onto the floor.

She didn't reply.

"There's no goddamned way around it, either," he continued after a moment. "There's no other way to present the evidence, to nail it down. I've got to question him about it—damn!" He glared at her, and she couldn't meet his eyes.

"OK, I'm sorry," she said finally. "You want me to catch up with him? To take back the promise?"

Granger thought about it, then shook his head. "No," he said finally. "No, that would make it even worse. We do need him to talk about the gun. Without him we can't put the gun in Tobin's hands. He's right that Charleston will make it look as though he had more to do with it, with the gun. So he won't talk about it unless he feels he's getting something in return."

He sat suddenly. "OK, you were right. But I hate it."

"Me too," Josalyn said. She picked up the bag of Simon's new clothes and sat across from Granger.

"So where does this get us?" she asked, lifting the corner of the bag. Between them lay increasing mountains of bound briefs and opened law books.

"Let's trace it out," said Granger. "We know three things about the gun. First, it belonged to Daryl Barnes. We've got the registration papers, all that. Second, Zack was keeping it in his office. We've got Simon's testimony on that. What a break that was! OK, Simon Lee tells Tobin about the gun. According to Ruby, that gun, or a gun, was in Tobin's paint closet before the murder."

"So Tobin must have stolen it from Zack's drawer," said Josalyn.

"That's the way it looks."

"But what was Zack doing with his cousin's gun? Why did he have it in his office drawer?"

"I don't know. But Charleston will say that Zack stole it, with the intention of using it against her client."

Josalyn rattled her pencil against her notepad. "OK, it all works. I just wish I felt more confident about our witnesses.

Simon's a loose cannon, I can feel it. And Garcia, after what she said at the prelim. . . ."

A little silence grew while they thought about that.

"Have you talked to Yvonne Barnes yet?" Granger asked.

Josalyn shook her head. "Not beyond the basics. I'll say this for her, the lady's good. You ask her a question she doesn't want to hear, and she just doesn't hear it. I don't dare pry and badger, or she'll clam up entirely." Josalyn looked disgusted. "There are times when I wish I could get that lady drunk, but I'm not sure alcohol would have any effect on her."

Granger smiled faintly. "Yeah, I know the feeling."

Silence settled while Granger stared at the window and thought not of the case, but of Marian and Jemma. He'd called his own lawyer this morning and now, like so many clients, he just had to wait, and wait, and wait. And in the meantime, the trial hung over him, and the prospect of losing his daughter hung over him, and he could no more ignore one than ignore the other. Any more of this, he thought, and he'd be back to the bottles of Mylanta.

"Sterling, are you OK?" Josalyn asked suddenly.

He brought himself back to the moment and looked at her across the landscape of paper.

"Yeah. Yeah, it's just . . . yeah, I'm OK," he said and smiled.

She looked at him with those fine eyes, obviously not buying it, but she didn't press. She gathered up her notepad and stood. "You need to talk, I'm just down the hall, boss," she said. "I'm going to put Mr. Lee's testimony into the computer, then I'm heading out. You need dinner?"

Granger shook his head. "No. No, thanks, I've still got a lot to do."

He gestured vaguely around the office, and she nodded at him and left. It was only after the door clicked shut that he realized that she had, for the first time, used his given name.

Twenty-Two

Looper-Go-Round

Inspector Looper had been following the papers and found herself suddenly a celebrity. Not the best kind of celebrity, true, but a celebrity all the same. A person or two recognized her in the grocery, and one of these had approached her.

"Hey, aren't you the lesbian cop that arrested that artist because he wanted to sleep with your girlfriend?"

"I wouldn't put it that way."

"No?"

"I don't think so."

"Can I have your autograph?"

Looper took the pen and signed.

Her bed might be empty, she might be on forced leave (something Chief LoBianco had done the day after her testimony at the prelim, and she was still ticked off about it), she might not have a job to go back to when this was all over—but hell, people recognized her red head bobbing down the street. Life was swell.

Granger scheduled her for testimony the first week. On the big day she dressed up as though she were going to a Baptist church, pushed past the reporters, and took the stand.

During her first afternoon of testimony, Granger covered the same ground they'd gone over in the preliminary, only in more detail. He concentrated on the physical evidence. He had her pick up and examine the crowbar with Tobin's prints, then insert it into the doorjamb to demonstrate that it was the same crowbar used to pry the door. He instructed her to hold up the cash box that had been discovered at the scene. He asked her to identify photographs of the broken glass scattered under Barnes's body. All of this to suggest how Tobin had carefully choreographed the scene to make it look as though Barnes had been killed in a robbery during a struggle with an armed intruder.

After that, Granger went over the transcripts from her interviews with Tobin, sifting through the contradictions.

Granger kept her on the stand the better part of three days. It all went well enough, Looper thought. Then Cynthia Charleston swaggered up for the cross, her head tilted, her cheeks painted with blush, smiling a smile that made Looper want to reach out and smack her face.

"Inspector Looper," said Charleston, "will you describe your own state of mind when you arrived at the crime scene?"

"I don't understand the question."

"That morning at the gallery, were you feeling fatigued?"

"No."

"The day before the shooting, how late did you work?"

"Untill about nine-thirty."

"Was that unusual?"

Looper reflected a moment. "It was a long day, but not that unusual. Just another twelve-hour day in the city."

"You were working on more than one case then?"

"Yes. I think it was the Baker case, the day before. It had just gone to trial."

Granger cut in, objecting. "Relevance?" he asked.

"Your Honor, the defense is trying to establish the inspector's state of mind at the time of the investigation," said Charleston. Her voice draped over the courtroom like a silk sheet. "It has a bearing on competence."

Judge Wagner made a noise deep in his throat. He did not look well. He coughed, then stared a long time at the top of his desk. Finally he ruled for Charleston. "Proceed."

"The evening before the shootings, did you go out after work?"

"To dinner. At La Rondala. I had the combination plate."

"What did you have to drink?"

"Two beers. And part of a third."

"That's a very precise answer. Far more precise than at the preliminaries. Has something in the meantime occurred to enhance your recall regarding your drinking habits?"

"No. I'm just trying to answer your questions the best I can."

"What time did you finally get home that evening?"

"A little before midnight."

"Were you tired the next morning?"

Looper was getting weary of this woman and waited before she answered. "No, I wasn't tired," she said at last. "I was chipper as hell."

"Your Honor, the defense seems to be reaching here," protested Granger. His eyes, though, were on Looper, warning her to keep it under control. She touched her wild red hair and bit her lip.

"Let's see where this goes," said the judge.

"Is it true you were tired, depressed over the Baker case? That you conducted the investigation in a way that was not entirely—"

"Objection. Leading the witness."

"Sustained."

Charleston paused, restarted. "Inspector Looper, what was your mood that morning?"

"Objection," said Granger. "We've already been over this ground."

"I'll decide that," said Judge Wagner. "In the meantime, the witness will answer."

Looper hesitated a beat. Charleston seized the moment, sheathing her voice in condescension. "The witness seems confused. I'll repeat. Inspector Looper, what was your mood the

morning of the shooting, when you walked into the Barnes
Gallery?"

Looper had had enough of Cynthia Charleston. "You know
how it is, Cynthia," she said. "Another day, another murder—and
I couldn't find my designer jeans."

Judge Wagner brought down his gavel. "Enough of this, both
of you. Inspector, restrain your sarcasm. And Ms. Charleston,
please put your questions into the scope of direct. I'm not in the
mood for this kind of silliness."

"Yes, Your Honor." Charleston tugged at her jacket, then
shook out her hair. She studied the back of her hand, as if
admiring her long, thin fingers. Vain behavior, overtly feminine,
calculated, exaggerated, designed to irk Looper. "Did you talk
to my client, James Tobin, on Saturday morning at the Barnes
Gallery?"

"Yes."

"Was he wounded and bleeding?"

"Yes."

"Did he tell you at that time that Mr. Barnes had attacked
him and a violent struggle ensued?"

"Something like that."

"At the gallery that day, did you notice any evidence of such
a struggle?"

"I try to be a good detective, and not interpret the evidence
until after it has been collected."

"I see. In your investigation, did you make note of a broken
chair?

"Yes. It was noted."

"Did anyone make note of torn clothing?"

"Yes, but those tears appeared to have been—"

"A simple yes or no, please."

"Yes."

"Did photographs of James Tobin—taken shortly after the
incident—reveal bruises on his body?"

"Yes."

"Do you consider yourself an expert on homicide investigation?"

"I know what I'm doing."

"Your Honor, am I to consider that an affirmative answer, or is Inspector Looper here for our entertainment?"

"Inspector," said Wagner. "Please answer in a straightforward manner."

"Yes. I'm an expert."

"In your expert opinion then, did the various evidence at the scene—a broken chair, broken glass, torn clothing, bruises on the defendant—did these suggest some sort of violent struggle had taken place before the shooting?"

"I can't bring myself to jump to that kind of conclusion, Cynthia."

"Only for the prosecution, then, will you jump to conclusions?"

"Objection!" shouted Granger.

"Sustained. For the last time, both of you, I have had far too much of this behavior. Inspector Looper, simply answer the questions. This is not a comedy show."

Charleston strolled back to the defense table and glanced a moment at her notes. Granger shook his head. Looper knew he thought she should know better. She had let Charleston get too much under her skin.

"Inspector Looper, is it true that you were acquainted with James Tobin before the incident on March twentieth of this year?'"

"I met him once. I wouldn't describe him as an acquaintance."

"Where did this meeting occur?"

"Several years ago. At a gallery opening."

"Do you feel this earlier acquaintance with my client colored your view of him, that morning when you arrived at the scene of the shooting?"

"The earlier meeting was far too brief to have much influence on me," said Looper. Looper knew, like Granger knew, what was coming next. The two of them had gone over it in detail. Charleston was going to dwell on that meeting. Get it out in front of the jury. This time Looper would respond differently. She would yes and no her to death. One-word answers. Elaborate as a barbed-wire fence.

"Who was with you during that earlier meeting?"

"Luisa Brown."

"And what was your relation to Luisa Brown?"

"A friend."

"Wasn't she also your lover at the time?"

"Yes."

"So she is your former lover now?"

"Yes."

"After you met Tobin, did you and Luisa Brown discuss Tobin?"

"I don't recall."

"Did she tell you that she found him attractive?"

"Objection," said Granger.

Wagner hesitated. "Overruled."

"I don't recall," said Looper.

"Is it true that Luisa Brown is bisexual?"

"Objection!" Granger was on his feet now. "I don't see the relevance of this third party's sexual orientation."

"Sustained. Ms. Charleston, I have been lenient in this line of questioning, but you don't seem to be going anywhere. Please tie this up."

"Yes, Your Honor." Charleston tugged at the hem of her jacket again. She glanced in a rather deliberate way at the camera, smiling to herself, then continued. She clearly enjoyed this. "After you and Luisa met the artist James Tobin at the gallery, were you jealous of the conversation that went on between them?"

"I didn't have any reason to be."

"Inspector Looper, is it true that the evening you first met James Tobin, at the gallery opening in the company of your lover, Luisa Brown, that at that time, Luisa Brown propositioned James Tobin?"

There was a lull. The jury was leaning forward in their seats. Charleston had played a trump, and all bets were off.

"I don't understand the question," said Looper.

"I'll try to make it plainer. In your presence, that day when you first met my client, did your girlfriend ask James Tobin to have sex?"

"Objection!" Granger shouted again. "Your Honor, I have strenuous objections. This is outrageous grandstanding."

"I'm going to allow," said Wagner. "If there was a prior relationship between the arresting officer and the defendant, it's relevant. Please answer the question, Inspector Looper."

Looper took a breath. Tobin was watching her. He wore a royal blue jacket and a crisp white shirt. His tie couldn't be any more precisely knotted, and his hair was perfectly combed, except for a large, rather deliberate-looking black curl that fell over his forehead. He kept his face expressionless, a regular poker face, but Looper could see, she thought, a smug turn to his lips.

She considered lying. There weren't many people who understood Luisa, her sense of humor, how she would say things just to pull someone's tail.

"No," she said.

As soon as she did, though, she remembered it hadn't just been Tobin in that little circle of people. There'd been a couple of others within earshot. Whether Charleston had access to them as witnesses, Looper had no idea.

"No?" asked Charleston. "She didn't proposition him? Is that what you are saying?"

"That wasn't my understanding of her statement. Luisa was joking."

"Joking? Please explain."

"Luisa has a strong sense of irony. The truth is, she was mocking him. I know. She found James Tobin repulsive."

"Really?" asked Charleston. "And you—did you share Luisa's opinion?"

Looper glanced again at Tobin. His smirk was all but apparent now, as if inviting her to insult him. As much as she would have liked to oblige him, she held off. This whole thing had gone badly enough.

"I hadn't formed any opinion of him."

"I see. Now, on March twentieth, when you encountered my client at the Barnes Gallery, did you recognize James Tobin as the same man you had met earlier, in the company of Luisa Brown?"

Again Looper wished she could somehow get away from the truth, but it was impossible. She had mentioned their earlier meeting at the murder scene, in front of the magenta-haired paramedic. She was stuck.

"Yeah. I recognized him."

"While you were interviewing him, did you happen to remember the sexual innuendo that passed between your ex-lover and James Tobin?"

"It wasn't an innuendo. And it wasn't on my mind."

"Later, while you were charging James Tobin with murder, did this earlier flirtation come to mind?"

"No."

"Inspector Looper, is it possible that, when you saw James Tobin at the scene of the shooting, it was jealousy, the memory of an old wound, that motivated you—consciously or unconsciously—to manipulate the evidence in such a way—"

"Objection!"

"Grounds, Mr. Granger?"

"Inspector Looper has answered this question already. The defense is simply attempting to demean the witness's professional and personal integrity by repeating these ridiculous allegations over and over."

"Sustained."

"I apologize," said Charleston. "I don't mean to deride the inspector. I am sure she is normally a very competent police-woman."

Then, smiling like a shark, she brought up the issue of bagging hands.

TWENTY-THREE

୧୬ ୧୬

MISSING MINUTES

After a protracted campaign on Josalyn's part, Yvonne Barnes had agreed to meet her for coffee on Monday evening at an out-of-fashion place tucked into the first floor of an old hotel on Cathedral Hill. It was a yellow brick building in a row of other brick buildings. The places had been respectable enough once, though they were a little shabby now, inhabited for the most part by pensioners and retirees too stubborn for rest homes, many of whom struggled every day up the long hill to one of the seven cathedrals that had given the district its name. San Francisco's topography did not make religion easy. Sometimes, Josalyn Williams thought, San Francisco didn't make anything easy. Some would-be parishioners got no farther than the liquor stores advertising themselves in ancient neon on every corner.

She pushed through the doors and spotted Mrs. Barnes in a back booth, staring unhappily into a coffee cup. Badly lit, casually dressed, no makeup, and the woman still looked good. Josalyn shook the thought away and crossed the room.

"Thank you for seeing me," she said, holding out her hand. Mrs. Barnes shook it automatically and let it fall, and Josalyn slid into the banquette bench across from her.

"Your case isn't going very well," Yvonne Barnes said abruptly.
Josalyn just blinked at her, and Yvonne's lips tilted into a tiny,
cold smile. "Charleston cut a lot of holes in Looper's testimony,
didn't she?"

"She cast doubt on some irrelevant issues," Josalyn replied
smoothly. "The detective's love life has very little to do with your
husband's murder, Mrs. Barnes."

"Perhaps," the widow responded. "But what about my hands,
or Ruby's hands? Can you prove that one of us didn't shoot
somebody that morning?" Her chin rose as she stared at Josalyn.

"No, we can't prove that," Josalyn said. "Did you shoot someone that morning, Mrs. Barnes?"

They stared at each other for a moment. Then Yvonne Barnes
said, "No, of course I didn't," and stared into her coffee cup.

"Because there is something I think Cynthia Charleston will
bring up, and we need to prepare for it." Josalyn centered her
notepad on the table in front of her. "There are about fifteen
missing minutes, Mrs. Barnes, between the time Ruby dropped
you off and the time she reached the gallery. You've said before
that you saw Tobin in the alley. He ran in and locked the door.
You had to find your keys and unlock the door. We've done a
recreation and timed it, and all that doesn't take more than two
and a half, maybe three minutes. You ran inside and saw your
husband, and you said you tried to revive him. OK, maybe
another three minutes there."

"How can you say that?" Yvonne demanded. "I spent the
entire time—"

"Doing something else," Josalyn continued without heat.
"Ruby Garcia says that when she arrived, you were bent over
Zack, trying to revive him. According to the coroner's office,
there were no signs that anyone had administered *hard* CPR—no
sign along the ribs of someone trying to pump the heart, no
blood blown hard into the lungs where someone tried to do
artificial respiration for a lengthy amount of time." She glanced
up. Yvonne Barnes looked a bit pale, and Josalyn, who had

toughened herself, knew that Mrs. Barnes was reacting to the ugly picture of someone performing artificial respiration on a man whose throat had been blown away.

"Somehow," Josalyn continued, "it's hard for me to imagine you spending nine or ten minutes just patting your husband's face. That's a long time, Mrs. Barnes. Enough for one segment of a sit-com and an entire commercial break."

Yvonne turned her face away. Josalyn watched her with cool sympathy.

"Yvonne?" she said finally. "What were you doing?"

Yvonne Barnes's shoulders slumped. She put her hands around the coffee cup, as though her fingers were cold, and looked bleakly up at the attorney.

"It's about the gun," she said quietly. "It's about me and Zack and the gun."

The story was fairly simple. Yvonne Barnes reminded the lawyer that a rapist had been active in her neighborhood in late February and early March, and it scared her. All too often Zack worked late and she was alone, or she worked late and came in alone. Parking in San Francisco was so difficult that even an expensive condo didn't necessarily come with a parking place. Usually Yvonne had to park one or two blocks away and trudge home through the midnight streets.

She knew that Daryl, Zack's cousin, collected guns, and one day while she was watering his plants she tried to get into his gun collection.

"It's not something I'm particularly proud of," she told Josalyn Williams. "Mayor Jack McKinney may be pro-gun, but I'm not, although it's not an opinion I broadcast. I don't like them, and I don't like having them around. But I was frightened, especially after those speeches Jack made about crime in the city and the citizens' responsibility to stop it." She shrugged. "In any event, I felt that I needed a gun. I thought that instead of buying one, I'd borrow one from Daryl. He wouldn't miss it; he wasn't supposed to be back in town for months. And as soon as the rapist was caught, I could put the gun back."

But, she said, the gun cabinet was locked, and the key well-hidden. Then she remembered that Daryl kept another gun, for protection, on the top shelf of his bedroom closet.

It took only a moment to find it and another to wrap it in her handkerchief and shove it down into her purse. Then she carefully watered her husband's cousin's plants, and went home.

"But it kept bothering me," she said. "My cousin Byrum, back in New Orleans—he kept a gun, and someone broke into his house one night. Byrum went after him, but the burglar took the gun and shot Byrum instead. Killed him." She stirred her coffee. "I kept thinking that, this rapist, he hadn't killed anyone. He frightened women, and he tied them up and raped them, but he hadn't killed anyone. But what would happen if somebody pulled a gun on him? They never found the man who killed Byrum, you know. And I couldn't carry it with me. I don't have a permit, and can you see the headlines if I'd been stopped and it had been found? MAYOR'S PRESS SECRETARY FOUND WITH ILLEGAL WEAPON?"

She smiled without humor. "It got to the point where I was more afraid of the gun than I was of the rapist. So I took it out and gave it to Zack. It was still in my handkerchief. I'd never even unwrapped it."

"I see," Josalyn said, writing. "He knew about it?"

"No, not before. He said he'd take it back to Daryl's, but it was eight-fifteen in the morning, and I had to get to work and so did he. But I told him that I didn't want it in the house, so he said he'd take it with him and drop it off at Daryl's later in the day."

"OK," Josalyn said. "When was this?"

"About a week before . . . before he was killed," Yvonne Barnes said. "And when I went into the gallery that morning, and I touched Zack and knew he was dead—and Tobin was lying on the floor holding his leg and yelling—and I saw the gun, just lying there near Zack, that's when I remembered, when I thought about the handkerchief." She looked at Josalyn, eyes wide and clear. "I guess I was in shock, some kind of shock, because I thought if the police found that handkerchief, if it came out, then Zack would. . . I might lose. . . . Oh, God, I barely know what I was thinking anymore." She drained the coffee cup and put it down.

"So I went to the cash drawer. It was open, like someone had wrenched it out of the desk with a crowbar. But I didn't even think about that. I found my handkerchief, in the back of the drawer, and I took it out and put it in my pocket."

She reached into her purse and drew out a folded square of linen with the initials YB embroidered into one corner.

"Here it is," she said simply.

Josalyn Williams looked at it without touching it. Granger had his provenance now, she thought. A clear line tracing the gun from Daryl Barnes's closet to Yvonne Barnes's purse to Zack Barnes's briefcase and cash drawer to James Tobin's paint closet to James Tobin's hand. Granger would be pleased.

But Josalyn, looking from the handkerchief to the mayor's press secretary, couldn't shake the feeling that Yvonne Barnes was still holding something back.

TWENTY-FOUR

❧ ❧

THE TESTIMONY OF SIMON LEE

Tuesday and most of Wednesday were devoted to the criminalists and the coroner, who walked the court and the jury through the scene. It was sometimes fascinating and sometimes distressing, as when the medical examiner produced photographs of the victim, but in the end it was picky and detailed and boring and necessary. Josalyn Williams handled these witnesses with speed and dispatch, and Cynthia Charleston did her best to oppose, question, and cast doubt. But that, of course, was her job.

When he was finally called to the stand late on Wednesday, Simon told himself he would cooperate as best as he could. He did not want to tell how he'd gone along with everything Tobin had asked him to do. It made him look stupid, like he didn't have a mind of his own. Either that or he was a two-timer, someone who had gone along with his boss while the going was good but now was bailing to save his own skin.

Neither of those things was quite true, he didn't think, but he had to testify the way they wanted.

Still, Simon felt uncomfortable. He felt Tobin watching him. Every once in a while he would catch the older man's eye. He would remember how Tobin had been good to him, hiring him,

taking him into the scene. He felt like a son of a bitch for screw-
ing him the way he was getting ready to do.

At least they're letting me slide when it comes to talking
about the letter, he thought, so Ruby won't know how I opened
it and showed it to Tobin. Simon had tried to hunt Ruby down
these last few days, but her line was disconnected. He'd tried to
drum her out at Tobin's old place, too, but she wasn't there.

Granger took him through it slow. The attorney started way
back, August of last year, the day Simon had first met Ruby out
front of the gallery. That was the day Tobin hired him.

"Did you enjoy working for Tobin?" Granger asked.

"Yeah."

"He was a good employer?"

"He paid me regular. He let me work my own hours."

"Did he ever get angry with you?"

"I don't know if I would put it that way."

"How would you put it?"

"He liked things done a certain way. He'd tattoo you sometimes, if you didn't do it like he wanted—but hell, it was his art."

Tobin grinned at him. Simon felt this was not going so bad.
He knew he was supposed to hammer his old boss, but he didn't
want to seem ungrateful. Also he wanted Tobin to know the stuff
coming was nothing personal. Meantime, the jurors looked a
little sleepy, like they'd all done quaaludes the night before. Judge
Wagner nodded his head too. The fat bailiff held his hands in his
pockets, scratching his balls.

"Do you recall a show at the Barnes Gallery last December
entitled *The World Is Burning*?" asked Granger.

"Yeah."

"Do you recall the reviews of the artwork that came out in
the paper the evening before?"

"Uh-huh."

"Do you remember the substance of those reviews?"

"They were pretty bad."

"And how were sales?"

"Objection," said Charleston. "This witness isn't qualified to comment on sales figures at the gallery. He was merely an assistant." She snapped the words out like an angry dog, but when she turned to face Simon she smiled at him, as if to say that she was angry at Granger, not at him. But it stung anyway, saying that he wasn't qualified. He didn't smile back.

"I'll rephrase," said Granger. "Mr. Lee, to your knowledge, how many paintings were sold the night of the opening in question?"

"None. They didn't sell a darn thing."

Simon said it to get at the woman because she had attacked him that way, but he saw Tobin wince too. Granger kept coming, leading him over the same ground Josalyn had taken him during the practice sessions. He asked him about a remark he'd heard Tobin make in passing, regarding the insurance company.

"He made some kind of joke," Simon said.

"What was that joke?"

"That the paintings were pretty well-insured so maybe it would be OK if somebody came along and stole them."

"Did anybody laugh?"

"No."

Simon didn't look at Tobin anymore. He knew his old boss was throwing daggers at him now. Simon wanted off the stand, but Granger dwelled over each detail. How Simon had overheard him one day talking finances, complaining the place was going downhill. How late one night he'd come across Tobin removing his paintings from the gallery. And how later he'd told Tobin that Zack was keeping a gun locked up in the drawer of his office desk.

"You received a bonus in your pay envelope a few days after the theft?"

"Yes."

"Who did that bonus come from?"

"I didn't know."

"Who did you think it came from?"

"Both of them. Tobin and Zack. I thought they were both in on it together."

Granger nodded and leaned against the low wall surrounding the witness chair.

"Did the defendant ever ask you to keep tabs on Zack?" he asked, one friend to another.

"Yeah," Simon said warily.

"What did he say?"

"He said he was afraid Zack was losing it. And maybe, if I saw Zack doing something funny, I should let him know."

"Did you perform this service for the defendant?"

"A couple a times."

"Mr. Lee, you mentioned earlier in your testimony that you were friendly with Ruby Garcia, the defendant's girlfriend."

Simon tightened up. Granger's demeanor had gotten more aggressive, and Simon wasn't quite sure what to expect anymore. "Yeah," he said.

"Did she ever talk to you about her relationship with Zachary Barnes?"

"She did," he said.

"What did she say?"

"That she liked him. She had a thing for him."

"Did she mention to you that she had slept with Zachary Barnes?"

"Not in those words. But I knew something was going on."

"Objection!" Charleston said. "Conclusory on the part of the witness."

"Sustained," said Judge Wagner. "The clerk will strike the witness's last remark from the record."

Simon did not fully understand, but he was relieved. He didn't want to talk about Ruby and Zack anyway, and he worried they were moving toward the subject of the letter. Granger took it in stride.

"Did you ever talk to Zack about this affair?"

"Not exactly."

"What do you mean, 'not exactly'?"

"Well, one time Zack called me over to his house." Simon felt uneasy. They were on the edge of it now. They'd told him that they might have to bring up the letter, but he wouldn't have to say how he'd given it to Tobin.

"Did Zack explain to you why he called you over?"

"Yeah. He had a letter he wanted me to deliver to Ruby— and he didn't want Tobin to know about it."

"And what did you do with that letter?"

Simon had an awful feeling in his gut. It was the point Granger had promised not to push. Yet here it was, right in front of him. Simon wondered if maybe he'd gotten it wrong. Maybe Granger had said he had to ask, but it was OK for Simon to lie.

"Please answer the question," said the judge.

"I'll repeat it for the witness, Your Honor," said Granger. Then he bore down. "Mr. Lee, please, did you tell the defendant about the letter Zachary Barnes told you to deliver to Ruby Garcia?"

"No." Simon spoke the word with his head tilted to the floor, speaking so low he barely heard it himself. Judge Wagner made him repeat his response, louder, so the jury could hear. Simon didn't glance that way, but he could feel the cold eyes of the Court TV cameras on him and, behind that, the soft, brown eyes of Ruby Garcia.

Granger strolled back to the lawyer's bench. Simon thought for a minute that maybe this was over, that Granger was satisfied.

"Your Honor," said Granger, "I'd like to approach the bench."

"Permission granted."

Granger talked to the judge. They kept their voices low, muttering indecipherably like two old dogs in private conversation. After a while Charleston came up, and the two attorneys took turns trying to persuade the judge about something. At the end of it all, Judge Wagner addressed the jury.

"The prosecution has requested permission to treat Mr. Lee as a hostile witness, due to the fact that some of his testimony has contradicted information received in pretrial conversation.

"I have decided to grant that permission," the Judge continued, "as it will give the prosecution freedom to broach the witness on some prior inconsistencies. Please proceed, Mr. Granger."

It took Simon a little bit to realize what had happened. He lashed out.

"Hostile! What do you mean hostile? I've answered every question the way you said. . . ."

Wagner came down hard with his gavel.

"Young man, do not speak out of turn in my court!"

Simon fell silent. They were a bunch of bastards, all of them. Each out to prove their own points, advance their own agendas. He took a glance at the bailiff, who had taken his hands out of his pockets and was eyeing him up and down, as though he'd be happy to toss him in the slammer.

"Mr. Lee, I believe we skipped part of the story," said Granger. "In regard to the letter?"

"I'm not sure what you mean."

"The letter from Zachary Barnes to Ruby—when you picked it up, did you notice if it was sealed?"

"No. It wasn't sealed."

"Did you happen to open that letter and read it?"

Granger was going to drag the whole thing out of him, he could see. He could see Josalyn Williams too, sitting at the prosecution table, her face empty, studying him as though he were some kind of speck on the window. It angered him, but he didn't see any way out.

"Please answer the question," said Judge Wagner, talking to him like he was nobody. Simon spat it out.

"I glanced at it."

"Why?"

"I told you. Tobin asked me to keep an eye on Zack. Things were pretty tense."

"What did you do next?"

"I took it to the loft."

"And did you give it to Ruby Garcia?"

"Yes," Simon said, and didn't say anything else.

Granger just looked at him for a moment. "Were you jealous?" he asked.

"Me?" He hadn't expected a question like that. This lawyer was a son of a bitch. He glanced again to the prosecution table. Williams wasn't even paying attention; she leaned over a piece of paper, scribbling. The judge started to cough a little bit; it didn't last long, but it sounded bad, like he had some kind of weight on his chest.

"Were you jealous?" Granger repeated.

"No way."

"Mr. Lee, isn't it true you had a crush on Ruby yourself—and were jealous of the fact that she ignored you for these older men?"

"I told you, no!" Simon yelled and glanced at the judge. The man gave him a stern look but said nothing. Instead, Judge Wagner held his hand to his mouth, struggling to hold back his cough. Granger pressed on.

"Is that why you told Tobin about the letter? To punish Ruby?"

"No."

"And is that why, two days later, you told Tobin about the gun locked in the deceased's office? Because you were jealous of Zachary Barnes?"

Simon's eyes opened wide. "That's not why. It's because I had seen the gun, and was afraid of what might happen."

"Mr. Lee, please. You ran into Tobin on the staircase, right after you gave the letter to Ruby Garcia. Is that correct?"

"Yes."

"And you told him about the letter. Is that correct?"

Simon drew a breath. The people in the courtroom were looking at him, Tobin was looking, the television cameras, everyone in the world. He could feel the impossibility of the situation.

The judge was still struggling with his cough. "Mr. Lee," the judge said. "Please. . . ."

"Just tell me what you want me to say," Simon yelled. "And I'll goddamn say it. My job's gone. Zack's dead. My boss is a murderer. I don't give a rat's ass anymore."

"Objection," shouted Charleston.

Judge Wagner whacked his gavel on the desk. He started to shout, but the words came out in a sputter, and he fell into a horrible fit, coughing, struggling to speak, his face red, then coughing some more.

Awed, Simon and the rest of the court watched Judge Wagner's struggle for breath, and his clerk handed him a glass of water. Eventually the judge caught his breath and, in response to Granger's question about whether they ought to recess, insisted that the examination proceed.

But Granger said he had nothing further. Then Cynthia Charleston stood up and approached.

She introduced herself, smooth as silk, and spent a few moments in what seemed like idle chitchat, until Simon realized that he had just told her that the prosecution had bought his nice new clothes.

"But I don't know if I get to keep them," he said hastily, afraid of what would happen to him for keeping clothes that, presumably, the taxpayers had paid for. "I mean, Mr. Granger made me leave them before trial, so I wouldn't mess them up."

To his surprise, the audience laughed and even some of the jury grinned. Cynthia Charleston gave him a warm smile. She took him through his prior testimony about the gun, steering clear of any questions about Zack and Ruby and the letter. Simon began to relax.

"So you told Mr. Tobin about the gun in Mr. Barnes's cash drawer," she said. "Tell me, Mr. Lee, did you know whether the gun was loaded or not?"

"No, ma'am, I didn't," he said.

"Would it surprise you to learn that the gun wasn't loaded?" she said.

Simon looked at her, his mouth a little loose, while he remembered.

"Mr. Lee?" she said.

"I don't know," he said, refusing to look at James Tobin.

"OK, fair enough," she said calmly. "Two days after you told Mr. Tobin about the gun, did he ask you to run an errand for him?"

Simon thought he knew where she was heading, and it confused him. It couldn't possibly help Tobin any, but he answered the question.

"He always had me running errands for him," he said.

"This particular errand was on March sixteenth. He asked you to go to Oakland. He even let you use his car."

"Oh, yeah. I remember."

"Where did you go, Mr. Lee?"

Simon named a sporting goods dealer near the Oakland Coliseum, one that specialized in guns. A furtive glance at the prosecution table showed Granger and Williams looking intent and curious.

"And what did you pick up there?"

Simon shrugged. "I dunno. It was a small box, wrapped in brown paper and, you know, all taped up. I didn't open it."

"OK. Who paid for it?"

"I did," Simon said. "Tobin gave me the money before I left, and I paid for it."

"Good," she said, still calm. "When you got back to the gallery, who did you give the box to?"

"Tobin."

"Did he say anything about it?"

Simon wrinkled his forehead, thinking hard. "Yeah. He said something like he didn't know what Zack wanted it for, but he guessed that was Zack's business. And he showed me a note, yeah. From Zack. It said to pick up the stuff in Oakland." Simon looked at her in sudden understanding. "Oh, that's why you . . ."

"Thank you, Mr. Lee," she said quickly. "Do you know what happened to that note?"

"Yeah. Tobin tossed it in the garbage, and I emptied it out that night 'cause the garbage men, you know, they were coming the next day."

"Good. Now then, after you gave the package to Mr. Tobin, what did he do with it?"

Simon stared at her. "He opened it up."

"He opened it up, in your presence?"

"Yes ma'am."

"And did you see what was in the package, this package that Zachary Barnes had left a note about?"

"Yes ma'am."

She took a breath. "Could you please tell the jury what was in the package for Mr. Barnes, Mr. Lee?"

"Bullets," Simon Lee said. "Thirty-eight caliber bullets."

"Thank you, Mr. Lee," Cynthia Charleston said. "I have no further questions."

TWENTY-FIVE

⤳ ⤳

WHITE, WITH PEARLS

Ruby liked her new place, even though all she could afford was one room in a decaying Edwardian in the old flatlands below Dolores Park. The streets were full of hustlers and hipsters and drug freaks, but there was a vibrancy to it all. She heard Spanish spoken in the streets, too, like in the old barrios of San Jose. She began to feel close to something she'd deliberately left behind and wondered, maybe, if that's what she'd been searching for all along.

It was what Zack had suggested she do. Find her roots, her subject, and plunge into her art. She only wished that she had done it before all this happened.

Her new space was small, but the place had big French windows that opened over the alley. She had found an old wardrobe at a flea market and dragged it home. It contained all her clothes—she'd given the tiny closet over to art supplies which were, after all, more important than jeans and shirts and socks.

At the moment her daybed was littered with clothes. Tomorrow was her day in court, and she had to decide what to wear. Something serious or something delicate. Something professional or something plain. She tried on the white blouse and the white skirt that almost matched it, and slid a string of fake pearls around her neck. It made her look like some kind of virgin bride, she thought with disgust.

She had caught Simon's testimony. Afterward, he'd even come around Tobin's place looking for her. She'd been over there gathering up some stuff when she heard him pull up on his motorcycle. She hid in the back until he went away.

She was too angry to talk to him. They had been buddies; she had confided in him. Then, like some conniving little prick, he told Tobin about the letter from Zack.

The jerk, she thought. The stupid nobody.

If he had minded his own business, then Tobin wouldn't have found out about the affair. He wouldn't have socked her around. Maybe everything would have turned out different. She didn't know if she really believed that, and she didn't guess it was fair. Still, she needed someone to blame, and it was easier, for the moment, to blame Simon than herself.

She slid off her skirt. I should wear a darker color, she thought. Maybe also a vest with the blouse. She stood at the mirror and held a pleated skirt to her waist. Then the phone rang, and all her anguish returned.

Granger and Charleston had been calling her constantly the last few weeks, each of them wanting to get her alone, to firm up her testimony. She'd done that once already with Charleston, and met briefly too with Granger. She felt a bit of a thing for him. It was silly, she knew it, but he had a bashful way of looking at her and reminded her of Jimmy. He was about his age, though without the edge. She had to put that out of her head, though; it was just like her to jump to some older guy just as she was getting herself straight. He was the enemy, anyway.

The phone stopped ringing just before the answering machine clicked on. Ruby had been ignoring phone calls from both camps. Their messages filled the machine.

The phone started ringing again.

Ruby hesitated, then decided she couldn't let the murder rule her life. She picked up the phone. It was Charleston.

"The prosecution is bringing you on the stand tomorrow, you understand that?"

"Sure. I got the message on my machine. I let them know I would be there."

"You want to come down and go over your testimony one more time?"

"No. I understand pretty much how it's going to be."

"Are you sure?"

"Yeah."

"You saw what Granger did to Simon Lee, didn't you?"

"Yeah."

"You understand Simon Lee was a friendly witness. And you can see how they treated him. Don't think they'll treat you any different."

Ruby didn't say anything. Until a few days before, she hadn't known the difference between a friendly and an unfriendly witness. She'd only known that she was on the prosecution witness list, and that it was her turn to go up tomorrow.

"The DA's office, with the politics of this case, really needs that conviction. Granger's on the spot, you know. He'll do anything."

"It seems like anybody will do anything."

"Has he threatened to charge you as an accessory if you don't cooperate?"

"No," she said. "Because I'm not an accessory."

Now that Charleston mentioned it, though, Ruby remembered Granger bringing up the possibility. In a calm way, almost fatherly, as if warning her of consequences she might not have anticipated.

"If Tobin goes down, there's a good chance you'll go down too," said Charleston.

"That's silly. I haven't done anything."

"They have to release their evidence to me before it's presented to court. It's pretty clear, their strategy."

"What do you mean?" Ruby was skeptical. She did not altogether trust Charleston. Ruby had seen the woman operate, and she knew how deceptive she could be. Still, she feared what the attorney said might be true.

"Granger's going to say you and Jimmy were working together. You seduced Zachary in order to get him to go along with the fraud. Then when Zack refused, the two of you planned his murder."

"That's crazy."

"Maybe, but think about Simon," Charleston said. "Think about what they got him to say against Jimmy, and how they turned it against him. Think how bad he looked."

"I'm not Simon."

"You don't care about going to jail?"

"That won't happen."

"You don't care about Jimmy?"

Ruby didn't answer right away. She did care about Jimmy, she guessed, or she used to care anyway. Since the murder, though, she was afraid of him now in a way she had not been before. She wanted to escape the gallery and her life there.

"Of course I care about him," she said at last.

"OK. Then let me tell you something. I know Granger's an attractive guy. I know you like talking to him. Am I right?"

Ruby felt her cheeks flame up, like she'd been made a fool. Charleston went on. "So go ahead. Flirt all you want. But if you play footsie with the prosecution on the witness stand, Jimmy could get the death penalty. Or life imprisonment. How would you feel then?"

Ruby despised the way Charleston treated her. She wished she had the nerve to tell her to go fly away, but she didn't.

"Don't worry," Ruby said. "I won't say anything to hurt Jimmy."

"All right then. Are you sure you don't want to come down and go over the testimony again?"

"Not tonight. I have to get ready for tomorrow. To clear my head."

"OK, well you go clear your head," Charleston said. Her voice was like a real estate agent's: agreeable, but with a touch of condescension. "But show up tomorrow in my office at seven."

Despite herself, Ruby agreed. Like her mother, Charleston knew how to handle her. Make her feel guilty, like it was her fault, and it was easy to get your way.

"By the way, what are you wearing?" asked Charleston.

"I haven't decided." Ruby was still standing in front of the mirror. Her skirt lay on the bed, and her blouse was unbuttoned.

"Wear white," she said. "Nothing low-cut. Nothing higher than the knees. Nothing slutty, if you know what I mean."

Ruby felt a burst of anger, but her tongue flustered up in her mouth, and she could not speak.

"And also," said Charleston. "Maybe try a strand of pearls."

TWENTY-SIX

⌒⌒ ⌒⌒

RED RUBY, RUBY RUBY RED

Granger was concerned. Since the night Ruby first called him, she had been elusive, hard to pin down. She'd flirted with him a little, he thought, but frozen him off on her testimony. Then, that morning when she was scheduled to testify, he'd seen her coming into the building accompanied by one of Charleston's aides. Ruby settled into the stand dressed in white, her hands folded carefully in front of her. She avoided his eyes, then cast a nervous smile in the direction of her boyfriend. Granger's lips tightened—Charleston had gotten to her.

He couldn't be sure, though. Either way he had little choice but to proceed as he had planned. To go at her gently, establish a rapport. Let the jury see her as another person deceived by Tobin. Unlike Simon, she would not respond to being pushed. He needed to cajole her, flatter her, yet not so much that she suspected his sincerity.

A tough balancing act. Maybe even tougher now, if Charleston had managed to poison the well.

"Counselor," prodded Judge Wagner, "are you ready to begin?"

Granger took her through the formalities first. Her occupation, where she had met Tobin, when, how long she had lived in the gallery. Ruby answered politely. Even so, as the testimony moved into the substance of events, he was still unsure what to expect.

"Ms. Garcia, you are aware of the fact that a number of the defendant's paintings were stolen from the Barnes Gallery on February fourteenth of this year?"

"Yes."

"Do you recall your whereabouts that evening?"

"I was asleep."

Someone in the courtroom chortled. Granger pretended not to hear, but he took a careful look at the jury. They sat as expressionless as ever.

"What time did you go to bed?" he asked Ruby.

"About eleven. I lay down and turned out the lights."

"Where was the defendant?"

"Jimmy was taking a shower. He came into bed just as soon as he was done."

"Did anything out of the ordinary happen before you retired for the evening?"

"No. Jimmy was painting all day, and I was at class. I came home about six, like every Tuesday. Jimmy went back to his studio for a few hours. He's obsessive about his work."

"Do you remember what time he came out of his studio?"

"About nine. I remember because. . . ." Ruby faltered. She put her hand up to her chin, playacting, it seemed, though not very well.

"Please continue, Ms. Garcia."

"We made love," she said. "On the couch." She gave a quick, shy glance to the jury, then a longer look at the defense table— at Tobin. Granger feared another disaster, the preliminary hearing all over again.

"What happened next?"

"We talked."

This was getting away from him. He didn't want to declare Ruby a hostile witness, like he had done with Simon, and lose her cooperation forever. Still, the picture she was painting was far too sweet.

"Did he discuss with you the paintings that were about to be stolen?"

"Objection," said Charleston. "The prosecution is leading the witness. Our client could not have known paintings were about to be stolen."

"Sustained."

Wagner barely lifted his head. Granger didn't bother to rephrase. His object here was not to get answers, but to sow suspicion. To let the jury know that Tobin had plans to steal the paintings.

"Did the defendant mention to you anything about an insurance policy that had been taken out recently on the paintings?"

"Objection, Your Honor," Charleston said. "It's fairly apparent what the prosecution is up to here. His innuendo is not very subtle."

"Sustained."

Granger tried again, the same tactic from another angle. "Isn't it possible, Ms. Garcia, that the defendant could have gotten up in the middle of the night and left the loft without your knowledge?"

"Objection!" shouted Charleston. She was on her feet now. "This is pure speculation."

Wagner's face fell in a grimace of irritation. "Mr. Granger?"

"Yes?"

"Knock it off. Objection sustained."

"I'll rephrase, Your Honor. Ms. Garcia, do you recall the defendant leaving your bedroom at any point during the night in question?"

"No. He had his arms around me all night. There's no way he left."

Granger turned his back on Ruby. He caught a glimpse of Tobin, smug as a crow in a cornfield, his head raised, surveying the horizon as though nothing in the world could harm him.

One of the jury members shared the expression. Granger grimaced. It was time to slice to the heart of the matter.

"Did you ever know the defendant to have a gun in his possession?" he asked.

There was the smallest beat, the briefest of hesitations, and in that hesitation he thought maybe Ruby would tell the truth.

"No," she said. Her face seemed empty of all expression.

"Did you ever see a gun in his workplace, or in your apartment?"

"No."

"Did you ever see a gun on his person, or hear him talk about obtaining a gun?"

"No."

"Are you sure?"

"Yes."

"Ms. Garcia, do you remember a phone call that you made to my office during the preliminary hearings?"

"Yes." Her voice shifted tenor, but she kept her eyes straight ahead, vacant as they could be. It was an act, though, he was sure. She was a smart girl, and she knew what was going on. He tried to reach her. "At that time, didn't you tell me that you'd seen a gun in Tobin's work closet, in your loft apartment, three days before the murder?"

"Yes, I said that. But after I talked to you, I went back and looked again. I made a mistake. It wasn't a gun. It was a pair of pliers."

"You mistook a pair of pliers for a gun?"

"I guess so."

An odd silence filled the courtroom. Granger had heard that silence before, during the Hayes Valley fiasco last winter, when he'd had one of the rape victims on the stand and she had frozen up on him. Now this case was slipping away too. He had been counting on his gut feelings, his belief that Ruby wanted to tell the truth. Apparently he was wrong. He had failed with her on two important subjects. First the theft. And now the gun.

All that was left was Zack—and the letter the dead man had written her. It was Granger's last hope. He remembered how she had reacted when he told her about the letter: how much it had interested her and how badly she had wanted to see it. He had held off on showing it to her then. Maybe now was the time.

"Ms. Garcia, were you acquainted with the victim in this case, Mr. Zachary Barnes?"

"Yes, I was." A faint sheen illuminated her eyes.

"Is it true you had an intimate physical relationship with the deceased?"

"No," she said, but her voice seemed to catch, and the sheen grew brighter. Granger could not believe her answer. He leaned into the witness box and spoke in a voice as measured and even as he could make it. He wanted to be sure she understood. "Ruby, are you aware of the consequences of perjury in the state of California?"

"There's no need to threaten me." She snapped, coming back at him with surprising force. "When you interviewed me at my loft, I was extremely upset. You pushed me into saying a lot of things I didn't even mean, just to get rid of you. . . . And that's the truth."

"Are you saying, for the record, that you didn't have an intimate physical relationship with this man?"

"We had sex, if that's what you mean. But it wasn't intimate. It was just a one-night stand."

Granger nodded. "OK, Ms. Garcia. About when was that?"

"When was what?" Ruby said suspiciously.

"When was the one night of your one-night stand?"

Charleston flew upward, objecting.

"It goes to motive, Your Honor," Granger said blandly.

Wagner glared at him, then nodded. "Very well, Counselor, I'll allow you to proceed. But cautiously, do you understand?"

"Yes sir," Granger said, and turned back to Ruby. She stared at him, wide-eyed.

"Now, just when did you sleep with Zachary Barnes?" he said.

It had started a couple of weeks before the murder, maybe, when Jimmy went down to Los Angeles. She knew the real reason he wanted her to stay behind—some woman, some floppy hat gallery type in LA, or an art student, someone to ooh and ah and make him feel good, the way Ruby used to. The way Ruby kept trying to. But Ruby didn't want to think about that, about how distant Jimmy was starting to be, about how half the time he held her so close she couldn't breathe, and the rest of the time he was so far, so very far away.

But that time, in late February, it just made her mad. San Francisco was foggy and rainy and gray and cold, and she was fed up. Angry and fed up.

If Jimmy can do that kind of stuff, she'd thought, then so can I. Two can play at that game.

So she had gone over to Zack's place that night. Though Zack was Yvonne's husband, and Ruby was friends with Yvonne, she couldn't help herself. There'd been some long looks between them lately, a sexual vibe. Also Zack had taken an interest in her work, not just gushing, or running his eyes over her breasts, but giving serious advice, recognizing the bad parts as well as the good. He was a nice guy, that Zack.

So she had gone over to his house wearing a bright blouse, holding a bottle of tequila. He opened the door with something like a look of surprise, his beautiful lips opening like a flower.

"I'm blue," she said, making talk like some broad in an out-of-date movie. Zack seemed to like it.

"Not so blue as me," he said. "I've been trying to balance the books. But come in anyway."

"Is Yvonne here?"

"No. She's working late. Some press stuff with the mayor."

"Oh," said Ruby, subdued now, acting like she hadn't known all along that it was Wednesday and Yvonne was working late. "I thought, maybe, I don't know. Maybe the three of us, we could make some Mexican and have something to drink."

"It sounds good."

"Too bad Yvonne isn't here."

"Yeah."

Once inside, Ruby felt the fool. The Bearden on the wall. The African masks. The polished ebony and the colorful wall hangings. All of it arranged, carefully positioned, almost more like a gallery than the gallery. Yvonne's gallery, careful and cool. Ruby felt she did not belong. She tried to think of some graceful way out, but nothing came. The truth was she liked being near Zack, who was already clearing some papers off the kitchen table.

"To hell with work," said Zack. "Let's make ourselves some food."

They got out the spices and fired up the stove. Ruby fixed them each a tequila. She drank it the hard-core way, rubbing salt and lime in the hollow of her hand. Zack drank it that way too.

After a while they were laughing, and every once in a while she would bump up against him while they were cooking. Accidental, shy little bumps. They drank until they were loopy. The room became warm, and they confided in each other, Ruby saying how Jimmy was changing lately. They talked about money troubles at the gallery, and Zack told her how Yvonne seemed to be driven, almost beyond any sense, by her job at the mayor's office. He hardly saw her anymore, he said.

Occasionally, Ruby would glance up at Zack, at those brown eyes of his, studying his dark and wonderful skin, the sweet pink of his lips. He studied her too. They went up to the front room, big and sparse, lined with these high, thin windows that in daytime let in a wild flood of light but now were filled with a kind of velvety dark. They sat down on this big couch. They kissed. She pulled him down onto her, wrapping her hands up around his haunches. Though for an instant it seemed as though he might try to resist, lifting his head, he soon gave up any pretense of that. He burrowed himself into her, pulling up his shirt and hers too, so it was skin against skin. She loved the look of that, her light brown skin against his skin so black. She loved looking at him and feeling at the same time the crush of him against her and the wild movement of his hips and the taste of his tongue, ferocious and sweet inside her mouth.

And he murmured her name so that he took her with his body and his voice both. Murmured her name like a chant, like something hypnotic, like a dance. "Ruby," he said, breathing it into her ear. "Red, red Ruby. Ruby Ruby red."

As soon as it was over, the regret flooded her. Zack was her boyfriend's business partner. And Yvonne too, who had been good to her after all. Who'd treated her like a sister. Zack seemed embarrassed. He turned away from her, tucking in his shirt tail.

"I love my wife," he said.

So I made a mess of things, Ruby thought. I seduced my boyfriend's longtime buddy, screwed my girlfriend's husband. All because it would be nice to have someone talk to me straight-up, one-on-one, to touch me and admire me. Someone who doesn't hit.

And now Zack was dead.

A giant wave of emptiness washed up into her gut, a great ocean of blackness. The fact of his death hurt her so much that she bent over and held her stomach, trying to keep the sobs down while her throat filled with tears.

Granger handed her a box of tissues and waited, and after a moment she straightened, gulping air, conscious of the judge and the jury, the filled courtroom, and the cyclops eyes of the cameras. She put her shoulders back.

"Ms. Garcia," Granger said gently. "I'm going to ask you a few questions again. Do you understand?"

She just stared at him.

Granger said, "Isn't it true that on the evening of April fourth you called my office?"

She looked at Tobin, then wet her lips.

"Yeah, I called you," she said.

"And isn't it true that you told me that you saw a gun in James Tobin's work closet?"

Still looking at Tobin, Ruby said, "No."

"And isn't it true that you told me that it was bigger than a derringer?"

"No!"

"And isn't it true that you told me that it was silver, with a black handle?"

"No!" Ruby was almost shouting, but she was shouting not toward Granger, but toward the defense table.

"And isn't it true that, when you called me on April fourth, that you told me that the gun wasn't in the closet anymore?"

"No!" Ruby screamed.

Granger waited for a moment, letting the echoes fade.

"No further questions, your honor," he said, turning. As he did, he glanced at Tobin.

The defendant stared at Ruby Garcia, his expression icy and rigid.

I just hope, Granger thought, taking his seat, that Court TV gets a good shot of that.

TWENTY-SEVEN

࿊ ࿊

CHINESE TAKEOUT

That evening Granger sat alone in his office, surrounded by cartons of Chinese food. He stared at the small television set bracketed by his large feet.

It was too easy, in court, to get caught up in the give and take of testimony, in the fluid strategies of prosecution and defense, and to forget about the cameras and microphones and reporters. Sometimes it was a shock to come out of the courtroom to the noisy shoving of the media, and a greater shock to find one's own face plastered over the afternoon papers and looking out of the television set.

On a good day, he could ignore the whole thing or pretend it was something happening on the sidelines, something that didn't really have anything to do with Sterling Granger. On other days, it seemed like a hideous intrusion. It was intrusive today and served only to remind him that regardless of how the trial was going, his own job, his own neck, was still very much in the public eye, and very much on the line.

And the trial was not going well, he thought over a bite of Hunanese eggplant salad. The prosecution had not managed to neutralize the damage done by Looper's mistake in not bagging Garcia's and Yvonne Barnes's hands, and the testimony about the bullets had come as a rude and horrible shock. Granger, Williams, and Wong had spent two hours shouting over that on Tuesday night, after Simon Lee's testimony. But short of being psychic there was no way they could have anticipated that, and there seemed to be no way to neutralize it, either. And Ruby's refusal to testify about seeing the gun in Tobin's work closet just contributed to the picture Cynthia Charleston was building in the jury's mind, the picture of Tobin defending himself against the furious and armed Zachary Barnes.

The paper evidence, he thought, was not much better. He finished the eggplant salad and reached for the carton of hot and spicy scallops, which he emptied into the half-full carton of steamed rice. For meals like this, Granger gave up on chopsticks and used instead a huge tablespoon.

Pieces of paper and files on a computer disk. Financial summaries, mostly. Business records of the Barnes Gallery, Tobin's bank statement, Zachary's personal accounts, the flow of money back and forth.

The auditors had not turned up much out of the ordinary. The only thing clear was that both men were up to their ears in debt. The Barnes Gallery, like a lot of galleries, had boomed during the eighties, when art investors were bidding up prices. In the nineties, everything had gone flat. There was plenty of motivation, then, for either man to defraud the insurance company. Motivation enough for both, actually, and that was the problem. The evidence cut two ways.

Even so, they had come across some useful scraps. One of Granger's busy law clerks had discovered a receipt for a cash withdrawal from Tobin's account for fifteen hundred dollars. It was dated February fifteenth, the day after the theft, about the time Simon had received his payoff money. Following that lead, the clerk then secured an invoice from a motorcycle shop in San Bruno. Simon Lee had spent the same amount, fifteen hundred bucks, two days later on a used Kawasaki. Looper had told him that they might find that trail, and he was happy that her information had worked out.

But the information had come too late for Simon's testimony, and the kid was too volatile to risk recalling. It might be useful, though, if Charleston put Tobin on the stand. There was no telling if she would, but one fact worked in the prosecution's favor: Tobin was claiming self-defense. Defendants with that claim often ended up on the stand—that is, if the prosecution could muster its half of the case.

There was also the matter of the gun Tobin had taken from the locked drawer in Zack's office. Granger's examination of Ruby had not gone well, but he still hoped, on recall, she would admit seeing that gun in Tobin's paint closet.

Josalyn Williams tapped on the door.

"Will litigate for food," she said and came in holding a fork. Granger pushed a couple of cartons along the desk, and she sat opposite him and picked one up.

"Hunanese," he warned her. "I like it spicy."

"You know," she said around a bite of harvest pork, "for a white boy, you're not too bad."

For a while they just ate. Granger wondered if Josalyn had a boyfriend, or someone who waited for her at home. Or didn't wait for her.

He had talked to Jemma during a break in court that afternoon, and his daughter had sounded so frightened and alone that it broke his heart. His own lawyer could offer no positive news about any custody hearing. Marian had not yet filed, and Granger's lawyer didn't think that a preemptive filing would help him out at all.

"I want to see you, Daddy," Jemma had said, her voice breaking. "Mom says you don't want to see me."

Granger clamped down hard on his anger and kept his voice smooth and gentle. "Do you believe that, sweetheart?"

"No! But why don't you come see me?"

"Honey, I can't, not for a few more days." Jemma started to cry. "Baby, please, as soon as I can get away—you know I love you, don't you? You know it's just this trial. As soon as I can get away. . . ."

He wondered now if his excuses had sounded as lame to her as they did to him. And what, in the end, really mattered? Justice? Yes, justice mattered, but did it matter more than one heartbroken eight-year-old girl?

"What happened with Ruby Garcia?" Josalyn said into the quiet.

Granger shook himself mentally and looked at her. "I don't know," he said. "I let her slip away, I guess. Or maybe she was never that solid."

Josalyn picked up another carton. "You didn't give her Zack's letter."

"No. Things were going too badly. Her mood was wrong. I decided to save it."

"For when?"

"I'll bring her back up to the stand later. For now, we have to concentrate on other things."

"What do you have in mind?"

"Expert testimony. Contradictions between the various stories Tobin has told and the reality of the physical evidence. If we can build a strong enough case out of the circumstantial, maybe Charleston will put Tobin on the stand. Then we can trap him in his contradictions."

"The circumstantial isn't strong enough," said Josalyn. "Not the way the testimony has been going."

She was right, but hearing the words did not fill him with joy.

"Do you have any ideas?" he asked.

"There's always Yvonne Barnes."

They looked at each other.

"What about the mayor?" he said finally, playing devil's advocate.

"What about him?" Josalyn countered. "Have you been listening to the black media recently? If James Tobin walks on this one, this city's in trouble. Nobody's out there talking riots yet, but nobody's discounting it, either. McKinney's already got an image problem with the city's minorities."

"He knows that," Granger said. "Whatever his personal feelings may be. But he doesn't want Yvonne Barnes on the stand. And I get the feeling that putting her on the stand is not going to be a healthy decision."

"Even if she agrees?" Josalyn said.

"She won't," Granger said.

"I think she will," Josalyn replied. "I was just on the phone to her. She's been watching the trial on TV. She's no dummy, she knows things aren't going real well."

A small silence grew between them. "And what happens," Granger said finally, "if we put Mrs. Barnes on the stand, and she discovers she doesn't like it? What happens if we interview her before her testimony, and we need to push her? What happens if we're both mild as milk and sweet as pie, and Cynthia Charleston takes her apart and eats her for lunch?"

Josalyn didn't reply. They both knew what would happen. The only question was which one of them it would happen to.

TWENTY-EIGHT

❧ ❧

YVONNE

T he courtroom had an electricity that had been missing the last few weeks. It was supplied not so much
by Barnes and Williams in and of themselves, but by
the chemistry between them, a tension that was not
altogether amiable. It suggested they were both there for their
own reasons, that it was as likely as not their spirits might collide.
Also the women looked good on television. Yvonne Barnes,
with her high-mannered sophistication, her dark skin, and the
face of the grieving widow, was at once unapproachable and
beautiful. Then there was Josalyn Williams, a few years younger,
buoyant, hard-edged and precocious, standing up there in her
gray pin-striped skirt cut at the knees, her professional blouse,
her hair in carefully defiant cornrows.

Josalyn quickly established Yvonne Barnes's identity, then
moved on.

"Mrs. Barnes," Josalyn asked, "were you in attendance at James
Tobin's most recent gallery opening?"

"Yes, I was there."

"When did that opening take place?"

"December last year, a few weeks before Christmas."

"Was it typical for you to assist your late husband with the business end at such openings?"

"Yes. I helped Zachary keep track of sales."

"How many sales did the gallery typically make at a Tobin showing?"

"Well, a few years back—when James was a rising star—we'd sell eight, ten paintings. You couldn't keep people away."

"And what did these paintings typically sell for?"

"Anywhere between five and eighty thousand dollars, depending on the nature and size of the paintings."

"I understand," Josalyn said. She faced the jury, and Granger could see she had their attention. Working a jury, Josalyn had a certain vulnerability about her, but also a certain intensity. Together with Yvonne—aggrieved, yet startling in her composure—the two had a presence hard to deny. "And how many paintings did the gallery sell this particular evening?"

"None," said Yvonne.

Josalyn looked surprised. "None?" she echoed.

"That's right, none," Yvonne repeated.

She didn't look at Tobin, but Granger did. The defendant looked like stone.

"Did you speak to the defendant about this lack of sales?"

"Yes," Yvonne said. "Afterwards, at the reception. We were joking around, and someone said, 'All we need is an earthquake, a real mother shaker, and our troubles will be over.' It was a joke, you know, because the insured value of the paintings was so high."

"Objection," Charleston said. "I don't see the relevance." She leaned back in her chair. Her manner suggested a bemusement at this younger lawyer, but Granger knew it was all a pose. Charleston was a media hog and did not like being upstaged.

"Overruled," said Judge Wagner. "The witness will continue."

"How did Mr. Tobin react to that?" Josalyn asked.

"After that remark, Tobin says, looking right at Zack, 'It wouldn't take much brains to pull off a theft around here.'"

Josalyn paused just long enough to let this sink in.

"Did you get the impression that this, too, was intended as a joke?"

Yvonne Barnes shook her head. "I didn't laugh. No one else did either. In fact, there was something about his tone that seemed very inappropriate."

Charleston shot to her feet. She was dressed in maybe the hottest pink Granger had ever seen; in the midst of the courtroom's grays and browns, she resembled a tropical flower, or maybe an exotic weed. The effect was calculated, no doubt, as her wardrobe always was.

This time Wagner ruled in Charleston's favor, but Granger knew it was of little consequence. Josalyn had accomplished what she wanted with her opening line of questions. Not only had Yvonne's story helped bolster Simon's earlier testimony, but it helped establish the financial motive, the fact that Tobin was struggling, frustrated, prepared to act desperately. Josalyn moved on.

"Did the gallery have an alarm system, Mrs. Barnes?"

She said that it had and gave the name of the alarm company.

"And was the gallery alarm system functioning at the time of the theft?"

"No. It had been turned off," said Yvonne.

"At whose direction?"

"Mr. Tobin's."

Josalyn again paused fractionally. Granger glanced at the jury. They were listening intently, and most of them were taking notes. He didn't smile, but he felt like it. So far, Josalyn was doing very well.

"Did the defendant give you a reason for turning the alarm off?"

"James claimed the alarm went off sporadically, without cause. He said it was a nuisance."

"Mr. Tobin lived upstairs from the gallery, didn't he?"

"Yes. Zack let him use the loft apartment."

Josalyn nodded. "And that was without charging him rent?"

Yvonne nodded as Charleston jumped up, objecting that they were going over old ground. Josalyn apologized, but Granger was starting to recognize that satisfied little expression at the very corner of her eyes.

"Did you, or your husband, have the alarm system checked subsequently?" she asked.

"Yes. After the theft."

"What, if anything, was discovered to be wrong?"

"Nothing."

"Nothing?"

"The system checked out fine. The repair woman tried for four hours, and she couldn't get it to malfunction."

Josalyn Williams stood with her arms akimbo, a stance Granger had seen before, aggressive but attractive too, taut, as though her whole body were absorbed with the concerns of the moment. Granger worried a bit—he knew juries had a nasty habit of punishing the overconfident. Regardless, she had moved her line of attack forward. Having first established Tobin's motivation to steal the painting, she had then shown how he arranged for the alarm to be disconnected.

She had to realize, of course, this was not enough. Charleston would challenge Yvonne's credibility. The defense attorney would do her best to make Yvonne look like a jealous wife searching for someone to blame—the grieving widow who hated Tobin so much that truth was the least of her concerns when it came to exacting vengeance.

Josalyn returned to the theft.

"Did you ever hear your husband and the defendant discuss the theft which took place in the Barnes Gallery last February?"

"Yes."

"When did this discussion take place?"

"Tuesday, the week before the murder. Zack and I had plans for dinner, so I stopped by the gallery."

"When you walked inside the door, what did you see?"

"My husband stood at the far end of the main room and James stood at other end, much closer to me. There was a wooden chair, broken, lying on the floor between them."

"Do you recall Mr. Tobin looking towards you, or otherwise recognizing your presence in the room?"

"James had his back to me. I don't think he knew I was there."

Granger had been watching Tobin. The man could have been a statue, staring directly ahead of him, not reacting to Yvonne's testimony at all. Beside him, Cynthia Charleston leaned over to whisper something, but he ignored her.

"Mrs. Barnes, could you please tell the jury what James Tobin said to your husband at that time?"

"Objection!"

"It speaks to motive, Your Honor," Josalyn said without missing a beat.

"Overruled," Wagner said. "The witness will answer."

Yvonne looked at him, then said with distaste, "He said, 'You go public with the insurance fraud, you black son of a bitch, and it will be the end of the gallery.'"

"What, if anything, did your husband say in response?"

"Zack said, 'The gallery will survive.' I remember the calm in his voice."

"What happened next?"

"James stepped forward, pointing his finger. He said, 'No, Mr. Barnes, the gallery won't survive. Because you won't live to run it.'"

Another pause. The jury looked rapt.

"Those were his exact words?"

"Yes."

"Then what happened?"

"I stepped between them. I wanted Zack to come home."

Josalyn nodded her understanding. She came back to the prosecution table and picked up a notepad—just filler, Granger knew. Something to give the jury time to catch up on its notes, to take in the implications of Yvonne Barnes's testimony thus far.

"Do you have any idea why Tobin might have threatened your husband's life?"

"Objection! Speculative and conclusory," said Charleston. She spoke vigorously, as though she knew she were going to be upheld on this one. It was a misstep by Josalyn, or so it seemed, because it gave Charleston a chance to break up Yvonne's testimony. To dispel the vividness of her description, the image of the broken chair and James Tobin threatening the life of Zachary Barnes.

"Sustained," said Judge Wagner.

Charleston stayed on her feet. She tried to take her small victory another step forward. "Thank you, Your Honor. Also, I would like to challenge the admissibility of this whole line of questioning. I suggest it be struck from the record. Not only do I have severe doubts as to its veracity, but the prosecution here is raising issues beyond those mentioned in the disclosure statements."

"Your Honor," Josalyn argued, "the questioning of this witness has been well within all the usual parameters. This is somewhat absurd."

"I agree," said Judge Wagner. "Please sit down, Ms. Charleston."

Charleston hunched down into her seat, disturbed. Not so much because she had been overruled, Granger thought. It was the judge's tone. Wagner usually treated each side with equal disdain, gruff and ugly. Josalyn Williams, though, he regarded with his head up, his eyes following her face. She had won the judge's favor.

Josalyn took no notice, or so it seemed. She plunged back into the examination. "Mrs. Barnes, you testified earlier regarding an argument in which you overheard the defendant threaten your husband's life?"

"Yes."

"Did you and your husband ever discuss this incident?"

"Yes. That night when we got home," said Yvonne.

"What, if anything, did your husband say about the alleged theft of James Tobin's paintings?"

"Zack told me that James himself had arranged the theft, in order to collect the insurance."

"Did your husband ever mention going to the authorities with this information?"

"That was his intention."

Yvonne Barnes held her head yet higher. She was a beautiful woman, even when she was uncomfortable. Granger feared Josalyn was leading the witness into a territory she did not want to explore.

"Mrs. Barnes, wasn't your husband's gallery co-beneficiary in the policy that covered Tobin's paintings?"

"Yes."

"What was the amount of payment he was scheduled to receive?"

Yvonne lowered her head and cradled it between her hands. Though she straightened almost instantly, and her face resumed its composure, it was clear she was struggling. Either that, or it was a good act. She had worked as a TV anchor, after all.

"Please answer the question," said Judge Wagner.

"My husband already lost his life," she said clearly and with dignity. "All that's left is his good name. You can't force me to speak against him."

Josalyn looked at her evenly, and Granger bent quickly over his notepad, jotting aimlessly. The witness had turned, somehow Josalyn had lost control, and Yvonne Barnes was closing up, retreating. If this continued, the case could be lost.

"Ms. Williams," Judge Wagner said, "this is your witness. Decide what you want to do."

"Yes, Your Honor. I'll withdraw the question."

The jury watched. Josalyn seemed to be contemplating the far corner of the room, beyond the camera. She turned. Her eyes met Granger's. No doubt she saw his concern, just as he saw hers. He was tempted to signal her. Return to the prosecution table, let's talk it over. With the jury watching so closely, though, he did not want to undermine her, and she did not return on her own. Perhaps hers was the right move. Just catch your rhythm, he thought. Go right back to work.

"Mrs. Barnes, in your earlier testimony, you indicated that your husband meant to turn James Tobin in for his role in an alleged insurance fraud?"

"Yes, that's correct."

"Did you ever hear your husband make these intentions known to the defendant?"

"Yes."

"When?"

"During the argument. When James threatened to kill my husband."

"Now, in regards to the insurance policy your husband had taken on the missing paintings, what was the dollar amount to be paid to the defendant?"

"Two hundred thousand dollars."

"And since they were co-beneficiaries, your husband would have received that same amount?"

Yvonne hesitated. It was the same line of questioning that had gotten her upset. This time, though, Josalyn had come around the back door. Granger felt his shoulders relax a little bit. Josalyn was good.

"Yes," Yvonne said at last.

Josalyn nodded, satisfied. "When your husband threatened to expose the alleged fraud, what—if anything—did the defendant say in response?"

"He accused my husband of trying to ruin his career."

Josalyn took another pause, then seemed to move into a different line of questions.

"Mrs. Barnes, you've known James Tobin for quite some time, haven't you?"

"Yes." She sat back, her hands folded in her lap. "I first met him when we were both in high school."

"In New Orleans?"

"Yes, but different schools."

"In fact, James Tobin introduced you to Zachary Barnes, did he not?"

"Yes, he did," Yvonne said with composure, but her shoulders tensed and Granger wondered if she was twisting her fingers together, hidden there in her lap.

"Would you say that, overall, your relationship with Mr. Tobin has been a smooth one?"

"Objection, Your Honor," Charleston said with feigned weariness. "This isn't getting us anywhere."

"Sustained," Wagner said. "Ms. Williams, I remind you that the day is drawing on."

"Yes sir," she said, smiling quickly at him. "Thank you." She turned back to the witness chair. "So, Mrs. Barnes," she said in the same calm voice, "your opinion of Mr. Tobin is based on a long acquaintance. In light of which, do you feel that, in order to protect his career and his financial interests, as well as to hide his role in the theft, that James Tobin was the kind of man who would kill?"

"Yes!" Yvonne said loudly, just as Charleston yelled, "Your Honor!" and leaped from behind the defense table. The camera swung to her. Granger imagined how her pink suit filled the screen.

"Sustained," the judge said.

Yvonne Barnes paid no attention.

"Yes I do!" she continued. "I know James Tobin killed my husband. I am absolutely convinced of it! Who else was in that room with him? Who else had gunpowder stains all over his hands?"

It was an emotional moment. It was, in fact, just the kind of reaction that Josalyn had been building toward. Wagner pounded his gavel. The cameras zoomed in tight on Yvonne's face. Charleston protested the outburst, asking that it be stricken from the record.

"Agreed," said the judge. "And if the counselor cannot keep her witness under control, then I will issue contempt citations. To both witness, and to counsel."

"Yes, Your Honor," Josalyn said humbly, but she had won another battle. Though the outburst might not stay on record, it had changed the balance of the courtroom. The jury had been scintillated. Josalyn stretched out the moment. She crossed to the prosecution table, picked up a stack of papers, then slowly turned back to the witness.

"Mrs. Barnes, I have here tax records for the Barnes Gallery. These records show that your husband lost a great deal of money during the last three years."

"I'm familiar with those records."

"Did your husband ever speak to you about these losses?"

"Yes."

"What did he say?"

"He was afraid, if things continued, he might lose the gallery."

"When the paintings were stolen, did he speak to you regarding the financial condition of the gallery?"

"He told me the insurance money might save the gallery. But he wouldn't touch that money."

"Why not?"

"He told me James had defrauded the insurance company. The money was dirty."

"Mrs. Barnes, was your husband involved in a scheme to defraud the insurance company?"

Josalyn asked the question quickly and boldly, with such suddenness Yvonne did not seem quite sure how to react. The testimony was back to that place again, where Josalyn kept bringing it, to Zachary's involvement with the fraud. Granger knew this had been the one point that Josalyn would not cede to Yvonne in their earlier conversations. Josalyn had been stubborn about it. Yvonne needed to admit her husband's weakness, she said, his temptation to become involved. It gave her testimony more power. It explained Tobin's calculated need to remove this man who, in his eyes, he could no longer trust. Yvonne had seemed torn, just as she seemed torn now, between her desire to convict Tobin and to preserve her husband's dignity, as well as her own.

Yvonne stammered. "You have to understand, my husband loved that gallery. And he would do anything to save it."

Josalyn paced away. It was apparent Yvonne was on the verge of admitting something she had not admitted before. Yet there was still some impediment that needed to be knocked away.

"Mrs. Barnes, this is a murder case," said Josalyn. "If we are to receive justice, I must insist you answer the questions as put to you. I know you understand this. Please put aside your fears and tell the jury: was your husband involved in the defendant's plan to defraud the insurance company?"

"Yes," she said. "At least, at first he was. Then he changed his mind."

Yvonne closed her eyes. She seemed broken, as though to admit this about her husband was too much. From a practical viewpoint, too, Granger realized, this not only threatened her image of herself, but possibly her career as well. The mayor's press secretary did not need to be so close to scandal. Then Yvonne opened her eyes, looking about the room, raising her gaze to meet the jury's. The dignity seemed somehow to come back. Her husband had been only human, after all. She had only been trying to protect him.

"Take your time, Mrs. Barnes," Josalyn said and turned toward the bench. "Your Honor, I have more questions, but since it's almost noon. . . ."

Wagner nodded, banged his gavel, and recessed the court until two o'clock. Josalyn came back to the prosecution table.

"I need to talk to her," she said quietly to Granger. "There's something she's holding back."

Granger snapped the locks on his briefcase. "You collar her, I'll call the office and order in some sandwiches." He paused. "Good job, Williams."

"Thanks," she said, flashing him a grin. "But I think I'll pass on the sandwiches. Barnes is still pretty skittish. Do you mind?"

"No," he said, although he really did. He watched Josalyn and Yvonne talk for a moment, their slender bodies bending toward each other. Then Josalyn led the way out.

TWENTY-NINE

❧ ❧

YVONNE AFTER LUNCH

I t was Tobin's idea,"Yvonne said after lunch. It was two-thirty by the time the court was ready to proceed, and cool afternoon sunlight flooded the windows. Granger hadn't had a chance to talk to Josalyn after the lunch break, and he wondered what she and Yvonne Barnes had discussed, and what really lay behind their two perfect, composed facades.

"You mean the theft at the gallery, correct?"

Yvonne nodded. "Yes."

"How did Zachary react?" Josalyn prompted.

"He agreed to go along. Later he regretted it, and at the last minute he changed his mind. By then it was too late. Tobin went ahead without him."

"When did your husband tell you this?"

"That evening, after the big fight between them, Zachary told me everything. He had hinted at it before, but that's when I learned the whole story." She paused. Regal, it seemed, with all her old beauty flush in her face.

"I insisted he go to the authorities," she went on. "You see, earlier that same day I overheard a message on the phone machine. It upset me so much that I took the tape out of the machine and stuck it in the bottom of my dresser drawer."

"Do you still have this tape?" asked Josalyn.

"Yes. I do," said Yvonne. She reached into her pocket and took out a manila envelope. "In fact, I have it with me here in court today."

The courtroom buzzed. Granger couldn't help but stare in amazement. Charleston was up again, protesting more furiously than ever.

"This is a cheap stunt! Your Honor, the prosecution cannot be allowed to sneak in this unreviewed evidence. This is obvious grandstanding, a violation of the disclosure rules. I insist not only that this tape be ruled inadmissible, but that the prosecution be censured."

"Calm down, Ms. Charleston," said the judge. He turned to Josalyn. "What's the story here?"

"Your Honor, this tape is as much a surprise to me as to the defense."

There was a stirring in the courtroom. Wagner banged his gavel.

"Order," he said. "The witness will surrender this tape, and the court will recess to consider its admissibility. I would like counsel to meet me in chambers."

Judge Wagner's chamber was silent except for the whirring of the tape machine. The attorneys refrained from posturing for the moment, and Judge Wagner cleared his throat and pushed the off button. He took the cassette out and laid it carefully on the desk in front of him.

"Well, there seems to be some relevance," he said.

"If it's authentic," said Charleston, "but I maintain that relevance isn't the issue here, Your Honor."

"Then what is the issue?"

"As I said in court, it's apparent the prosecution kept this evidence secret, then revealed it today in a grandstand gesture. All in an attempt to startle and impress the jury. This is a clear violation of the disclosure rule."

Wagner turned to Granger. He was the lead prosecutor. Ultimately the burden of explanation fell to him.

"Is that true, counsel?"

"No," said Granger. He was going out on a limb here because he did not know what had transpired between Yvonne Barnes and Josalyn Williams. "To be honest with you, Mrs. Barnes has not been a terribly cooperative witness. It was only in the last week in which we have been able to carry on any serious conversation with her at all."

"This is old-fashioned horse manure," said Charleston. "Your own records indicate a May interview between Ms. Williams and Mrs. Barnes."

"Which was not particularly productive," Josalyn said.

"Believe me, if we had known about the tape, we had no reason to keep it hidden."

"You perhaps had no reason to keep it hidden," said Charleston coldly. "But perhaps you are not so fully in control of this case as you'd like to think."

"I resent that remark, Your Honor. Ms. Charleston here is constantly pushing the brink of decorum."

"Stop it, both of you," said Wagner. He turned to Josalyn. "Ms. Williams, at what point did you become aware of these tapes?"

"Just today in the courtroom, Your Honor. I had no prior knowledge."

"That's inconceivable!" said Charleston. "She's been tampering with Yvonne Barnes!"

"Be quiet!" Wagner said. "Let me ask the questions here."

Charleston settled uneasily under his glare. Wagner did not like being told what to do, and she had pushed him hard, ignoring the risk that he might rule against her out of irritation if good reason failed.

"Now, Ms. Williams, at what point did you go over testimony with Mrs. Barnes?"

"I talked to her once, briefly, right after the funeral. That was merely a sympathy call, and we did not go over the details of the case."

"And later?"

"We met earlier this week, Tuesday night. She finally agreed to talk to us, and Mr. Granger asked me to handle the pretrial examination. I have my notes from this conversation if the court would like to see."

"That won't be necessary." Wagner lifted his head as he spoke, as if clearing his nasal passages. "Ms. Williams, you are aware of the rules of disclosure."

"Yes. I am also aware of how any violation on my part would not only jeopardize this case, but my own career." Josalyn smiled. "And if Your Honor would allow me to be honest, I am very ambitious—as no doubt you have read in the papers. It's very unlikely I would do anything to endanger my career."

Granger laughed; he couldn't help himself. A smile shuddered too across Wagner's enormous jowls.

"If you'd like to call Mrs. Barnes and speak to her. . . ."

"No," said Wagner. "I've decided how I want to handle this." The smile was gone now, if in fact it had ever been a smile. "I don't see any evidence that disclosure has been violated here, and I am going to rule the tape admissible."

"Your Honor, I strongly urge you to reconsider," said Charleston. "The court should investigate the dubious nature of Ms. Williams's relationship with Mrs. Barnes these last few weeks. This tape may well have been doctored by the prosecution, cut, and spliced. These voices could be those of actors for all we know. To expose the jury—"

"Please," said Wagner. "Do you seriously believe that Yvonne Barnes had the technical wherewithal to doctor this tape?"

"We all know she worked in television. She could've secured assistance. Or the prosecution, as I said, may have used its own technicians."

"I doubt it," said Wagner. "Because you know and I know and they know how clearly such tampering can be detected by experts with the right equipment. Just the same, I am going to make my ruling of admissibility subject to independent verification of authenticity."

"Your Honor," Charleston insisted. "If you will allow me, please, to return to the issue of admissibility and the violation of disclosure."

"No!"

"You are opening yourself to challenge on appeal."

"Then appeal, Ms. Charleston. I have made my decision."

The matter was finished. The tape would be admitted, Granger knew, and it would be found to be genuine because Yvonne Barnes was too smart to try to doctor it.

So Tobin's motive, and his intentions, would no longer be simply a matter of testimonial evidence. The jury would hear Tobin threaten Zachary over the insurance money. The media would hear it too. The voices on the tape would be broadcast over the radio and the television. Legal analysts would talk about the impact, and Josalyn Williams would emerge as a new personality. Charleston would try to undo that damage. She would try to blister Yvonne into looking like she had made it all up, but the tapes gave Barnes a new credibility. Attacking the widow would run the risk of making the attorney look callous, insensitive.

Yes, it was a step forward, Granger thought, despite all his misgivings. Still the case wasn't won, not yet, and Yvonne still had to finish her testimony.

"Congratulations," he said to Josalyn as they filed out the door.

"Thank you," she said, but her face was turned away from him, and her thoughts hidden.

THIRTY

❧ ❧

THE GLORIOUS
FOURTH

I t was almost a week before experts had authenticated the tape and it was played in court, a week before Yvonne finally retook the stand. June ended during that week, July began, and the nation celebrated another birthday. San Francisco, too, celebrated in its usual way, with an evening fog bank that rolled in through the Golden Gate. But San Franciscans were used to enjoying smudgy, soft-edged fireworks. They gathered on the margins of their cool bay and oohed and aahed as though they could see every single spark.

During the interim, the courtroom proceedings had been loud and furious, with legal wrangling, motions made and argued and dismissed, sanctions threatened, and evidence proposed and tossed out or severely limited—a part of the trial that Granger knew was important, but which this time around seemed like nothing more than gamesmanship. The jury, for the most part, had been saved these quarrels and histrionics, although he was afraid that they were growing increasingly bored. At least they weren't sequestered, he thought with gratitude, remembering one jury in Eureka which, in frustration, had actually taken apart the jury room and held a bailiff hostage for three days. Not a pretty sight.

Outside the courtroom, Charleston had been running a full-out media campaign to challenge Yvonne's credibility, implying she was involved in her husband's death. Josalyn reported that Mrs. Barnes was holding up well, especially when Mayor McKinney, in a major show of support, asked her to resume her duties as his press secretary. He made sure that she had plenty of public exposure, even if it was limited to announcements about ribbon cuttings and other noncontroversial subjects.

Although Granger and Josalyn Williams spent their days together in court, and often shared meals during the lunch breaks, they spoke only of the day's happenings or of preparation for Charleston's next grandstand attempt. He had questioned her about the tape only once, its sudden appearance and why Yvonne Barnes had not mentioned so damning a piece of evidence earlier. But Josalyn made it quickly obvious that she did not want to discuss the matter, and in the press of other business, Granger let it slide. It puzzled him because he thought he and Josalyn had developed a closer working relationship. He had even hoped that it might blossom into a friendship, but Josalyn seemed to have retreated. And now, in mid-trial, was not the time to bring the issue up. Julie Ann Wong was still breathing down their necks at least once a day, and if Josalyn wanted to protect her private life as strongly as she seemed to, he could not object.

Meanwhile, Marian had finally filed her motion for sole custody of Jemma and to end Granger's visitation rights. His lawyer successfully argued for a continuance until the Tobin trial was over, and the judge granted it. More importantly, in the absence of solid evidence to the contrary, the judge decreed that Granger's current visiting schedule was not a detriment to Jemma and that it should remain in place pending a hearing on the custody motion. Granger suspected that Julie Ann Wong had called in some favors to secure that decree. He was grateful, even suspecting that she did it only to keep her lead prosecutor on the job.

And so it was that Granger and Jemma spent July fourth together. He packed a picnic lunch, and they drove across the hills
into the warmth of the East Bay and Tilden Regional Park, high
above Berkeley. Jemma rode the carousel, and after lunch
Granger hired two horses so they could take a leisurely loop
along the hillcrest, caught between the folded, golden hills and
the sky. In the evening they went north into Marin County to
watch fireworks unbeset with fog. They lay on a hillside, Jemma's
head cradled on his arm, and watched with sleepy contentment.

She fell asleep on the way home, after tucking herself into a
neat, tight ball in the Mustang's passenger seat. She looked small
and pale against the dark strap of the shoulder belt. Waiting at
the Golden Gate Bridge toll plaza, Granger touched his daughter's
wild curls. He had not seen her in more than two weeks. Suddenly it seemed as though nothing could make up for that long
a drought.

THIRTY-ONE

༖ ༈

THE TAPE

On July sixth, Yvonne Barnes again took the stand. She looked cool and in command, except for the small white handkerchief that she clutched in one hand. Granger looked at that handkerchief dubiously and hoped that Josalyn Williams knew what she was doing.

Instead of starting with the tape, Josalyn chose to pursue another avenue of questioning. She quickly took Mrs. Barnes through questions designed to awaken the jury's memories of previous testimony, then deftly questioned her about the gun.

"I'm the one responsible for that, as much as I hate to admit it," Yvonne Barnes told the court.

"Please explain," said Josalyn.

"I borrowed it from Zack's cousin Daryl."

"When did you borrow it?"

"Wednesday, March ninth, I think it was. Though maybe borrow isn't the right word. Daryl was on vacation. I was watching his house for him, and I took it from his bedroom."

"Why?"

"Self-defense. A woman had been raped in the neighborhood, and I was frightened."

The attorney and the witness regarded one another, and Yvonne told the court the story about her fear of being alone in the evenings and of taking Daryl's gun, wrapped in her own monogrammed handkerchief, from Daryl's apartment to her own home.

"Did you ever unwrap the gun?" Josalyn said.

Yvonne Barnes almost laughed. "Unwrap it? I never even looked at it. I didn't . . . I don't have a permit, you see, so I was afraid to carry it with me, and afraid to leave it at home, too."

"Why?" Josalyn said.

Yvonne Barnes explained about her cousin Byrum and his untimely death at the hands of a burglar and the muzzle of his own gun. Granger checked the jury. They were taking it well, and two of the women were nodding.

"Finally I told Zack about it, one morning before work," she said.

"Can you remember when that was?"

"Yes," Yvonne said. "That would have been Friday, March eleventh."

"When you told your husband about the gun, how did he react?"

"He wasn't pleased," Yvonne said. "But he said he'd take it back to Daryl's. Except that we were both late for work. So he put it in his briefcase, and we both left the house. That night he said he'd left it in the cash drawer at the gallery, the one he keeps locked."

Josalyn nodded. "And was it still wrapped in your handkerchief?" she said.

"I don't know," Yvonne replied. "But Zack didn't give me my handkerchief back, so I thought that it might be."

"Did you ask?"

"No," Yvonne said. "I have more handkerchiefs."

It broke the tension, and a light chuckle ran around the courtroom. Josalyn bent her head over her notepad, letting the moment of lightness play itself out. Granger nodded to himself. She was acting like a pro, and he felt a small twinge that, to his own surprise, he identified as pride.

"Mrs. Barnes," Josalyn continued, "did you know whether the gun was loaded?"

Yvonne shook her head emphatically. "No, and I wouldn't know how to check, either."

She went on to testify that she didn't believe Zack would ever purchase bullets for the gun, or ask anyone else to do it for him, that it was entirely out of character. This wouldn't carry much weight, Granger knew, coming from the man's widow, but it had to be said.

"OK, Mrs. Barnes. Did Zack ever tell you that he had returned the gun to Daryl Barnes's apartment?"

"No," Yvonne said. "I never asked him. I just wanted to forget about the whole incident. It certainly isn't something I'm proud of." She paused. "I just assumed that Zack had taken care of it."

"I see," Josalyn said. "Now, just to be certain, to the best of your recollection, you took the gun from Daryl Barnes's closet on March ninth, is this true?"

Mrs. Barnes indicated that it was and agreed that she had given the gun to Zack on the morning of Friday, March eleventh, and that he had taken it with him to the gallery. The next time she saw the gun was March twentieth, after the shooting. Then Josalyn took her through the moments after she had come into the gallery, including when she took the handkerchief from the broken cash drawer.

"But why did you do that, Mrs. Barnes?" Josalyn said, feigning puzzlement, acting as the voice of the jury. "You must have known that you were disturbing a crime scene."

"I don't know if I did," Yvonne said, looking straight at Josalyn. Then she turned slightly to look straight at the jury. "I was thinking so many things that I really don't know what I had in mind. Zack, and the gallery, and my job, and Tobin screaming and cursing. . . ." Her voice shook suddenly and she ducked her head, and Josalyn requested, and got, a short recess.

When they reconvened, Josalyn finally moved to introduce the tape. Both Tobin and Charleston sat stiffly at their table, shoulders tight, frowning, and Granger almost felt a moment of pity. It was like they were seeing a train coming and not able to get out of the way.

"Mrs. Barnes," Josalyn said. "Before the holiday, you testified that you had overheard a conversation between your husband and the defendant, a conversation that had been recorded on your home telephone answering machine. Is that correct?"

The jury leaned forward avidly.

"Yes."

"And you further testified that you had taken the tape from the machine and hidden it in your dresser drawer. Is this also correct?"

"Yes," Yvonne Barnes said firmly. "The tape frightened me."

"I understand. You testified that you had brought the tape with you into court. Is this the envelope you produced on that day?"

She handed a manila envelope to Yvonne Barnes. Yvonne identified it and, at Josalyn's request, took out the tape cassette and identified it, too.

Josalyn played out the business of producing a tape machine, setting it up, and making sure that it was connected to the courtroom speaker system. Charleston tried a few objections, but even she knew they had no merit, and Wagner snapped at her.

Finally, Josalyn had Yvonne Barnes press the play button, and the courtroom filled with the hiss and squeak of the tape.

"Zack, this is James. If you get this message before. . . ."

A fumbling noise, then some heavy breathing, like a man out of breath.

"Sorry, I was at the other end of the house." Zack's voice, a pleasant voice. A bit winded though, as if he had hurried to answer the phone.

The machine whirred.

"Listen, Zack, you can't do this. If word gets around, it won't just be me in trouble. As far as the art world goes, we'll both lose everything."

"I told you not to go ahead with the theft, James. I told you I changed my mind."

"Just take your share of your money and shut up."

"I can't do that."

"Zack . . ." Tobin's voice, full of menace, measured, a bit staccato.

"Yes?"

"I'm telling you, I absolutely will not allow word of this to get out. Don't get self-righteous with me. I'm telling you, you'll pay a dear price—and it's not just money and prestige I'm talking about. I want you to get down here so we can talk about this. I don't want to have to kill your ass."

"Don't get hysterical. I'm on my way."

"I am not hysterical. I'm dead serious."

Then there were no more voices, only the sound of the machine humming in the silent courtroom.

The rest of the direct examination would have gone quickly, except for Charleston's constant peppering of objections. Josalyn Williams took Yvonne Barnes through the morning of March twentieth, to Ruby leaving her at the gallery's side entrance and her seeing Tobin at the back door, through finding the body, calling 911, and the arrival of the beat cops. Then the attorney gave her a warm smile, raised her eyebrows, and turned away.

"No more questions, Your Honor."

THIRTY-TWO

❧ ❧

CYNTHIA AND YVONNE

For the first time, Cynthia Charleston looked like she thought the case was in serious danger. There had been a wet eye or two in the jury box while Yvonne Barnes described finding her husband's body, and the jurors appeared to regard James Tobin with increasing disdain. But Charleston was a pro. She hid her worries well as she rose to approach the witness. Charleston kept the preliminaries short and sweet and plunged right into it.

"Mrs. Barnes, you testified that you 'borrowed' a gun from your husband's cousin?" asked Charleston.

"I said that, yes."

"Did you ask permission?"

"No. He wasn't home. As I already explained." Yvonne had gone back to her haughty and injured look, and the jury regarded them both quizzically. Charleston must have known she was skating on dangerous ground, attacking a widow, but she had to take her chances. And the haughtier Mrs. Barnes looked, the more Charleston could get away with.

"Mrs. Barnes, you worked as a reporter for a number of years, did you not?"

"Yes, that's true."

"When you reported on a criminal case, and someone took something without permission, did you describe that action as 'borrowing,' or as stealing?"

"Objection." Josalyn stood up, apparently ready to explain her displeasure at length. Wagner sustained her, though, so she settled back into her seat. Charleston was unconcerned. Granger knew that her point had been to show the jury how this woman used language to her own end. Getting it on the record would have been nice, but it was secondary. And she was succeeding in rattling Yvonne Barnes.

"Mrs. Barnes, when did you discover that your husband was having an affair with Ruby Garcia?"

"Objection!"

"It's OK, I'll rephrase," Charleston said easily. Yvonne Barnes had flinched—precisely why Charleston had asked the question the way she did.

"Mrs. Barnes, we have heard testimony that your husband was having an affair with Ruby Garcia. When did you learn of this affair?"

Yvonne Barnes regarded her with cold contempt. Granger bit his lip, and although Cynthia Charleston didn't smile, her body language spoke volumes. The jury had been sympathetic toward Yvonne Barnes, the grieving widow, and would forgive her much; they would be far less generous to Yvonne Barnes the Ice Queen.

"Mrs. Barnes?" Charleston prompted.

"Ms. Garcia characterized it as a one-night stand, Ms. Charleston. I agree with her," Yvonne said.

"Whatever you wish to call it, Mrs. Barnes, could you please tell us when you found out about it?"

"I don't remember the precise date," Yvonne said, still cold.

"I see. Was that before or after borrowing the gun from Daryl Barnes?"

The jury, along with everyone else, jerked back. Granger heard the cameras whir as they zoomed in to handle this one in close-up.

"I don't remember," Yvonne Barnes said.

"Were you jealous? Do you remember that?"

"I didn't regard it as significant."

"Your husband had frequent affairs then?"

"Objection," Josalyn said angrily.

"Overruled," said Wagner. "The witness will answer."

"No," said Yvonne. "That's not what I said."

"Then you were jealous?" Charleston kept the pace up, not giving Yvonne a chance to think.

"I'll admit to some jealousy. I loved my husband very much."

"In this jealous mood, did you take the gun from the residence of Daryl Barnes?"

"The two incidents aren't related."

"Mrs. Barnes, did you have that gun in your possession the morning your husband was shot to death in the Barnes Gallery?"

"I resent this! My husband was murdered in cold blood, and to suggest that I pulled. . . ."

Wagner interrupted. His voice was loud and gruff. "Mrs. Barnes, answer the question."

"The answer is no!" she shouted. "I did not have the gun in my possession!" She had lost her composure, and in that instant you could see the rawness in her face, the pure anger, and you wondered, indeed, why she had taken the gun.

Charleston let the echoes die away, then leaped into it again.

"How long were you alone at the crime scene that morning, before Ruby returned from parking the car?"

"Ten minutes. Maybe fifteen."

"You are aware that Ruby Garcia has testified to a much longer period?" Charleston was bluffing, again. Ruby Garcia had said no such thing.

"She's mistaken," Yvonne said, and then her venom got the best of her. "Or else she's lying to protect her boyfriend."

Charleston also let this moment linger, letting the image imprint on the jury: Yvonne Barnes the Ice Queen, alone at the crime scene with a gun in her hand.

Then Charleston seemed to change the subject. She paced back to the defense table and picked up a short stack of papers. Granger watched her suspiciously, and beside him Josalyn's fingers tightened around her pencil. Charleston moved back toward Yvonne Barnes.

"Mrs. Barnes, you have testified that you've known Mr. Tobin since high school, isn't that correct?"

Yvonne said that it was, and Charleston guided her through testimony outlining her original meeting with James Tobin, and the fact that for three years they had run with the same circle of friends. For some reason, this line of questioning seemed to make Yvonne Barnes more and more unsettled. Josalyn's objections about relevance were overruled.

"And, in fact, you were more than just friends, weren't you, Mrs. Barnes?" Charleston said smoothly.

"I don't know what you mean," the Ice Queen said. Granger briefly closed his eyes, afraid of what was coming.

"Isn't it true, Mrs. Barnes, that you and Mr. Tobin dated throughout your senior year?"

"No," Yvonne said. "We went out once or twice, but I wouldn't call that going steady."

"I didn't call it that, Mrs. Barnes," Charleston replied. "Your maiden name was Yvonne Bateau, wasn't it?"

"Yes," she replied curtly.

"And isn't it true that after graduation, Mr. Tobin began dating someone else?"

Yvonne Barnes's jaw tightened. "I wouldn't know," she said.

"I see," Charleston said. "Perhaps this might help your recollection." She held up another piece of paper.

"Your Honor, this is a copy of a police report," she said.

Yvonne Barnes closed her eyes, and Granger felt like doing the same as Charleston read a report about an incident involving a nineteen-year-old woman named Yvonne Bateau, another young woman named Charlene Hughes, and a young man identified in the report as James Michael Tobin, also nineteen.

According to the report, Bateau had discovered Tobin, her boy-friend, in flagrante delicto with Hughes, Bateau's best friend, a white woman. According to the report, Bateau had been pressing Tobin to go public with their relationship, and Tobin had refused. She accused him of being a liar, and a two-timer, and a racist, and, according to the report, Bateau had threatened the lives of both Hughes and Tobin.

After that, it was difficult to dispel the notion of Yvonne Barnes as a vindictive and jealous woman, and Charleston did all she could to cement that picture for the jury. Josalyn Williams's objections stemmed the tide a bit, but the impression was firmly set.

Then Charleston, smiling, turned back to the murder.

"You blame James Tobin for your husband's death?" she said.

Yvonne Barnes looked like she would refuse to answer, and Granger prayed under his breath. Then, finally, the Ice Queen said yes.

"But you were the one who took that gun without permission, who gave it to your husband, introducing it into an explosive situation when you knew of the ongoing contention between your husband and James Tobin?"

"Yes," she said again, uneasily.

"Mrs. Barnes, who was the last person you saw in possession of that gun?"

A long pause ensued while Yvonne Barnes first looked like she was trying to remember, then like she was struggling with what that memory brought forward.

"Mrs. Barnes?" Charleston prompted. "The last person you saw with that gun?"

"My husband," she said. Then she buried her face in her hands, more fully than before and with greater abandon, a dramatic gesture Granger did not fully believe.

"No more questions," Charleston said quickly, dismissing the witness before she had a chance to recover so that the jury could see her befuddled, lost, no chance for excuses.

Granger and Williams shared a deadpan glance as Yvonne Barnes left the witness stand. Under the flat expression, Granger cursed with steady fury. Yvonne Barnes's testimony was effectively undercut, and there was little that the prosecution could do to repair the damage.

The Ice Queen had frozen herself into a trap. The thought brought with it no consolation at all.

THIRTY-THREE

❧ ❧

GRANGER

Granger sat behind the prosecution table in the empty courtroom, with his opened briefcase on a chair beside him and a legal pad on the table. But the pad held only blank, lined paper, and the pencil in his fingers just tapped an aimless rhythm against the sheets.

It would be another long night, he already knew that, and knew with a sinking feeling that he had no choice. Marian's lawyer was pressing for an immediate change in his visitation schedule, and the heart of her argument, it seemed, was Granger's job. The hours. The unreliability. The stress.

He could argue, in return, that Marian's unwillingness to compromise was only making things worse. He could argue that her contentiousness damaged Jemma much more than it damaged himself. But he knew that the core of her argument was sound, and he had no idea how to deal with it.

More and more, he was forced to choose between his career and his private life. And he could no more face that choice than he could face losing an arm.

He pushed the issue aside, cursing silently, and reviewed his case.

He almost had his provenance. He could prove the trail of the gun from Daryl Barnes's closet to Yvonne Barnes's home to Zack Barnes's briefcase. The jury had heard Simon Lee tell about seeing Zack put the gun in the locked cash drawer, and about telling James Tobin. The gun's last move—into Tobin's hand—had been outlined by the criminalists back at the trial's start, with their testimony about gunshot residue and bullet markings. The only missing move was from the cash drawer to Tobin's paint closet— a vital move because it spoke to premeditation. Ruby's move. He had tried to patch it into the record during her testimony, but he wasn't happy with the result.

And motive? By Yvonne Barnes's testimony, Zachary was about to expose Tobin as that most pathetic of artistic practition- ers, the failing artist forced to steal and burn his own works in an attempt to see some profit from them. The media had been having a lot of fun with that one, and for a man of Tobin's ego- ism it must have made things even worse. He had killed Zachary Barnes to avoid exposure. He had killed Zachary Barnes in a fit of jealousy over the affair with Ruby. He had killed Zachary Barnes in a dispute over the insurance money.

Granger shook his head morosely. Instead of one or two clear, persuasive, proven motives, he had a bundle, and none of them, he thought, was solid enough to convince the jury. Especially when so much of the rest of the case was seemingly built on sand.

Charleston may have sacrificed some media and jury sympathy this afternoon during her cross-examination of Yvonne Barnes, but she had gained something far more precious: for the first time, she had a reasonable explanation of the events of March twentieth, an explanation that bolstered her client's assertion of self-defense. Any implication that Yvonne Barnes had shot her husband was, of course, nonsense—and they could, if necessary, get the criminalists and Looper back on the stand to prove it. But Charleston's revelations about Barnes's past were incredibly damaging. Over and over, Granger heard an infuriating, singsong voice in the back of his head that kept repeating, "Reasonable doubt. Reasonable doubt." He tried to push the voice away.

And then there was Looper. That was a whole other problem, Granger thought unhappily. He tossed the pencil down and stretched his arms over his head.

Charleston still threatened to put Luisa Brown, Anita Looper's ex-lover, on the stand to testify about her prior meeting with James Tobin. Her testimony would not prove that Looper had manufactured, or rearranged, any of the evidence; bad feelings between the investigating detective and the defendant did not automatically mean that evidence tampering had happened. But then it really didn't need to prove anything. All it needed to do, in the mind of only one juror, was to provoke a reasonable doubt. That's all. That's what Cynthia Charleston would be gunning for.

Anita Looper said that Luisa Brown had turned the entire meeting into a joke. Granger only hoped that Luisa remembered that joke and would be willing, on the stand, to share it with the jury.

Granger stood and paced for a moment. Simon Lee's testimony about the bullets was the real killer here. Yvonne Barnes had sworn that Zack would never have bought bullets, or arranged for anyone else to buy them, but she couldn't prove that he hadn't done it. Simon said he saw a note with Zack's signature on it, and that the note went into the garbage. Could Tobin have forged the note? Could they prove it? Could Charleston prove that he hadn't? Granger and Williams and Wong had gone round and round and round on the issue, without arriving anywhere.

According to the police search report, no bullets of any sort had been found in the gallery, in the loft apartment, in the cars of either defendant or victim. It was as though the box of bullets had disappeared into thin air.

But there was one person who might help. One person who had been close to Tobin, one person whose testimony, if given honestly, might finally put his prosecution over the top.

Granger suddenly tossed pad and pencil into his briefcase and snapped it shut. It was time to interview Ruby Garcia again.

THIRTY-FOUR

❧ ❧

RUBY, AGAIN

Granger waited in his car, in the dark, parked in a small alley off Guerrero Street down in the Mission District. He sat just a dozen or so paces away from the door that led up to Ruby Garcia's apartment. He had been waiting for more than an hour and was prepared to wait several more. His intention was to call Ruby back to the stand, but before he did so he needed to impress upon her a certain understanding.

Another hour passed. Granger grew a little weary, a little hungry. He decided to chance walking to El Toro, the taqueria place at the end of the block. It wasn't far. If Ruby did come home, she would no doubt turn on the lights inside her place. He could always just walk up and knock.

Just as he got out of the car, though, Ruby stepped around the corner. She recognized him. He thought for a minute she would bolt, but instead she just stood there.

"You want to talk to me?"

"I do."

"I don't have much time," she said. He had never really seen her in quite this posture before, standing full figure. She was a

215

lanky girl, a thin shadow wavering in the dark. "I'm going out again in a few minutes."

"You been following the trial?" he asked.

"Yeah." She glanced nervously upstairs, as if ready to ditch out. She hung loose, though, curious. He felt a familiar pull inside the hollow of his chest, an ache. "I guess Yvonne really shook things up," she said.

"It's not enough, though. Your boyfriend's going to get off. And Charleston, she's trying to make it look like Yvonne pulled the trigger."

Granger was trying to appeal to Ruby's sense of fair play, her discomfort at Yvonne being handled the way she was. Because Ruby knew, like he knew, that the gun had not been in Yvonne's possession that morning, or in Zack's.

"Did you come down here to try and drag me back into this? I've done what I've done."

"You know it isn't right for Yvonne to take this kind of stuff. To hear her husband implicated," he said. He edged forward. If she tried to run, he was going to reach out and grab her and make her listen. "You have to tell the truth."

"Listen, I'm trying to get away from all that. That whole scene. It was a mistake, and I don't want to think anymore about it. I mean it was glamorous to me." The light from the arc lamp up above fell on Ruby's face and illuminated her. She looked innocent and young. "Tobin and the gallery and all the people and the money. I was sucked in. Maybe you don't know anything about it. Maybe you have never been tempted because you always had everything, got everything you want."

For one terrible moment Granger was tempted to tell her about Jemma, but he pushed it ruthlessly aside.

"The truth is what's important here," he said. It was a platitude, but it was his job to say such things. Maybe it was his job to believe them, too.

"The truth? The truth is I can't go anywhere without people looking at me. Talking. Wondering. That's why I got my own place. To search it out for myself. To do my work, away from the scene. It's what Zack would have wanted."

"So this is how you repay him?"

"What kind of thing is that to say?"

"You loved him, didn't you?"

Ruby glanced away. Her features got lost in the darkness, and he couldn't see her anymore. "I don't know. We shared something, that's all I know. Then everything turned out rotten, the way it always does for me. I just want to get clean of that whole scene."

"The way to get clean is to tell what really happened."

"It's too late for that," she said.

"No, it's not too late."

"What do you mean?"

Granger paused, looking at her. "I'm recalling you."

"What?"

"I'm bringing you back to the stand."

"Goddamn you," she said, and turned away. He was ready. He grabbed her by the arm. The light fell full on her face now, and on his own too, and he could feel the two of them caught in this moment, together, and knew this was his last chance.

"You may not regard law as an art, but I do. At least sometimes. And like any artist you have to ask yourself a simple question."

"What's that?" she asked, furious.

"You have to ask yourself if you want to build your vision out of something true and beautiful. Or out of lies."

In the silence that grew between them, he could hear a Muni bus growl by on Guerrero, and the sound of salsa music from a nearby bar.

"It isn't always so easy to tell the difference," Ruby said finally.

"Deep in your heart, you know," he said, and then he let her go. In another instant she was up the stairs, behind the door, closing it, and Granger stood on the dark sidewalk wondering if he had done any good at all.

*   *   *

The next day Ruby returned to the courtroom. Granger resumed his examination with the letter from Zack. He asked the clerk to give the witness the evidence labeled "People's Eleven," and asked Ruby to read the paper.

"Out loud?" she asked, as if wanting to keep it for herself.

"Out loud."

She cleared her throat and looked nervously around the room. Tobin, his face closed and cold, offered no help.

"'Dear Ruby Red,'" she began, her voice trembling. "'I want to talk to you about what happened last night between us. The feelings are so strong I can't think of anything else.'"

She paused. The sheen was in her eyes again, but the defiance of her earlier testimony was gone.

"Go on," said Granger. "Read."

"'What I said last night was true. I have very deep feelings for you. All right, I love you. I've said it.'"

The slope in Ruby's shoulders deepened. She held the letter away from her and touched at her eyes. He thought she would cry, but instead she went on reading, this time without his prompting.

"'But what I am telling you is not right. I love Yvonne. And James is not such a bad guy. You should try and work it out with him, if that's what seems right. No matter what happens, though, there's one thing I don't want to see get lost in all this. Your work. That's all that's really important. You're a good artist, and I mean that. Forever yours, Zack.'"

She broke apart now and pushed the letter aside. Granger let the courtroom sit in silence.

"I lied," Ruby said.

She said it softly. The courtroom seemed to have fallen yet more silent than it was before. Granger could have sworn he heard the whirling of videotape inside the cameras.

"Excuse me, Ruby. Could you please speak a little louder?"

"I lied," she said again. "I've been lying all along. About everything."

"Your Honor," Charleston said, on her feet, "this witness is distraught. I'm not sure she realizes the consequences of what she has just admitted—let alone the consequences of perjury. I move we adjourn so she can compose herself and consult with counsel."

"Ms. Garcia," said the judge. "Do you wish a recess?"

"No."

"Proceed, Mr. Granger."

Granger directed his energy back at Ruby. She met his eyes this time, and he could not help but think of the evening before and how she'd looked with that white light falling in her face. He asked her where she had been the night Tobin's paintings were stolen from the gallery.

"I was at home. That part of my story was true, at least."

"You were home the entire evening?"

"I came home from school about six. Jimmy was acting a little short, you know. . . nervous. Pacing around. He didn't want to talk. And he didn't eat much dinner."

"Did the defendant leave the loft after dinner?"

"No. Jimmy disappeared into his studio, like he does, and I studied for class. We ended up in bed at eleven."

"Do you recall the defendant leaving the bedroom at any point during the night?"

"Yes."

"What time was that?"

"About three in the morning. I woke up. Jimmy was coming in the bedroom door. He was in street clothes—and he had one of those wool caps on his head."

"So, in truth, James Tobin did leave the apartment the night of the theft?"

"Yes."

Granger nodded, letting the pause happen, then moved back into his questions.

"Did you ask him where he'd been?"

"I did, but he wouldn't tell me."

Granger glanced over at Tobin, deliberately, knowing the jury's eyes would follow his own. He stared straight ahead, as if he did not notice the attention, as if all this had something to do with someone other than himself.

"Ruby, did you ever see a gun in the defendant's possession?" asked Granger.

"Not in his possession, no."

"Did you ever see a gun in his apartment?"

"Yes, I did."

The courtroom stirred. The jury moved in their seats, onlookers whispered, and a reporter jockeyed in closer with his notepad. Meanwhile Granger guessed the camera was tightening on Ruby. Time for an extreme close-up on her pretty face, her dark eyes.

"When did you see that gun?"

"A few days before the murder."

"Could you describe the weapon you saw?"

"Yeah. It was the color of stainless steel, and it had a black handle. I remember, I was in Jimmy's work closet looking for some paint thinner. There was this gun behind some paint cans on the upper shelf. I didn't know what to think. It really upset me, just seeing it there."

"This work closet, it's the same work closet you described earlier? In your previous testimony?"

"Yes."

"Didn't you say at that time that you had not seen a gun at all? That what you had seen was a pair of pliers?"

"I was lying."

"Why did you lie?"

"I was afraid of Jimmy."

Granger nodded. "Can you tell me why you were afraid?"

She shrugged uncomfortably. "Jimmy, he's got a temper, you know? Like, the night after the opening, after he didn't sell any paintings? He got real mad. And when he found out about me and Zack, when he read that letter. . . ." She shrugged again.

"What did he do, Ruby?" Granger asked gently.

"He hit me," Ruby said matter-of-factly. "That's what he does, you know. He hits."

"And why are you telling the truth now?"

"Because," Ruby hesitated. Tobin had his head bowed, and his hand on his forehead.

"Why, Ruby?"

"Because I couldn't go through with it. Jimmy killed Zachary Barnes, and he should be punished."

"Objection! That is conclusory on the part of the witness."

Wagner sustained, but it didn't matter. The jury had heard. The news crews had their sound bite. The cameras were cutting from Ruby to Tobin, his livid posture and startled eyes.

The second damning bit of testimony was almost a gift, and certainly nothing Granger expected.

He had routinely taken her testimony through the evening of March nineteenth, just to make sure they had all the bases covered. Ruby told about the *rellenos con arroz* she had prepared for dinner, and Tobin's comment that as soon as the insurance money came in, they wouldn't have to eat poor anymore. Ruby had resented the comment; she was proud of her cooking skills.

"So after dinner I emptied the garbage, 'cause otherwise we got roaches. Those old loft buildings, they're all over the place. And something rattled around."

Granger happened to be facing the defense table when she said it, and saw Tobin's face suddenly pale. Keeping his eye on the defendant, he said, "Something rattled, Ms. Garcia? Was this normal?"

"No," she said. "So before I turned the can over into the big dumpster, you know, I took a look. We used the dumpster over behind the next building, 'cause that way Jimmy didn't have to pay for garbage pickup. Anyway, I took a look."

Tobin stared hard at her, his eyes almost wild.

"Can you tell us what you found, Ms. Garcia?"

"Sure. I found a box of thirty-eight bullets. I know 'cause that's what it said on the box. And the box, the seal on one side, it was broken, like the box had been opened already."

Granger turned from Tobin to look directly at Ruby. "Did you open the box, Ms. Garcia?"

"Hell, no," she said. "I threw it away. I didn't want bullets around my place."

"Did you tell Tobin about it?"

"No," she said.

"Why not?"

She just shrugged and, when pressed, said, "I don't know." Granger decided not to push her. He knew that Charleston would do enough pushing during her cross-examination. She'd call Ruby's motives and memories into question, she'd do her best to neutralize the testimony.

But Granger knew that the jury had been watching Tobin, just as he had been.

It was five o'clock, and Wagner called for recess.

The guards led Tobin away. The courtroom emptied; Josalyn congratulated Granger and went outside to deal with the press. Granger was slow in leaving, and as he gathered his papers Charleston edged by him.

"You're going to get your wish," she said. She looked weary from the long day. He knew the feeling. In other circumstances, attorney to attorney, he might have bought her a drink.

"What wish is that?"

"Looks like I'll have to put my boy on the stand."

She put one hand on her hip and with the other dragged up her suitcase. It was unlike a defense attorney to admit it when they were against the wall. Possibly she was deceiving him, but Granger smiled anyway. Because somewhere in his gut he felt a surge of pleasure, and he knew Tobin's last gambit was coming soon.

Thirty-Five

◌◌◌ ◌◌◌

The Defense

During the next few days, Granger did what he could to wrap a ribbon around the prosecution's case. He brought in an expert in the analysis of blood spatter patterns. Another to demonstrate the position of the two men when the gun was fired. A third to discuss the results of the bag tests. A fourth to analyze the trajectory of the bullets.

For every expert he produced, the defense produced another with the opposite opinion. Even so, he was feeling better about the case. The prosecution had established a motive. They had tape-recorded evidence of a death threat. They could show step-by-step how the murder weapon had been brought to the gallery and how it ended up in Tobin's possession. They could use the material evidence to show how Tobin had planned to cover up his crime. And they could use Tobin's own admission to show how he'd attempted to cover it all up by wounding himself, claiming self-defense.

Even the tone of the press coverage had changed. A few weeks before, the case had been a hopeless fiasco. Now the prosecution had redeemed itself. The person responsible for this redemption, according to the commentators, was Josalyn Williams. Her examination of Yvonne Barnes had been the pivotal event.

The critics were less certain about Granger. He had done well enough with Ruby the second time around, but his big battle lay ahead with the defendant, James Tobin.

A legal analyst on channel seven suggested he give the task over to Williams. Another commentator urged him to come out swinging. And a San Francisco department store called to see if he would sponsor their cologne.

Though at least partly tongue-in-cheek, the offer rankled Granger, perhaps more than it should have. He was also rankled by the constant attempts of the media to place him and Josalyn Williams at odds.

Although Josalyn had retreated into silence since her examination of Yvonne Barnes, she was not challenging him. But she wasn't offering much help either. Her job was finished, she seemed to have figured, though she also seemed uncomfortable with the way things had gone. As for the reason for that discomfort, Granger could only guess. At least she was quiet too with the press.

Then, somewhere in the middle of all this analysis, the prosecution rested its case.

Charleston moved the defense quickly. Character witnesses. Experts. A reexamination of the financial records. She did not return to the notion of alternative suspects and sloppy police work, nor did she call Luisa Brown to the stand. Looper's former girlfriend must have chosen to stand by her after all. But Charleston did remind the jury that no evidence supported Yvonne's claim that Tobin was carrying a yellow bundle of bloody clothes. The defense stood firm. The killing was self-defense.

Tobin had to testify.

He was carefully groomed. His suit looked professional, though not too businesslike, a careful shade of blue that brought out the vulnerability in his eyes. His hair had been recently cut, though not too close, so that his black curls were still thick and lush. He did not look like a man who belonged in jail. When he raised his hand to take the oath, though, there seemed a touch of arrogance, the slightest smirk. But it was gone as quickly as Granger noticed it, replaced by something else, an earnestness, an innocence in the face of justice.

For her part, Charleston had varied her motif. Her skirt, her jacket, her shoes—all were a muted white. "James," she asked, "could you tell the jury when you first learned that your girl-friend, Ruby Garcia, was having an affair with the deceased?"

"In February, I think." Tobin's voice was light, full of air. Gone was the disturbed man recorded on tape. "A couple weeks before Zack died."

"How did you find out?"

"Ruby told me. She said that she and Zack had fallen in love."

"Did she say anything else?"

Tobin seemed reluctant, as if something ugly needed to be said, but he was too nice a guy to say it. Granger guessed their strategy. They would paint Ruby as the wild one, Tobin as the earnest boy, the faithful friend.

"She said they planned to run off together after the insurance money came in." Tobin's face held a look of distress, his brow furrowed.

"Were you jealous?"

"I was fond of Ruby. I thought I had been good to her. But to be honest, she is a disturbed girl from a very rough back-ground, and my feelings for her as a partner had worn thin. I realized it wasn't going to work out. So when she told me that, I was more concerned for Zack."

Tobin made eye contact with the jury. He touched his fore-head, accidentally mussing his hair. Or perhaps it was not acci-dental. That black curl teasing across his forehead gave him a look of boyishness and made his story somehow more believable.

"Why were you concerned for Zack?"

"We'd been partners for a number of years, but lately he'd gotten self-destructive. I thought maybe it was just some midlife thing. I hoped he'd pull out of it before he ruined his marriage. And our business."

"James, did you and your partner ever discuss financial concerns?"

"Yes. The Barnes Gallery was in financial trouble."

"Were you worried?"

"Of course." Tobin smiled, self-assured, pleasantly cocky. A smile, no doubt, that had helped sell a painting or two. "But as an artist, I've had lots of financial ups and downs. You get used to it. Zack, though, he was taking it hard."

"Can you describe his reaction?"

"He was at wit's end, and he had this idea. He wanted to arrange a theft. Of my paintings, from his gallery. Then we would collect the insurance money together."

"Did you agree?"

"No."

Tobin was persuasive and relaxed. He told the story from the opposite vantage point as Yvonne did, using the same events to implicate not himself, but her husband. If not for all that had gone before, his might seem a credible version. It still might seem that way to the jury. Charleston would do her best to keep that illusion going. That meant dispelling the testimony of Simon Lee and Ruby Garcia. She moved in that direction now.

"James," she said, "you've heard the prosecution witness Simon Lee claim that he saw you cut the paintings out of their frames. Is that what happened?"

"No."

"Then what did happen that evening?"

"Well, I woke up about two in the morning. I'd heard a noise down in the gallery, and I decided I better go check it out. When I got down there, I found Simon Lee cutting my paintings out of their frames."

"Did you speak to him?"

"Yes. He told me Zack had put him up to it."

"So what did you do next?"

"I threw Simon out of the gallery, then I went back upstairs to bed. The next morning, I called Zack about it. By that time, though, he had gone ahead and finished the job on his own."

"What did you do next?"

"I didn't know what to do. We met later that day in his office, and he told me he had already destroyed the paintings. Then, right then, he called the insurance company to file a claim."

"Why didn't you tell the police?"

"I planned to, but I wanted to give Zack a chance to change his mind. We'd been friends a long time, so I told him that we should come clean with the insurance company. I told him this several times, but he didn't like hearing it very much. He told me that he was going to collect that insurance money, and if I tried to stop him, he would kill me."

Tobin had done it again. Told the exact same story as the prosecution, only changing the names, pointing the blame at Zack. He smiled at the jury now, a little more shyly, as if overwhelmed by the circumstances that had gotten him here, wrongly accused but still patient. Relieved to have this chance to show how the facts, if you looked closely, would exonerate him.

Charleston dimmed the lights so Tobin could identify some slides of the missing paintings. It gave him the opportunity to comment intermittently on his own work in a way that made it difficult for Granger to protest the relevance. The real point of the slide show, Granger knew, was to give the jury another glimpse into Tobin's life. To show him as an artist, up close and intimate. Tobin played it well, like a master regarding his art, modest but absorbed despite himself, and Granger realized that this was how the man regarded himself. A master. He did everything for his art, or for that illusion. Meanwhile, Charleston's manner was conversational and deferring. The two of them there in their fine clothes, regarding the illuminated images floating above them in the darkened room, looked like a picture from an elegant magazine. Eventually, though, the lights had to come back up, Granger knew, and it would be back to the grimmer realities of the trial.

It occurred to Granger that the defense had not shown the painting hanging at the top of the stairs at Tobin's apartment, the self-portrait. Because it was not among the stolen, maybe. Or because its image was too disturbing.

"James," asked Charleston, "were you aware that Zachary had been keeping a gun in his office drawer in the Barnes Gallery?"

"Yes. Simon told me. He also told me that Zachary meant to use that gun against me."

"What did you do when Simon told you this?"

"I removed the gun from Zachary's drawer. I put it in my paint closet upstairs."

"Did you bring that gun to the meeting between yourself and the deceased on the morning of March twentieth?" Charleston asked. The question did not surprise Granger. The defense's strategy had not been to deny the details of the prosecution's case, but to offer alternative explanations.

"Yes," Tobin said. "It was a mistake, I know that now, but I did bring that gun with me."

"Why?"

"I was afraid. I agreed to the meeting because I wanted to talk things out. Then I started to worry. Zack had threatened me already, and it occurred to me that he had arranged this meeting because he wanted to kill me."

"But didn't you have his gun?" asked Charleston. "The revolver was in your possession, was it not?"

"That's true, but I knew that Zack had access to his cousin's house, with the gun collection. I worried that he had found another weapon."

"What did the two of you discuss at this meeting?"

"I told him I couldn't go along with his scheme any longer. I was going to the authorities first thing the next morning."

"What happened next?"

"Right then, in the middle of our conversation, Zack reached into his office drawer, looking for the gun. When he couldn't find it, he got angry. He came at me, wild and crazy as hell. He had something in his hand. At least it seemed that way at the time. So I pulled the gun."

"Did the deceased say anything at this point?"

"No. He lunged at me, and he somehow got his hand up on my hand, forcing the barrel under my throat. He was trying to pull the trigger, to jam his finger up in there. I pushed back, and the barrel hit his chin."

"Then what happened?"

"The gun went off," Tobin said.

Tobin put his head down in a motion of despair. His body shook as he sobbed, and despite himself Granger felt that sob, awful and plaintive, as if it came from within. When Tobin lifted his head, tears were coming down his cheeks. "It was the worse thing that ever happened in my life," Tobin said. "It was an accident, I swear. I never wanted that gun to go off."

THIRTY-SIX

༈ ༈

REASONABLE DOUBT

Granger's job was simple. He needed to undermine Tobin, to show that his testimony was nothing more than a tissue of lies. The artist, though, was skilled at rearranging the facts to suit his version of events. Like others skillful at illusion, much of his ability no doubt lay in his own egoism, his belief in the fundamental validity of his perception, damned the details. Though Granger knew he was unlikely to destroy that underlying belief, he could at least point out the contradictions to the jury.

Still, that little voice kept ringing in the prosecutor's head, chiming over and over again, "Reasonable doubt. Reasonable doubt."

Granger approached the stand with more confidence than he felt.

"You testified earlier that you were fond of Ruby Garcia?"

"Yes. That's true," Tobin said easily, the good witness, secure in his honesty.

"She was your lover?"

Tobin seemed reluctant, as if suspecting a trap, and his brows came together. He did not look quite so handsome when he was suspicious. "Yes," he said at last. "I suppose you could phrase it that way."

"Mr. Tobin, did you become angry when you found out your lover was sleeping with your business partner?"

"No. Not really."

"No?" Granger stressed the disbelief in his voice. He wanted the jury to question the honesty of the man's emotions. "Your lover was sleeping with your business partner, but you weren't jealous. Not even a little bit?"

"Things between Ruby and me were over. I was not in love with Ruby Garcia."

"She was your lover, but you were not in love with her?"

Tobin faltered. "That's right."

It was a good way to set the tone. A start toward making the man look insincere, someone who used words, and people, according to his needs. Granger turned his back to the jury and gave the defendant a wry smile. If Tobin was unnerved, he did not show it.

Tobin was not going to be easy, Granger knew. He had glimpsed the man's nature somewhere in those pictures, the articles, the testimony of the other witnesses, his demeanor here in the courtroom. There was a flaw someplace, he was sure, a weakness in the man's rendering of himself. Even so, he was not quite sure what that weakness was, or how to exploit it on the stand. It seemed to slip away when he tried to articulate it to himself, to lie just beyond his reach.

"Mr. Tobin, are you familiar with a letter that Zachary Barnes wrote to Ruby Garcia a few days before the murder?"

"I've heard it discussed here in the trial."

Now Granger asked the judge if the clerk might come forward yet again with People's Eleven, so that it might be presented to the defendant. Wagner assented.

"In your testimony, you claimed that Zachary and Ruby planned to run away with the insurance money."

"Yes."

"Could you find the place, here in this letter to Ruby, where Zack makes mention of such a plan?"

Tobin read the letter to himself, making a show of it, moving his lips as his eyes rolled down the page. "He doesn't say anything like that here." Tobin pushed the letter away, dismissive.

"In fact," said Granger, "doesn't Zack say much the opposite? That he loves his wife and means to break off with Ruby?"

"That's how it appears."

"Yet, according to you, they were preparing to run off with insurance money?"

"Yes."

"Then how come this letter, written by Zack just days before his death, makes no mention of these so-called plans?"

No sooner had Granger finished his question when he realized his mistake. The question gave Tobin a chance to speculate on Zack's motives, a speculation that would not be kind.

"Maybe Zack was deceiving Ruby. Maybe he was lying."

Tobin shrugged, as if he did not enjoy such speculation, but there was a glint in his eye, an undercurrent of mockery. He knew that Granger had slipped. Granger felt his face burn. He thought of the analysts, how they relished pointing out his every mistake. This damage wasn't serious, though. It hurt his pride more than anything. He moved the testimony along.

"Earlier Simon Lee testified that he saw you in the gallery on the night of the theft. Is this true?"

"I saw him there, yes, but the circumstances were not as he claims." Tobin had gained confidence now, and with that his arrogance showed more fully. Granger wondered if the jury could see that arrogance too.

"Mr. Tobin, Simon Lee has also testified that he saw you with a razor knife, cutting the paintings from their frames."

"That's not true. Simon Lee was the one with the razor."

"Mr. Lee also claims you asked him to be quiet about what he had seen and that you paid him to. . . ."

"None of that is true." Tobin was assertive, still in charge.

"So Simon Lee was mistaken in his testimony?"

"Yes."

"All the details were inaccurate?"

"Yes."

"You did not pay him to be quiet?"

"Of course not."

Granger walked back to the prosecution table. He took his time, letting Tobin sit. At length he stepped forward with a piece of yellow paper. In his overconfidence, Tobin had given him an opening, and Granger meant to take advantage. "This invoice is from Mid-City Cycles in San Bruno, dated February eighteenth, four days after the theft in the gallery. It indicates that fifteen hundred and twenty nine dollars was received from Simon Lee as payment on a Kawasaki motorcycle. Did you give that money to Simon Lee?"

"No."

Granger went back to the prosecution table. Once again he dallied, fiddling around. This time he came forward with records from Tobin's bank. "Mr. Tobin," he said. "These records indicate you withdrew fifteen hundred dollars in cash on February sixteenth, two days before Simon Lee purchased his motorcycle. Let me ask you again, did you give that money to Mr. Lee?"

"No."

"What did you do with that money?"

Tobin hesitated, though only for an instant. "I spent it on paints. On canvas material. It's very expensive stuff." He smiled, pleased with his answer. A little too pleased, Granger thought. He saw a member of the jury stir in his seat, maybe thinking the same thing.

"Do you have a receipt for that purchase?"

"No," Tobin said, and smiled. "I'm an artist, Mr. Granger. I've always been bad about things like receipts and stuff. I just get too involved in what I'm doing. People are always yelling at me about keeping better records." He twinkled. "My tax preparer certainly does. So does—so did—Zack." The twinkle disappeared, and James Tobin looked genuinely distressed. Granger just looked at him, expressionless, then returned to his examination.

"On Tuesday, March fifteenth, you made a telephone call to Zachary Barnes. Is that correct, Mr. Tobin?"

"Zachary and I talked often on the phone. But I can't be certain about dates."

"Surely you remember this particular conversation. It was recorded on the phone machine and played back for us here in court."

Tobin looked annoyed. "Mr. Granger, every time you open your mouth, do you think you're going to have to explain it in court? I was angry, yes. Zack and I argued, yes. Haven't you ever argued with someone? And said things more strongly, maybe, than you really meant?"

Tobin had made a point with the jury, Granger thought, but he refused to allow that thought to slow him down.

"What about the theft, Mr. Tobin?"

"What about it?" Tobin retorted. "Zack made some accusations, and I chose not to answer them. That's not a capital offense, is it?" He paused. "I was trying to persuade Zack to withdraw the claim."

"You were? Mrs. Barnes testified that she overheard you threaten her husband's life later that same afternoon."

"I never threatened Zachary's life."

"So Mrs. Barnes was mistaken?"

"The whole time Zachary was alive, she tried to cover up for him. Now that he's dead she's still trying to protect him. And her own reputation, too. That's the bottom line with her."

After Charleston's cross-examination of Yvonne Barnes, Tobin's attack didn't seem as petty as it should have, Granger thought, and he felt something in him start to snap.

"Mr. Tobin," Granger said. "This version of events you are putting forth today, here on the stand—is it as accurate as the version of the murder you gave the police the day you were apprehended?"

Charleston shot to her feet, and Wagner's gavel beat down against the bench. "Objection!" Charleston shouted. "The state has no right to ridicule my client on the witness stand."

"Sustained. Mr. Granger, please refrain."

Granger stepped back. During cross-examination, he often found himself lost in the moment as he tried to appeal directly to the jury. He would get so involved that he noticed little else, not even his own people at the prosecution table. Now, though, he glanced at Josalyn. She had been watching him, of course, and she nodded to him, recognizing that things were going well. There was a certain reserve there, though, as there always was. The truth was he had not cracked this witness yet, and she knew that as well as he did. ˙

"After the murder," he continued, "Yvonne Barnes told Inspector Looper that she saw you in the alley behind the gallery. Could you tell us what you were doing in the alley?"

"I was not in the alley."

"Where were you?"

"I was lying inside on the floor, bleeding."

"By a gunshot wound from your own hand, isn't that true?"

"Yes."

"At the crime scene, you told Inspector Looper that Zachary had shot you in the leg. Yet later you changed your story. Why?"

"I panicked."

"Because you had murdered Zachary Barnes?"

"Objection!"

"Mr. Granger," said Judge Wagner. "Will you please approach the bench?"

Charleston started to approach too, but Wagner waved her back. "We've come a long way in this trial, and this kind of direct accusation doesn't score points with me," Wagner said. His breathing was wheezy and gruff, like that of an old dog. "So put it in your pocket, or I'll have this entire testimony stricken from the record. Do you understand?"

"Yes, Your Honor."

Granger took the warning seriously, but he realized too that Wagner had done him a favor. He had not upbraided him in front of the jury, nor in front of the accused. In fact, the pause had given him a chance to step back from his performance and see just how close to desperation he had come. "Reasonable doubt," the voice sang in his head, and he couldn't entirely push it away.

Granger returned to the task at hand.

"Mr. Tobin, you admit to bringing the gun to the gallery?"

"Yes," said Tobin.

"Where did you get this gun?"

"I took it from Zack's office."

"Simon Lee mentioned that the cash drawer was locked. How did you get the gun out?" Granger asked.

"I know where the key is kept," said Tobin. He brushed back the curl from his forehead, a practiced gesture that in a different circumstance may have been charming, the curl slipping through his fingers in that haphazard way. Except that in this instance the curl stuck up, making Tobin appear distraught, out-of-sorts. "You know that kind of thing when you work with someone long enough. It's the kind of drawer that locks automatically. You can't open it without a key."

"Never?" asked Granger. There was a contradiction here, Granger was almost sure. The key, the gun, the locked drawer. Something was skewed in the order of events.

"No. Never," said Tobin. "It can't be opened without a key."

"You've told several versions of what happened the day of the murder. In the most recent version, you were in the middle of a conversation when all of a sudden Zack went to the cash drawer and yanked it open."

"Yes."

Granger broke it off. "I'm sorry, I'm confused," he said. Then he turned to Judge Wagner. "Your Honor, if the court please, the prosecution requests the defendant rise from the stand so that he might demonstrate with his person the events of that morning."

Charleston edged forward as if she wanted to object, but there were no real grounds. She was the one, after all, who had put her client on the stand.

"Permission granted," said Wagner.

"One other request," Granger said. He came forward with a toy pistol in his hand. "For verisimilitude's sake, I'd like the defendant to have this in his possession during the reenactment."

"Objection!" Charleston said in desperation.

"Don't fear, it's rubber. A theater prop. No one will be shot."

"Permission granted," Wagner said again. The judge went on to explain to the jury, painfully, lugubriously, how the presence of the mock gun in the defendant's hand should in no way influence their opinion of his guilt or innocence. Then he directed the bailiff to examine the gun, to be sure it was a prop and nothing more.

Despite the judge's admonition, the innuendo inherent in the bailiff's precautions was clear. Before the defendant received a gun, even a toy gun, it needed to be checked carefully. A standard maneuver, but Granger was pleased nonetheless. Seeing the prop in Tobin's hand would make it easier for the jury to imagine him pulling the trigger.

Granger directed Tobin out of the witness box. The attorney paced off the distance between where Tobin had stood that day and where Zack had stood.

"Was this the approximate distance between yourself and Zack during your argument?"

"Yes."

"Where was the gun at that time?"

"In my pocket."

"Then please put it there now. In your jacket pocket, on the right-hand side. That's where you carried it the day in question?"

"Yes."

Tobin slid the rubber gun into his pocket. He raised his head a little when he did, trying to give himself some dignity. The effect was thuggish. Looking at him now, knowing that gun was in his pocket, it was hard to imagine it had ever been anywhere else.

"Now, Mr. Tobin, I am Zachary Barnes. I have just turned my back to you—and am reaching for the drawer." Granger turned around. He bent at the waist, as if going into the drawer. "Was this the point at which you pulled the gun from your pocket?"

"Yes," said Tobin.

"Now, please, do as you did then. Pull the gun. Point it at me."

Tobin obliged, though somewhat reluctantly. Charleston could not help him.

"This was how you stood then, the gun in your hand, pointed at an unarmed man, as he bent over a filing drawer?" asked Granger.

"I thought he was reaching for a gun."

"But you just told this court that you held that gun in your hand."

"I thought maybe he had another gun. He was reaching in his drawer for something, I know that."

"Didn't you just say that drawer was locked? That he couldn't get inside without a key? Didn't you say that?"

Tobin paused, and the tip of his tongue flickered out to wet his lips.

"Yes," he said finally.

"Then how did he get inside?"

For a moment Tobin said nothing. There was no good answer to the question, and Granger knew he had him. The man was lying, and the longer he stood there like that, holding the gun, the more apparent the lie became.

Then Tobin just shook his head, sadly.

"I keep trying to remember," he said. "And I just can't. It's like that time, those minutes, they're just entirely gone." He looked at the jury, still sadly. "It's like Yvonne said when she talked about that handkerchief. Sometimes you just can't remember."

"Can't, or don't want to?" Granger demanded.

"This whole charade is a farce, Your Honor!" shouted Charleston. She looked as if she were about to hemorrhage. "This is a shameless gambit designed to humiliate my client in front of the jury. I move to strike."

Wagner seemed to ponder her suggestion. Granger remembered the judge's warning of just a few minutes ago. He feared

Wagner might throw his cross-examination out. Judges were unpredictable, though, much like other human beings.

"Motion denied," he said.

Frustrated, with no recourse, Charleston asked for a word with her client. Granger made a fuss for appearance's sake, but in fact he had no objection. He knew it could do no harm for the jury to see the defense in disarray. To overhear the whispers, to see the frantic rolling of the eyes, the thin bead of sweat.

Charleston got her wish, but she had to know the sight was none too pretty. In the end, she walked away calmly, putting her best face on it.

"My client is ready to proceed," she said. Tobin, though, seemed more agitated than before. Granger approached him with a certain relish.

"Mr. Tobin, why did you shoot yourself in the leg?"

"I've explained that. I was afraid no one would believe Zack had tried to kill me. Not unless I could show them my wound."

"So your first thought—after you shot Zachary Barnes and he lay bleeding to death—was how to deceive people about what happened in that room?"

Tobin shook his head. "I wanted to dial 911, but my leg. . . . I couldn't walk."

"Mr. Tobin, you told one version of events to Inspector Looper at the crime scene. Then an entirely different version just a few hours later at the hospital. Is it possible you are getting these stories confused?"

The courtroom was dead quiet, waiting for Tobin's response.

"No."

"Then today you told a third version of events, here on the witness stand."

James Tobin did not respond.

"Mr. Tobin, the crowbar? How did those marks get on the gallery door and on the cash drawer?"

"I don't know."

"Yvonne Barnes has claimed she saw you outside the gallery holding a crowbar in one hand and a yellow package in the other. Was that package your blood-spattered shirt?"

Tobin's back straightened, and the trace of panic left his face. "There was no yellow package," he said with great conviction. "Zachary Barnes and I had an argument. He tried to kill me. In the struggle, the gun went off." He looked at Granger, his chin up. "My business partner, my old dear friend, is dead. This isn't going to bring him back. None of this is ever going to bring him back."

Tobin stared at Granger, and the corners of his eyes gleamed with moisture.

It seemed his final pose, and nothing Granger could do after that shook the facade of quiet grief that Tobin projected. Granger finished his cross-examination, Tobin stepped down, and the defense finally rested.

And all the time that little voice inexorably singsonged in Granger's ear.

"Reasonable doubt. Reasonable doubt."

THIRTY-SEVEN

❧ ❧

THE VERDICT

The jury was three days into deliberation when they reached a decision. Notice of it came into the DA's office first, bright and early, but the news leaked to the press almost immediately: they would reconvene to hear the verdict at one o'clock. By the time his office reached him at home that morning, Sterling Granger already knew. He finished his solitary meal, staring at the empty place where Jemma would usually have been, and wondered why instead of excitement he simply felt a sort of empty dread.

Ruby heard the news on the radio, in Spanish, while she sat in the morning sun on the fire landing outside her apartment. Her stomach tightened. By the time this day was over, she'd know if her former lover was a free man or a convicted murderer. She touched her ribs and closed her eyes for a moment in a silent prayer.

Yvonne, like Granger, heard it from the television. She had resumed her job with the mayor's office, but today she was dressed in mourner's black, except for a blood-red vest and a string of African jewelry. Mayor McKinney, passing her desk, told her she could take the afternoon off, and she knew he wanted her at the courthouse, playing for the crowd, McKinney's flunky on the spot. Dutifully she gathered up her purse and headed out. But she would have been in the courtroom anyway.

Josalyn Williams was down at City Hall, already at work, examining an upcoming docket. She took the message slip, read it, nodded, and reached for the telephone to call Sterling Granger. Then she stopped, her hand resting lightly on the receiver, lost in thought.

Simon Lee was fast asleep, plunged into a rowdy state of despair that had been with him ever since that day he'd learned of the murder. He did not find out about the impending announcement until almost noon, when he stumbled into the unwashed streets and saw a small crowd gathered around a flickering television inside the corner laundry. As soon as he learned, he fired up his Kawasaki and hurried to the Hall of Justice.

When he got there, the courthouse steps were filled with people, and the crowd spilled down the block. The atmosphere was oddly festive, and the press was everywhere. Simon pushed through the crowd until he came to a news truck monitoring the courtroom. The cameras showed Charleston at her table, Granger at his, and the bailiff leading Tobin down the hall.

Finally the jury entered too. Granger watched them intently, and so did everyone else. There are a million theories about how to read the faces of the jury, Granger knew. What it means if they nod to one another. If someone smiles to the defendant. If the jury foreman is left-handed. If one of the women wears a hat. Enough different indicators so that no matter what the outcome, one of them was bound to prove true.

The foreman was the shovel-jawed man that Granger and Williams had once nicknamed "Dudley Do-Right"—it seemed a lifetime ago. Today his jaw clenched with a seriousness that did not betray the secret written on that paper he held folded between his fingers.

"Have the members of the jury reached a verdict?"

"Yes we have, Your Honor," the foreman said. At that moment Granger thought he caught the faintest hint of a smile cross the face of a women juror. Innocent, he thought, and felt his heart beat hard twice, then seem to stop.

"What is that verdict?"

The foreman turned now and looked at Tobin. "On the count of murder," he said, "we find the defendant guilty in the first degree."

Tobin's head fell toward his chin. The cameras zoomed in tight, measuring his reaction. Meanwhile Ruby stood in the back of the courtroom. Tobin had lied about her on the stand, the son of a bitch, but even so the verdict left her cold. He deserved it, but she could take no joy in his defeat. She thought of Granger and searched inside for that attraction she had felt for him, however briefly, that night on the stairs. It was gone, and she was glad. Yvonne Barnes, meanwhile, had managed a seat directly behind the prosecution. When the verdict was read, she clutched at herself and felt a sudden release of the dark cloud within her; then Josalyn Williams embraced her over the banister. Granger felt nothing but relief. Charleston, he noticed, was leaning into Tobin, giving him the small comfort that defense lawyers gave their clients when all had been lost and the only hope was appeals, and more appeals. A long process of waiting, then waiting some more, which was perhaps as dreadful as any finality could ever be.

Wagner came down on his gavel, bringing the room to order.

"The next order of business is to schedule a time for sentencing."

They returned to the mundane details of the courtroom. There was always this business to go back to, the routines and the rituals. Then it was over. Tobin was escorted away, and Granger made his way onto the courthouse steps.

Outside, Yvonne Barnes and Josalyn Williams were center stage in a throng of media. Charleston stood not far away, in a smaller crowd, promising an appeal. Granger waited, and soon the press was on him too. He would say, of course, the words it was his job to say: "Justice was done, the guilty have been punished, the system works."

Predictable, of course, but he would say them with a particular pleasure this time, a feeling of vindication. Before the press closed in on him, he happened to notice Simon Lee up ahead, pushing through the crowd. He strained to see where Simon was going, but then the reporters were on him, and it was Granger's turn in the light.

Simon, for his part, had spotted Ruby. He could see her working her way down the far side of the steps, away from the crowd. He made his way toward her and stepped in front of her just as she hit the main sidewalk. She stepped back.

"Ruby," he said. "I'm sorry."

She regarded him, and for an instant she wanted to slap him, the little prick, for all the trouble he had caused her. But he looked so sorrowful that the urge quickly left her. Because what had happened wasn't Simon's fault any more that it was hers. Simon was just some hopeless kid, some wanderer, not so different from herself. She embraced Simon and held him close; then just as suddenly she pulled free. Simon watched her disappear. He had apologized, it was all he wanted. He knew he would never see her again, or if he did, they wouldn't have anything to say. Even so, he stood alone on the sidewalk for a long time after she was gone. After a while some reporter recognized him and asked for an interview. Simon told the little squirm to get lost. Then he jumped on his 'Saki and rode that bastard hard, wild, all through those twisted streets.

EPILOGUE

❧ ❧

SIX MONTHS LATER

It was late January, and the city's politically prominent were getting together for an inaugural party to celebrate the reelection of the progressive slate. Mayor McKinney had made it into a second term. Julie Ann Wong had won a new stint as DA. The Board of Supervisors had suffered one turnover but maintained its liberal majority. So most everyone was happy.

The party was held at McKinney's house in Forest Hills, a neighborhood of green lawns and stately houses built in an old eucalyptus grove above the fog belt on the city's west side. The mayor's house was made of stone, an oddity in this city of stucco and wood-frame houses. Like everywhere else in the city, though, the parking was tough, if not impossible, a situation aggravated by the fact that the mayor had scuttled the valet service. There had been a fuss after the last inaugural party, a stink over elected officials too lazy to park their own cars and a bigger stink over the awarding of the valet contract. The business ended up with three firms suing the city—one black-owned, one white, one Hispanic—because an Asian group had been awarded the deal. This time, in the spirit of democracy, the mayor had decided to scuttle the service altogether. Let the ruling elite park their own cars.

Granger arrived late. He wore a double-breasted suit and tinted glasses. The mayor shook his hand.

"Ah, living up to your new image."

Granger shrugged uncomfortably. The District Attorney had suggested the wardrobe—he suspected that she loved the idea of Granger as Media Star, even though he couldn't get use to it.

"Why not?" said Granger, unwilling to disagree with her. "An image is hard to come by."

"I know. I've paid thousands for mine. And no one will let it stand."

The mayor stood close and laughed his barrel-chested laugh. He pressed Granger's flesh again and slid off into the crowd.

A waiter came by with champagne. The mayor hadn't given up this amenity, Granger noticed, and he was grateful. The champagne man was white. The beer man was black. The woman with the Cajun shrimps was Chicano, and the one with the oysters Pacific Islander. On the surface, it looked a happy mix of the city's ethnicities, but Granger knew how much effort had gone into polishing that surface, just as he knew how bitter the bickering was underneath.

Though a lot of people might not like to think so, it probably wasn't different from the old days, a little patronage here, a little bit there, handouts to the Irish, Germans, Italians, Jews. The more people you had, the more money in your camp, the more you got. Old rules, new players. And there was always someone who got the shaft.

Granger caught a glimpse of Yvonne Barnes on the other side of the room, talking to a reporter over the chicharrones. She had come out of her shell after the trial and acted as the press manager for McKinney's reelection campaign. Granger had seen her on television, and she had handled herself with a kind of nobility and grace that made her interesting to watch. You could almost see the suffering on her face, and you knew that she was losing herself in her work. After the election, she had been profiled in several magazines, her virtues extolled: her professional toughness, her harsh and beautiful features, her devotion to the memory of her husband. It was rumored that she was being scouted to act as the lieutenant governor's press liaison, with a national career on the horizon.

Granger caught her glance, and though they had never been friendly, she nodded. In that instant, seeing her upturned face, the fiery glimmer of her eyes, he understood that the same grief and sorrow were still there and maybe always would be. They provided a heat in which she forged herself hard as steel.

All of the principals of the case, himself included, had reaped headlines in the aftermath of the case. A Career Resurrected. The Gilded Attorney. A Prosecutor Reborn. The stories all speculated on how long it would be before Granger would defect to private practice and a lucrative career as gentleman lawyer. They had not known, and Granger had not told them, that plans for such a move were already afoot.

Josalyn Williams, of course, had been profiled too, as an up-and-coming prosecutor. So had Charleston and Ruby Garcia. Ruby was still living in the Mission and working as an artist. The article Granger had seen was in an alternative paper; it profiled her work and mentioned the Barnes case only in passing. Simon, of course, had disappeared from view, vanishing back into the Haight. Judge Wagner was still presiding, still sick, still hacking away.

Meanwhile, Tobin was in San Quentin, busy forging his appeals. He claimed he was innocent, as cons always did, though he had another version of events now and was launching a new show of work he'd done in prison. But the insurance company was withholding payment on the theft, and rumor had it that Tobin had signed over the rights to all his works to Charleston to pay his outstanding legal fees and meet the costs of the appeal. Charleston, in turn, had sold reproduction rights to most of the works to a Madison Avenue firm, and Tobin's inoffensive renderings of poverty and homelessness were showing up in advertisements for expensive blue jeans and overpriced automobiles. In fact, that morning Granger had seen one of them in the business section of the *San Francisco Chronicle*. An unshaven homeless man, his belongings piled into a battered shopping cart, had stared out at him over the caption "This man wants your car." Tobin, it was rumored, was furious, and unable to do a thing about it.

Granger surveyed the crowd in front of him. It seemed everyone with a job in City Hall had shown up, and it was time for him to mingle. Just then, though, a voice caught him from behind.

"Hi, Counselor."

It was Looper, and Granger was genuinely glad to see her. She had finally learned of Charleston's original plan to put Luisa Brown on the stand and had been furious that Granger had not told her. But her temper did not last. Looper had a new girlfriend, or so Granger had heard.

"I hear you've turned down a transfer," he said.

Looper grinned her wolf grin. It was all politics, a lot of fuss over nothing, and she didn't want to talk about it. "I'd get another job if it weren't for how much I love corpses," she said, then took a gander at the crowd. "Looks like old home week around here. Oh, hey, congratulations. About the kid, I mean."

Granger smiled hugely. "Thanks. I just heard this afternoon."

Looper cocked her head, looking at him. "And that's why you look so relaxed. You gonna take a vacation to celebrate?"

For a moment Granger was tempted to confide in her. Late that afternoon, he had been granted sole custody of Jemma, after a battle noteworthy only for its initial bitterness and ending rapidity. Marian had found someone new, someone who was not all that interested, it seemed, in a ready-made family. The accusations and threats had disappeared abruptly, and while Granger was extremely grateful, he prayed that Jemma would never know how quickly her mother had given her up, and why.

In the meantime, the two of them were scouting for a new home, probably across the Golden Gate, and Granger had already told Julie Ann Wong that he would be leaving the department in March for that private practice the news analysts had always so confidently predicted for him. Wong had made him promise not to tell.

"No vacation until spring break," Granger said. "Until then, she studies and I prosecute, like I'm paid to do."

"Yeah," Looper said. Her voice was twinged with sarcasm, and she gave him a wink. "Good old Granger, always playing by the rules. In the courtroom, as in life."

He didn't follow her. "What do you mean?"

"You don't know?"

"If I did, I wouldn't ask."

"Come on," she lowered her voice now so only Granger could hear. "You knew about that tape at least a week before it came out in testimony. You violated discovery."

Granger frowned at her. "That's not true."

"Hell, maybe I wouldda done the same in your shoes. Except I wouldda been caught and investigated to beat hell."

"Detective," he said, "what makes you think I knew about that tape?" He had a feeling of dread in his stomach, a suspicion which—if he bothered to admit it—had been there all along.

"You want me to spell it out?"

"Yes."

Looper hooked her arm through his and drew him away from the crowd, through a set of French windows, and onto a small balcony. The damp January chill bit through his jacket.

"The day Yvonne testified, I saw her and Williams sitting in Williams's car, out in the parking lot. And since I'm a nosy type, I just cuddled back in a doorway and watched."

Granger didn't say anything, but he remembered the day, remembered his offer to get sandwiches for the three of them, and Josalyn's graceful refusal.

After a moment, Looper continued. "Our Ms. Williams had a little package in her hand."

"And so?" Granger said.

"And so, that evening on TV, I see Yvonne whip out the tape on the stand. She takes it out of a manila envelope, just like I saw your buddy holding in the car."

Granger closed his eyes. So that was the reason Josalyn had moved away from him, had let that small seed of friendship wither.

She had been right to distance herself. What she did certainly violated the spirit and the letter of the law. If it got out that the rules of discovery had been violated, then that was grounds for appeal. Tobin could walk. Guilty or not, he would be back in his loft, painting his pictures, and maybe even the insurance company would have to pay him for the missing paintings.

The only way that would happen, though, was if someone came forward with that information. Looper wasn't going to do that, Granger knew, because Looper didn't like Tobin. He was guilty as sin, and he had caused her too much trouble. Williams wouldn't say anything, of course, and neither would Yvonne.

That left only him.

And he realized, with a shrug, that he wasn't going to say anything either.

"Myself, I am glad to see that son of a bitch in jail. Who wants him out on some technicality?" said Looper.

Granger did not respond. He agreed with her reasoning, maybe, and for that reason would hold his tongue. Or maybe it was because Granger knew the furor that would result if he said anything at all, the careers that would be derailed, the muck that would be written about them. Tobin wasn't worth it, Granger thought. And as for the issues of discovery and disclosure, it was better to pretend that you just didn't know.

Just then, Julie Anne Wong entered the room; at her side was Josalyn Williams. Rumor was that Wong had taken Williams on as her protégé, that she would go after a higher office the next time around, and that Williams was being groomed for a run at the DA.

"Counselor," said Wong, taking Granger's hand. "I'm so glad you could make it."

"Yes, yes," Granger said. There were smiles and handshakes all around.

Silence followed, a moment of awkwardness. In that moment, a glance passed between them all. Granger realized that Wong knew the truth of the matter as well, that everyone knew, and they all averted their eyes. The same thought was running through all their brains.

Justice had been served, but not the law. The guilty man was in jail, but they had violated the rules to get him there.

But did it matter? Rules were written to be ignored. And who, after all, were such rules meant to serve?

If such issues were on their minds, however, no one raised the questions, and no one offered any answers. The champagne server approached, a tall white man in black pants and a red jacket. He bowed discreetly as each of them took a glass, and the idle chatter of the room seemed to increase. They made no toast, but each individually raised his glass to his lips. Granger held off a moment, watching the others. Then finally he too lifted his glass and tasted for himself that bittersweet champagne.